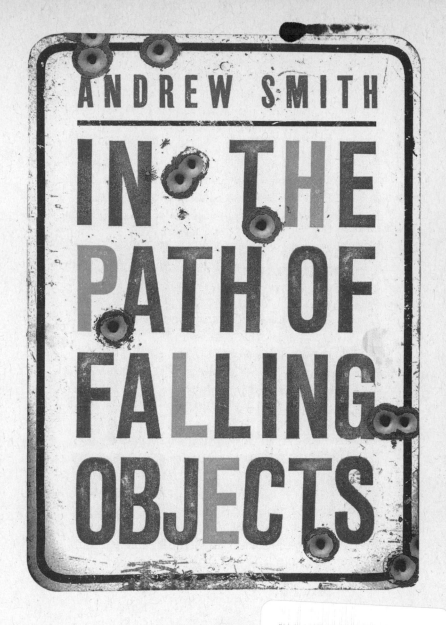

ANDREW SMITH

IN THE PATH OF FALLING OBJECTS

SQUARE
FISH

FEIWEL AND FRIENDS
NEW YORK

SQUARE
FISH

An Imprint of Macmillan

IN THE PATH OF FALLING OBJECTS. Copyright © 2009 by Andrew Smith.
All rights reserved. Distributed in Canada by H.B. Fenn and Company Ltd.
Printed in September 2010 in the United States of America by R. R. Donnelley & Sons
Company, Harrisonburg, Virginia. For information, address Square Fish,
175 Fifth Avenue, New York, NY 10010.

Square Fish and the Square Fish logo are trademarks of Macmillan
and are used by Feiwel and Friends under license from Macmillan.

Library of Congress Cataloging-in-Publication Data
Smith, Andrew (Andrew Anselmo).
In the path of falling objects / by Andrew Smith. p.   cm.
Summary: In 1970, after their older brother is shipped off to Vietnam,
sixteen-year-old Jonah and his younger brother Simon leave home to
find their father, who is being released from an Arizona prison,
but soon find themselves hitching a ride with a violent killer.
ISBN: 978-0-312-65929-5
[1. Brothers—Fiction.   2. Survival—Fiction.   3. Psychopaths—Fiction.
4. Vietnam War, 1961–1975—Fiction.]   I. Title.   PZ7.S64257In 2009
[Fic]—dc22   2008034755

Originally published in the United States by Feiwel and Friends
First Square Fish Edition: October 2010
Square Fish logo designed by Filomena Tuosto
Book design by Michelle McMillian
www.squarefishbooks.com

10 9 8 7 6 5 4 3 2 1

LEXILE 840L

For my brothers:

Patrick,

Stephen,

and William

The only shade there is blackens a rectangle in the dirt beneath the overhang of the seller's open stall. The girl stands there, behind a row of hanging wooden skeletons that dangle from the eaves.

"You like the skeleton?" the seller asks. "Give me a price."

"They look funny. Their arms are too long. They go down to their ankles," she says. "And where do you get wood from around here, anyway? There's not a tree for miles."

The seller shrugs. He doesn't understand.

Sometimes nothing is quieter than Mexico at ten in the morning in summer.

There is a statue of a knight made from tin. It stands facing the roadway.

The man standing next to the girl asks, "How much for that statue?"

"Give me a price," the seller says.

The man nudges the girl and says, "Want to see something you'll never forget?"

He presses a pistol barrel up beneath the seller's chin.

He shoots.

There are pictures I can draw out on the map of our life, words I scratch on this paper, the hollow parts filled in with nothing but my guesses after Simon told me what happened when we split up.

I can say this now.

I can give you this map.

scorpion

Our brother fell apart in the war.
Mother fell apart after that.
Then we had to leave.

Even in a perfect world the horse would not have carried me and my brother all the way to Arizona; it fell and died not ten miles away from our home in Los Rogues, New Mexico. And while I sat in the dirt and heat of the dusty road, looking at how my hands had been scraped when we fell, Simon, my stubborn little brother, tried to pretend he wasn't crying, but he cried anyway and pressed his face into the knees of his jeans, soaking the fraying denim with his tears for more than an hour before even looking up at me.

And I don't know what I was thinking. There was no way I could pull that dead horse out of the road, but I was so ashamed at leaving it there that I tried to anyway.

"What do you think you're going to do, Jonah?" Simon said.

And I kept pulling dumbly on the horse's leg, leaning my weight back as far as I could.

"We can't just leave it here. It's embarrassing." I could feel the sweat crawling down my face.

"No one ever comes down this road."

"Just our luck someone will today," I said.

So I jerked at my canvas pack, pinned beneath the hulk of the horse's flank, wiped my arm across my nose as I slung the pack over my shoulder, and tugged the dirty, sagging pants higher on my waist.

"We should go back home," Simon said, his throat still choked tight from the crying.

"We can't. Don't be stupid. We'll starve to death."

"I hate you, Jonah."

"So what?"

Of course I knew that Simon didn't really hate me. It's just something brothers say to brothers, sometimes. Because I always believed that Simon was my best friend. I still do believe it.

Mother and Matthew, our older brother, said we always fought when we were little, but I don't think that's true. But we did have some pretty good ones, at times, and Simon almost always ended up getting me in trouble. He'd always been good at that.

By the time Matthew was in twelfth grade, he began spending less time at home. I couldn't blame him. He'd gotten a job at the bowling alley, and he'd sometimes stay there all night, or sleep at a friend's house just to stay away. But he'd always come back, especially at times when our mother would leave Simon and me there alone. Matthew would bring us food wrapped in waxed paper from the bar at the bowling lanes. We never said it out loud, growing up, but Matthew and I understood that we were all we had, and the three of us brothers needed each other just to survive.

There's only one bed in our room, and when Matthew was home that meant Simon and I had to sleep on the floor with blankets, next to each other to stay warm. When it was real cold, we'd all three sleep in that bed. Sometimes I knew that Simon and I would lose patience with each other, too, because there's only so much you can put up with during the daytime from someone you have to sleep with every night of your life. At least, that's how I look at it.

And now Matthew was gone. Simon and I didn't talk much about where he was. The thought of losing him was more frightening than probably anything else. But we had also gotten used to his not being home, even if we'd never get used to the possibility of his not coming back. And there were things about Matthew that I knew, but never told Simon, and couldn't tell Mother because after we stopped getting letters from him, she just shut down and then she vanished.

Now our horse was dead, and I felt so lost and scared. But I didn't want Simon to know that, so I made him keep walking with me. He didn't have a choice. And he hated that.

So we walked, Simon dragging his feet in the dirt of the road, following three paces behind me. His shoes were too big and he never tied them, so his feet made this awful snoring sound wherever he went.

And I looked back only once, where the road broadened out, curving around a creek bed where cottonwoods picketed, trunk upon trunk, silver-dollar leaves clattering like teeth, but I couldn't see the horse.

"We're going to keep going anyway. I promise I will take care of you."

I knew Simon wouldn't reply, and my words sounded so strange and hollow in the quiet of the afternoon. I guess I hadn't really heard my voice in the past two weeks, or, at least, hadn't noticed it as much as I did out there on the edge of the desert. Mother had gone off with one of her men friends for Georgia, or Texas, or someplace, and Simon and I had been left behind, alone in the crumbling shack of our home.

The electricity had been gone for days.

I was sixteen that summer. My jeans were cuffed even though I was already nearly six feet tall, and where they were folded they had begun picking up dirt and twigs. They first had belonged to Matthew. The shirt I wore had been ordered from an Alden's catalogue; my brother had worn it, too, when it was new. The elbows were wearing through and I kept the sleeves rolled up, the tails tucked in tightly down inside my jeans, almost to my knees. It was too hot for flannel, anyway.

The last letter from Matthew came two months ago, at the end of the school year.

And all Matthew's letters to me were in our pack, ordered, tucked beneath the carelessly wadded clothes and the canteen of piss-warm water that tasted metallic, like it had been strained through the filth in the drain of the streaked porcelain sink basin in the kitchen. At the bottom, under our clothes, was the comp book where I drew my map, and a small pistol.

So Simon and I came down from the hills where we lived, where we had abandoned our horse, the trees thinning out to open on the vastness of the desert, the dirt road stretching in a narrowing line to disappear among the mesas in the distance, the stream becoming nothing more than dampness, shaded somewhere beneath the rocks strewn to mark its path, following the road, or the road following it. On the opposite side of the bed, a derelict trailer sat crookedly, one wheel missing, the blackness of its doorway yawning upward at the shadows of gathering clouds.

We said nothing to each other.

It would rain soon; I could smell it.

The rain came in relentless slate sheets. We saw its approach, a smoky drape across the desert, sweeping toward us like some monstrous black broom, the first spitlike gobs of wet streaking down through my hair and pasting my shirt to my chest. By the time we decided to go back to the doubtful shelter of the trailer, Simon and I must have looked like castaways climbing from the sea.

"Here." I interlaced my fingers to give a boost for Simon's foot at the edge of the trailer's doorway.

"Why do I have to go in there first?"

I don't know why I even put my hands down there. I should have known he would say something like that.

So I just looked at Simon, then, grabbing at either side of the doorway, heaved myself up into the dimness of that crooked trailer.

Water ran down from the top of the doorway, spilling across the blistered linoleum and pooling against the far wall, where gravity had pulled a collection of beer cans and other trash across the slope of the tilting floor. My wet hair hung down across my eyes and mouth. I swept it back over my head and reached a hand out into the rain to help my brother up into the trailer.

There was a door there, hanging open, but it was bent badly, and so I kicked at it until it finally wedged into the jambs and stopped the pounding rain from coming in.

"What if we can't get out?" Simon said.

"It'll open."

The rain was so loud inside the small trailer, roaring like an endless swarm of locusts hurling themselves against the rusted skin of its exterior. When the thunder came, the trailer seemed to lift in the air, and we both nearly fell down from it.

But there was enough light coming in through the two side windows that we could see where we were. A bed stretched across the width of the trailer in the back, the uncovered mattress yellowed and torn, offering up tufts of its innards where the cloth had worn through. And smeared all along the yellowing walls were handprints, stamped in the red dirt of the desert, probably made from someone drying themselves here during a rainfall like this one. I put the pack on what was left of a table, attached to one wall, but broken jaggedly across its middle as though bitten by some giant.

I opened the pack.

"It's still dry. We should put on some dry clothes, Simon."

"It stinks like piss in here."

"Least we're not out there."

We changed our clothes, leaving our wet things hanging wherever we could; from the splinters of the broken table, the knob of the door, the edge of the window; our shoes turned upside down at the upper edge of the floor where there wasn't any water. I pulled a tee shirt from the pack but it was Simon's, so I sighed and put it back. My nose was running, water dripped from my hair, and I realized I had nothing else dry to wear in the pack besides some underwear and one pair of jeans that were too big for me. I took out Matthew's letters and stacked them flat. Standing barefoot in the rusted water on the floor, I tossed a pair of socks to Simon, who had climbed up onto the bed.

"These are your socks," Simon said, putting them down, ignored, on the torn bedding.

"Wear them anyway."

I left the pack on the table and placed the bundle of Matthew's letters down on the bed next to Simon's feet. My brother scooted himself back and sat up against the rear wall.

Simon was fourteen then. He stood so close to me in size that people who didn't know us usually thought we were twins. So he was the unlucky third step in the clothes chain at our house, and that meant that, except for the shoes, his were almost always too small for him.

I liked to read. I liked drawing. But Simon liked everything physical, and was good at sports and made friends easier than I ever did.

Neither of us had cut our hair in months. We were both smart enough to know that back home we didn't live like other kids. Our mother was always gone, always going to church, and I believed she was embarrassed to be seen with us. Whenever she needed Simon to do something, she'd tell me, like I was some kind of translator or something, or like she couldn't even see him. I know I'd tried to protect him, growing up, and Simon could tell I was doing it, so he'd push back at me, and I'd fight, but I'd never give up on Simon.

And we were smart enough to know we had to stay close. Still, we both played at the game of pretending how opposite we could be; and so it was probably all we could do to tolerate one another as we tried to get somewhere together and alone out on that road. I wondered whether our frail peace would last.

I stood there, my feet cool in the stained water on that peeling floor, listening to the roar of rain, feeling the drips from my hair on my bare shoulders, just watching my little brother act so comfortable as he stretched out across the bed. I pulled my wet hair back and twisted it around into a tail.

The last time we had eaten anything was the day before we left. But we agreed to a rule, Brothers' Rule Number One, that neither of us would ever say he was hungry.

Below the edge of the carcass of the bed, a *Time* magazine sat atop the castings-off of previous tenants, splayed open with curled and desiccated pages. I picked up the magazine, closing it so I could see the cover, moved Matthew's letters to the side, and climbed up onto the bed next to Simon.

"No one's been here for a while, Simon. This is from last October."

I showed the magazine to Simon, who looked at it blankly, shrugging. The cover showed a checkerboard of square pictures, each alternating between the same repeated black-and-white image of

President Richard Nixon sandwiched between color photographs from the war in Vietnam; all of this beneath the banner WHAT IF WE JUST PULL OUT?

"Well, they could have left it a little nicer in here."

The rain continued to roar its drumming on the shell of the trailer.

I thumbed through the magazine. It was like a gift to have found something to read.

"Even if the rain stops soon, maybe we should just stay here for the night and then leave in the morning."

"And then where will we go?" Simon said.

"We already said we'd do this." I sighed. "Dad gets out in two weeks. He's all we got. We should be there."

Our father had been in and out of jail so much that I don't think either of us really could picture what he looked like. This time he was in prison in Arizona. That's what happens to heroin addicts. I guess it's one way of getting clean. Simon and I didn't talk about him much, but now that I look back on what happened to us that summer, maybe it was stupid of me to hold out any hope for things working out for us.

"You're insane, Jonah."

"What else can we do? We got ten dollars between us, and you know that any day they'd be coming to take us away. And most likely we'd end up separated. Then we'd have nothing left."

I had a ten-dollar bill in our pack. I won it months before from a poster contest at school and kept it hidden away, not ever telling any-one it was there, taking it out from time to time to secretly stare at it. Now it was just one of the things we carried or wore that belonged to the small list of everything we owned in the world.

Simon didn't say anything to that. He just sank down lower in his seat on the bed.

I read.

I heard Simon yawn.

"Do you hate her, too?" he asked.

I knew who Simon was talking about. Mother.

"Not really."

"She must hate us," Simon said.

"She does. I think so."

"Why?"

"'Cause we pinned her down there. And she wasn't good at it, so she just quit. That's all. Then Matthew," I said.

The rain pounded, making an angry noise.

"Really?"

"Yeah."

"And you still don't hate her?" Simon said.

"I gave up."

"When you gonna give up on this?" Simon asked. "On me, I mean?"

"Not gonna. So let's not talk about it anymore."

"Brothers' Rule Number Two," Simon said. "Don't be a quitter."

"Are you making that one up mostly for you or for me?"

Simon didn't answer that.

Thunder.

I listened.

And I said, "Sometimes when it rains like this it makes me feel like it's never going to stop. Like the world's coming to an end."

Dear Joneser,

I got my orders today and I'm going to be leaving on the 25th of this month. They're going to send me to Oakland and then I'll find out where I'm going for sure. Maybe they'll just leave me in Oakland (ha ha).

I'm really tired. I wrote four letters before this one, but I didn't want to forget my little brother. I should get some sleep I guess.

Hey.

There's a flight line of choppers outside my window, if you could call it a window. When they're taking off at night and in the day, it's a beautiful sight. They fly right over our window about 15 to 20 feet up. You would love to see that and hear it.

I thought it was funny how you said not to write to Mother till after September cause Dad might get out of jail then, and how Simon just said for me to not get killed. I will try. But you and me know why Dad keeps getting himself put in jail. Don't say anything to Simon.

Good night.

Love,

Matt

I never liked my name, so Matthew always called me Joneser or Brother Jones or something like that.

I liked how he did that. Everyone else just called me *Jonah*.

Simon fell to sleep, propped up against the wall at the back of the trailer, his head tilted over and his body leaned sideways. Eventually he slumped over and his head fell down onto my shoulder. At first I was going to push him off—he'd have done it to me—but I stopped myself and sighed.

I felt like crying. I guess I felt like giving up.

But Simon laid down a rule and if I broke it, that would be like letting him beat me in a fight.

The rain ended quietly before night came.

I fell to sleep.

Simon was already awake when I opened my eyes. It was late in the morning and the air in the trailer was becoming hot and thick when

I heard the soft rubbery thud of something dropping down from the ceiling and hitting the floor below the edge of the bed where we had slept. Then came the scraping-clicking of movement of legs along the linoleum.

"There's a big scorpion over there under that trash, Jonah."

It didn't really register. I sat up, letting my feet down onto the floor, and then, realizing what Simon had said, lifted them back up onto the bed.

"What did you say?"

"I saw a scorpion crawl under that trash there." Simon nodded his chin to show the direction, across the floor, the trash piled up on the other side of the doorway.

"It's really hot in here," I said.

"I think it's late."

I looked down at the floor once more, then swallowed and put my feet down and stood. I felt surrounded by an empire of angry and poisonous bugs, all hiding, watching, waiting to attack. I opened my pack with two fingers, and peered inside to be sure there was nothing alive there. I saw the shine of the pistol's barrel and the rest of our tangled clothes on the bottom, beneath the canteen. I shook out my shoes and slipped my bare feet into them, then cuffed my jeans and tiptoed to the door. When I tried to open it, the knob came right off in my hand and I nearly fell down, backwards, right on the spot where the scorpion was hiding.

"I told you you wouldn't be able to get that open," Simon complained. "Now what are we going to do?"

Sometimes, just the way he said things could make me so mad, and at that moment I wanted to throw that useless metal knob right at his head. But I knew I had to do everything I could to avoid fighting with Simon out on the road, even if he was always pushing at me. We didn't make a rule about it, but I think we both knew we didn't have to say it.

So I took a slow breath and bent to line my eye up with the rotten cavity where the doorknob had been attached. I poked a finger into the grease and rust of the hole, pushing and twisting at what was there, but nothing moved, and the door remained wedged tight.

Simon sat up, pulling straight the dingy tee shirt that had wound around him in his sleep. He was wearing my socks, and from the scattered and muddied papers on the floor he carefully picked his shoes, looking into them and shaking them out before slipping them loosely onto his feet.

I kicked the bottom of the door as hard as I could, denting its tin paneling and causing the top to buckle just a crack. It hurt my foot. I was hot, and so frustrated I wanted to scream.

"You're stupid," Simon said, goading.

And the scorpion emerged, flattening its yellow-brown body beside my foot. I jumped and stamped my heel across its abdomen, sending a spray of thick white slime several inches out on the floor. The stinger twitched and curled like a beckoning finger. I kicked the door again and raised my hand to punch it, but stopped myself. I didn't want to look at Simon. I know I would have hit him if he said anything to me; even—especially—if he said "nice job."

Sweating now, I pried at the top of the door, bending it slightly, but it began cutting into my fingers and would not move. I just stood there, sweat dripping from my neck, running down my chest. I stared at my feet, at the dead thing on the floor next to me, my hair, untied, hanging like blinders so I didn't have to look at Simon.

"We'll have to bust the window," I said.

"Do you want me to do it?"

He might as well have just called me *stupid* again.

I sighed. "I will."

And it felt good to break something, to hear the sound, the release of the glass snapping and popping beneath my foot as I balanced myself atop the splintered table, bracing with both hands pressed up against the smoke-yellowed ceiling of the trailer. I looked up and saw I'd left two sweat-grimed handprints over my head.

I thought maybe someday, someone would know I'd been here, even if they never knew who I was.

We gathered up the wet clothes we had taken off during the storm, and I threw them from the window, far enough so they would not land in the shards of glass on the ground below us.

Simon crawled out first, and I handed him the pack before following.

I brushed myself off and looked up at the sky, squinting, and judged that it was already nearly noon.

We walked out beyond the edge of the trailer's shadow and began picking up our wet clothes.

"We should just leave those here," Simon said, "they're too wet to put in the pack."

"I don't have anything else to wear. Except for some underwear, it's all your stuff in there now."

"Well, why'd you give me your socks then?"

"'Cause I'm stupid."

I stepped through brush, gathering our scattered clothes, shaking them out, draping them across the fold of the pack. I felt like an idiot. I stopped and let the pack fall to the ground, turning back to face my brother standing there in the shade of the crooked trailer.

"You left Matt's letters in there, didn't you?" Simon said.

And I didn't say anything. I just left the pack there in the dirt and walked back to the trailer, and boosted myself up on the naked wheel hub so I could squeeze my way back into the opening of the broken window. I felt the sting of a small cut on my belly when it raked across a tooth of glass. I climbed back into the hot trailer, watched as the blood slowly trickled, thick and dark, staining the

15

top of my jeans. I wiped it away with a rust-stained palm and pressed against the cut to stop the bleeding. It didn't hurt too bad.

I found Matthew's letters stacked on the bed where I had slept, where I had left them. The cut stopped bleeding. Frustrated and sweating again, I picked up the letters and went to the window to hand them out to Simon and just then the door swung open behind me, spilling the brightness of the sun and a few dirt-stained drops of water into the trailer.

Simon had gone around and, smiling, effortlessly, pushed the door open.

Simon loved pushing buttons.

And I felt so stupid and mad I just closed my eyes tight and said, "I swear to God I'm going to kill you today, Simon."

And Simon just stood there in the doorway, a crooked smile on his lips, watching me clutching those papers, sweating in the steaming heat of that crooked trailer, blood smeared like crusted paint across my tightening belly.

"Are those mountains Arizona?"

"No."

We had been walking on that dirt road away from the trailer for two hours. Shirtless in the heat, I tied my torn flannel around my head, draping the sleeves and tails over my burning shoulders. Our clothes, dry now, were stuffed into the pack again, and I stopped, looking back at Simon, who held a hand out like a baseball cap shading his eyes, dressed in jeans that were a good two inches too short and a graying tee shirt that was beginning to show small holes beneath the arms, dragging his feet in the dirt. I removed the canteen and took a mouthful of the summer-warm swill.

"Here."

I held the canteen out.

Simon tilted his head back and drank.

"That's the dirt track to Glenrio out there," I said. "It goes just about all the way to Texas."

"How far is it?"

"I don't know. Do you want to sit down?"

Simon corked the canteen and handed it back to me.

I kicked my shoes off, pushing my feet around in the warm sandy dirt of the road. It felt good, dry. I sat, legs crossed in front of me, and opened the pack. As Simon lowered himself to the ground to sit in the small shade I cast, I took a pencil and my comp book from the pack and began making my marks, scrawling my words.

"What's that?" Simon asked.

"I'm making a map."

"Of how to get to Arizona?"

"No." I said, "Of where we came from."

I kept drawing, writing notes beside certain marks: where the horse died, the trailer, the streambed. "In case we die out here and someone finds us."

Simon stretched a leg out, kicking up dirt.

"I'm not going to die."

"Okay," I said. "I'm not planning on it either."

"Then why are you making the map?"

I squeezed the pencil in my sweating grip. I almost wanted to break it.

"Did you mean it, Jonah?"

"What?" I said.

"When you said you wanted to kill me." He sounded scared, but I knew he was just testing me.

I stopped writing.

"I'm sorry, Simon. Sometimes you just make me so mad. You make me feel so stupid."

"You don't have to get so mad at all those things," Simon said. "About Matt. About Mother. Dad. There's nothing we can do."

Simon shrugged.

I sighed. "Well, if there was something, we sure didn't do it. Anyway, you said you hated me yesterday."

"That was yesterday. I don't hate you yet today."

"None of this is my fault."

"Do you think I don't know that?" And Simon leaned back, propping his loose shoulders up with his arms locked behind him, fingers scooping dirt beneath his palms. "Jonah, I'm really hungry."

He broke the first rule.

I sighed and waved my arm out at the road in front of us. "We have ten dollars, Simon. Pick any restaurant you see. And you broke your own stupid rule."

And I thought Simon would start crying, but he just looked up and pointed away in the distance and said, "I pick that one there," pointing nowhere, really, but when I looked down the road to where he was pointing, I could see the dust kicking up in the distance behind us, trailing like smoke, a reversed wave like the tail on a scorpion from a black car that was following the same road we were sitting on.

Just our luck.

gravity

Mister Jones,

I'm finally here. It took 18 hours. It rained last night. All it did was thunder once and before you could blink everything was soaked, it's really weird. It's really hot here, and it's wintertime. I don't think Hell is as hot as it is here. Right after I ate chow I went outside and in five minutes I was soaked.

About a week ago they mortared the airstrip here and killed 6 guys and wounded 14, but that doesn't happen often. Not every day or nothing.

Last night I went to a spa. I went in the steam room and it was so hot I could barely breathe. Then I went in the cold sauna bath then the hot sauna bath, then I took a cool shower and got a massage by a good-looking Vietnamese girl.

I like the Army a lot better here than in the States. They told me to tell you about hoax telephone calls and letters about my dying or deserting or something. A lot of people get stuff like that I guess.

But don't be scared. I don't think I am. I haven't seen or heard anything yet other than the strangeness of this place. It even smells weird. I bet you can even smell it on this letter. It smells like a funeral home.

It took me 18 hours to get here. It will take the mail 8 days to get to you.

Well I don't have anything else to say, so bye for now.

Love,

Matt

The car rolled toward us.

Thunderclouds balled black in the sky above.

"The monsoon rains are going to come again today, I think."

The car was a 1940 Lincoln Cabriolet, black and white with broad whitewall tires. Its top was down, and, as it neared, crunching and kicking back the dirt of the road, I saw a man at the wheel and a pretty yellow-haired girl sitting in the front, and there was also what appeared to be a third person sitting bolt-upright in the backseat.

It was as out of place in that desert as a sailboat would have been, and it was the kind of car you knew had to carry stories with it, but I had no intention of finding out what those stories told.

"Let's start walking," I said. "Just don't even look at them."

"We should ask them for a ride."

"No." I put my head down like I didn't even know or care about that car coming up alongside us. I began walking forward, just looking at the ground, listening to our feet, the scattering sounds of tires on the gravel and dirt of the road.

I warned Simon again, "Don't even look at them."

So I just concentrated on not paying that car any attention. I could hear Simon following along, scooting his feet in the rocks and dirt. And it wasn't until later, until it was too late for both of us, that I found out Simon was sticking a thumb out to beg a ride.

The car swerved out, passing us, giving us a wide share of the road. The driver never turned to look at us, but my eyes were drawn to the girl. I don't know why, but I couldn't stop myself from looking across at her as she sailed by us on that road, her hair swirling wildly in the wind, eyes shaded behind black glasses. And I could see she was watching us, her head turning farther around so she could look at us through the haze of rising dust as she passed. And as the car receded before me, the girl waved her open hands imploringly, saying something to the driver, and twisted around back over the seat and smiled at me and my brother before the car came to a stop a hundred yards in front of us.

Simon slid his hand in his pocket.

I stopped walking and watched.

The car's doors swung open, and both riders stood in the road, looking back at us standing there, watching them.

"They look like hippies," Simon whispered.

"They probably think we do, too."

I looked at my brother, but he kept his eyes fixed down the road.

Simon straightened himself, flicking his hair back over his shoulders with both hands.

The driver was thin, shorter than me, and had long and wavy black-brown hair that nearly reflected the sunlight. His face was covered with hair, beard untrimmed, and he wore low-cut bell-bottoms and an unbuttoned patchwork vest with no shirt beneath it, a fishing-line string of beads hanging down into the black hairs on his chest. Except for the uneven beard, he didn't look too old, maybe eighteen, maybe twenty. I guessed the girl was even younger than that.

She was taller than the driver, hair windblown and light, wearing jeans torn at each knee, and the sunglasses, and a tight pink tee shirt with three buttons on top, all unfastened.

They were walking toward us; Simon, squinting in the glare and dust at the driver, the car, the strange metal thing sticking up from the backseat, and me, dumbly mesmerized by the glint of light from the black lenses on the girl's glasses in the hazy fog above the roadway, the way she moved inside that pink shirt.

"Hey, Tom and Huck, aren't you a long ways from home?" the driver said, showing yellowed teeth and pivoting his head, birdlike, from me to Simon and back to me.

"Not that far," I said.

"Where are you boys going?" the girl asked.

"Nowhere."

"Arizona," Simon said.

"Either way," the driver said, punctuating his speech with the clink of a Zippo lighter he flicked open and shut with his thumb, "Arizona. Nowhere. They're both pretty far."

"Mitch," the girl said, "we could give them a ride."

I pulled the shirt away from my head. I was sweating, my shoulders and back were sunburned, and the air felt cool in my damp hair.

The driver looked right at me and said, "Do you want a ride?"

I shot a look at Simon, hoping to stop him from talking, but I knew it was already too late for that and Simon immediately said, "Sure! Thanks!"

And then Simon looked at me, grinning, and nodded in the direction of the girl, and the way she watched me made me feel like I was some kind of captured specimen. And Simon whispered to me, "Now go draw *that* on your stupid map."

The driver swept his arm in the direction of the open door.

"My name's Mitch," he said. "And this is Lilly. And the backseat's a little small 'cause of Don being with us, but you boys are pretty skinny, I'd say."

"I'm Simon Vickers. And the one there who doesn't want to talk is my brother Jonah. How far can you take us?"

"We're going to California, so I guess anywheres between here and there," Mitch said.

I didn't know what to do. I felt like I was being swept along by something that had already gone too far. I knew I didn't like Mitch from the moment I saw him, but there was something about that girl that just practically dragged me along with my brother's lead.

So I balled up my shirt and stuffed it down inside the pack, and Simon, acting so comfortable and relaxed, said, "We're practically starved to death."

He glanced at me. I guess it wasn't really breaking the rule to say it to someone else.

Lilly brushed her hair back and pulled her glasses away from her face, just an inch, so I could see her eyes, and said, "You just throw your bag in the trunk." Then she paused and I could hear her breathe, "Jonah Vickers. I'll get you boys something to eat."

I'd heard the stories about sailors who were lured onto jagged rocks by sirens. They must have sounded just like her when she said *Jonah Vickers*, I guess.

And I knew we shouldn't get into that car, but at the same time I wanted to say something to her, at least to say thanks, but I couldn't force anything out of my mouth and I just followed Mitch and Lilly as they led Simon and me toward that idling black convertible.

The thing I saw in the backseat was a man, nearly life-size and made from hammered tin, standing upright on a pedestal and holding a lance. He was clad with incongruous armor, an inverted plate of a hat tilted back on his head.

"That's Don," Mitch said. "He's been riding with us ever since we found him in Mexico. I hope you guys don't mind sharing the backseat with him. He doesn't say much."

I knew the statue was supposed to be a version of Don Quixote, and wondered why, across the sculpture's face, and fixed upon it with bands of black electrical tape, was a photograph, cut from a glossy black-and-white magazine page, a mask, the face of a man with black-rimmed glasses.

Lilly held before us both a feast—a closed box of Nilla cookies and a bag of Fritos.

"How about these?" she said, holding out the food for me, the colors nearly blurring my starved eyes.

My mouth hung open and I reached out for the cookies, fumbling, and dropped the box on the road in front of my feet.

"Ha!" Mitch laughed. "Isn't gravity a wonderful thing? It makes everything you could ever want drop right at your feet. What could be more convenient than that?"

I looked at him, and then bent over and picked up the box, saying, "Sorry," and thinking, *Simon, we should get the hell out of here.*

"This is just like *The Wizard of Oz*," Simon said. "Us being lost and following this road, and along comes the Tin Man."

Lilly pushed the seat on her side forward and said, "Come on. Get in before we run out of gas again."

Mitch shut his door and the car's wheels spun forward in the dirt. Simon and I sat on either side of the metal man with the paper mask, eating vanilla wafers by the handfuls.

Mitch began singing, "We're off to see the wizard . . ." and then stopped and said, "You boys aren't going to make me sing alone, are you?"

And he began the song again, this time with Simon joining in, smiling at me, trying to get me to sing, too, as bits of cookie fell out of his mouth and onto his lap.

"Oh brother." I rolled my eyes.

And neither Simon nor Mitch knew the words to the song, so

they just kept on repeating the first line over and over until I suppose they both got tired of singing it.

Even on that dry dirt road, in the heat of August, I was impressed by a certain remarkable beauty in this land, the slope of the road, the grasses gone almost white in the summer, the unexplainable rocks tilted every direction but flat, the redness of the mountains in the distance rising above the brush and occasional tree, the road so straight and wind-worn, the dry breath of the air cooling my skin, blowing the sweat-damp hair under my arm that lay bent across the rim of that open-top convertible while the car ground its way forward upon the gravel of our path.

I'd been this way before, but never like this. Not with Simon, alone, and knowing we were never going back. It felt like I was seeing the desert for the first time in my life.

I have to write this down. What this feels like to be out here with Simon, and those two up front that I'm not sure about.

I stared at her and listened to the road.

Our bellies were full. We drank warm 7UP and threw the bottles out over the back of the car when we were finished, and Mitch turned on the radio, but I could hardly hear it in the rush of wind through my hair, the crackling AM station playing "All Right Now," between the spastic bursts of static from the hills and dips in the road.

And Mitch just said, "Why?"

I looked at Simon. I thought he was only pretending to be asleep. He leaned against the side of the tin man so comfortably, the way he'd leaned against me the night before in the rain, in that trailer.

Mitch asked it again.

And I knew he was talking to me.

I said, "Why what?"

"Why are you going to Arizona? Who are you running away from?"

"We're not running away from anyone," I said. "We're trying to find someone."

"Well, you definitely found someone, man."

Lilly laughed.

"Our dad. He's in Arizona."

"This road go to Tucumcari?" Mitch had a slight accent; I thought he probably came from Texas; the plates on the car were from there, anyway.

"Yes."

"Hope we get there before we run out of gas," Lilly said.

"Thanks anyway. I mean for the ride," I said, and she turned back and looked at me, the faintest smile on her mouth.

And then I said, "Or hope we get there before it starts raining again."

"Why's he in Arizona when you're practically in Texas?" Lilly asked.

"It's a long story."

"So's this road," she said.

"Not that long."

Lilly turned around, propping her legs up on the bench of the white leather seat beside Mitch, letting her arm swing over the top, dropping her hand so smoothly to come to rest on my knee. For just a moment, I thought, she flashed a bit of anger and it nearly scared me, but I let it go.

"Look, sweetie," she said, and I thought, how condescending for her to talk like that when she was probably no more than seventeen herself, "if you don't want to talk, that's okay. I was just trying to be nice."

Then she rubbed my leg and turned back around, fixing her face forward.

I was embarrassed. I moved my hand to the place on my knee where hers had been. And I thought, *She's doing something to you. Don't let it happen. Don't be a sucker.*

Mitch didn't say anything, and Simon's eyes were still closed, but I knew my brother was awake and had been taking it all in. He did that kind of stuff all the time.

"My mother went off with someone and never came back. Our dad's in jail. He's supposed to get out soon, maybe he already is. I don't know," I said. "Our brother's in the Army. In Vietnam."

I watched Simon. He twitched like he'd been stung when I told Mitch about Matthew.

Mitch whistled.

"What's your dad in jail for?"

"You don't have to say, Jonah," Lilly said.

I didn't want to tell him anyway. I was mad at myself for telling them as much as I did.

I felt stupid.

I lowered myself into the seat, my left knee scraping against the tin statue, and Lilly turned around and looked at me again.

"So there. That's our whole story. We're all alone, and sometimes it's like we can't hardly stand each other anymore."

I didn't want to say it. I felt stupid, and hated myself for doing it. I wanted to get out of that car.

And I saw Simon's eye pop open for a moment.

"I'm sorry, Jonah," she said. "Let's forget about the whole thing. They're probably melted, but we got a bag of M&M's. Do you want some?"

"M&M's don't melt," Simon said flatly, hair hanging down in his face and trailing back in the wind, his eyes still closed.

"Thirteen," Mitch said.

"No. I'm fourteen," Simon said.

"Not you," Mitch said. "There." And he pointed at the sky. "There's thirteen vultures flying there."

I didn't say anything, but looked at the circling birds, overlapping, some blurring behind the others, wondering how Mitch knew there were thirteen of them.

"Mitch counts things automatically," Lilly said. "Just by looking at things, he can instantly tell you how many are there. It's pretty amazing. He's never wrong."

"How do you know he's never wrong?" I asked.

"You should test him sometime," Lilly said.

"Okay."

"You can test me, kid. Just don't try to mess with me about it. But you can test me, anytime. Sometime when we're not in the middle of a bunch of nothing." Mitch said, "Hey, Lil, would you grab me a cigarette?"

Mitch steered the car with his propped left knee and held his lighter out over the top of the steering wheel.

"Watch this, guys," he said, and with one hand he made a sweeping motion that simultaneously snapped the lighter open, spun its wheel, and produced a flame, ringing the bell of the cap as he did.

"Cool!" Simon said.

Lilly opened the glove box, and, leaning forward to watch her, I could see a shiny chrome-plated gun tucked behind two crumpled packs of cigarettes and wads of tissue. I was certain Lilly knew I was watching, could see the gun, but she just nonchalantly left the box open and went about lighting a Kool for Mitch and passed it across to him.

"Do either of you two smoke?" she asked.

"No," I said.

"I do," Simon said, putting his hand up on the back of the driver's seat.

I couldn't figure out what Simon was trying to do. Maybe, I thought, he was just trying to look cool in front of these two. Maybe he could tell I didn't trust Mitch, or he didn't like the way I kept my eyes on that girl, I don't know. Either way, it was just Simon being Simon, trying to push my buttons. Because I knew that while he may have smoked a cigarette or two back home with his friends in Los Rogues, he didn't actually "smoke."

And I watched as he took the lit cigarette from Lilly and leaned back in his seat and started smoking it, saying, "Thank you, Lilly," as she lit another for herself.

So I scooted over, and leaned my head around the chest of Don Quixote, peering around his lance and bringing my face just close enough so Simon could hear me say, "Pretty soon, I'm going to beat the crap out of you if you don't cut this out."

"I don't care," Simon mouthed, voicelessly, and turned away, exhaling a long cloud of smoke into the rushing air, tilting his head back against the seat top and slumping his shoulders. "'Cause you better watch out for yourself," he whispered. "That girl's messing with you. I can tell."

"I like the kid," Mitch said, tugging at his greasy beard between drags. "He's cool."

And part of me knew, because it was my job to be the grown-up one, that all of Simon's tests and jabs weren't pointed at me, they were aimed at the world and he had every right to be mad about what happened to us and how we were both so abandoned and adrift. But part of me wanted to be mad, too. I didn't like having to be the grown-up.

Still, I wasn't about to ever listen to Simon, or take any advice from him for that matter, when it came to a girl.

The music on the radio faded to nothing but epileptic sparks of static.

In the evening, before we came within five miles of Tucumcari, Mitch pulled the Lincoln off the dirt road, following another weed-grown track at a gray-rotted sign that read DRINKWATER FLATS. That's when Mitch told us that we would spend the night there and go get some gas and food in town the next morning.

"How many letters in 'Drinkwater Flats'?" Simon blurted out. I could tell he was counting, chewing his lip and rolling out his fingers on his lap, and Mitch instantly said, "Fifteen. Too easy."

Lilly laughed as Mitch slowed the car and parked it. "I told you."

Drinkwater Flats was a wide clearing in the brush at the base of a steep-sided mountain that seemed to be nothing more than three enormous red boulders tossed together in some ancient calamity. Mitch had stopped the car alongside the black mouth of a well made from a circle of stones piled about two feet high in most places. The sun was gone, the sky, cloudless, dimming above our heads as the first stars appeared.

"I want to see if there's any water in there," Mitch said. "The car could probably use some."

He opened the Lincoln's trunk and pulled out a coil of yellow rope. I followed beside him, and saw that the inside of the trunk was packed with suitcases and a cardboard shoe box sealed with masking tape.

"Can I get our pack?" I said. "I want to put my shirt on."

Mitch looked at me. Simon had gone off to the edge of the clearing, turned away. He was peeing in the bushes.

"You know, that war's a stupid thing," Mitch said, handing our pack over to me.

"I know."

30

"I hope you and your brother find what you're looking for."

In the entire course of time that I knew Mitch, that was the only thing he ever said to me that sounded close to being human. I know that now.

And for just a moment I thought Mitch was being sincere, that he really cared about me and Simon. But it was only just a moment, because I already had this nagging sense that Mitch was dangerous. And he had eyes like a statue's; like nothing that ever passed before them would really make him care about anything, or have feelings for anyone.

At least, that's what I saw when I looked at him.

"We have a canteen in the pack. You could use it."

"Good. I was thinking about tying Piss-kid over there onto the rope and lowering him down."

Mitch smiled, big dirty teeth. I didn't know if he was joking or not.

Simon came back, buttoning his jeans.

"Let's see what we have left to eat," Lilly said.

"Can I have another cigarette?" Simon asked.

"Sure, handsome."

I shook my head and rolled my eyes as Simon casually took a cigarette from Lilly.

The water in the well was good and cool. Once Mitch had filled the Lincoln's radiator, I took the canteen after him and drank, a little repulsed at sharing it with him. Simon and Lilly stood at the edge of darkness, the orange eyes of their cigarette tips winking in the nighttime, close together as the two whispered to each other.

I tried to guess at what it was that brought her along on this ride through the desert with Mitch, but everything I imagined didn't make sense. I could feel, in the way she talked and looked at him, the way she'd slide away an inch or two on that seat if Mitch looked at her or said anything, that there was something about him that she didn't trust, either; that she was keeping her distance. But it seemed like she was counting on him for something, too.

I wanted to ask her.

I wanted to talk to her so bad. But I just watched those fireflies of cigarette ends off in the distance.

There was no moon, no light, no sound out there on the flats, and the stars were thick and crowded splatters of white. The four of us sat on the edge of the well and ate, and Mitch found a Mexican radio station that broadcast only at night. It played "American Woman," and Mitch sang along, but kept changing the words to "American Lilly," and Lilly laughed and told him to quit it, but I don't think she meant it.

Mitch and Simon had taken Don Quixote out of the backseat, and he stood, like a guard, at the side of the Lincoln, his metal just catching the dimmest reflections from the night.

I gulped and looked at the girl.

"So who are *you* running away from?" I asked.

"Oh man!" Mitch laughed. "Everyone is after me and Lilly."

"Why?" I asked. "Is that car stolen or something?"

"That's funny," Mitch said, but I could see, even in the dark, he wasn't smiling when I asked it.

"That's Mitch's daddy's car," Lilly said. "He didn't exactly say Mitch could take it, but it's not exactly stolen. Mitch is just a spoiled rich boy, aren't you, Mitch?"

Mitch's eyes were cold. And he was looking at me when he said, "Lilly has a thing for poor boys, don't you, Lilly?"

Lilly shifted and looked away from Mitch, saying, "Jonah. That's quite a name."

I sighed.

"I suppose there will be all kinds of hell to pay if we don't get you all the way to Nineveh," Mitch said, twisting his mouth into a grin. His eyes still looked dead, still watched me.

I was sick of all the Bible stories, anyway, and how many times people would make the belly-of-the-whale jokes to me like I'd never heard them before.

"I don't think you have anything to worry about, Mitch," I said. "And besides . . ." But I didn't finish what I was thinking to say, that they'd probably end up throwing me overboard.

Simon cleared his throat. "Is she your wife?"

"That's even funnier," Mitch said. "Lilly? She doesn't belong to anyone. And good luck to anyone who catches her. She's pregnant, besides."

Lilly didn't say anything.

I looked at her. I guess I'd never really known a girl who was about my age and pregnant, too. I could see by her face that what Mitch said was true, and that it made her sad, too. And I felt sorry for her and wondered, again, why she'd ever gotten into that car with him in the first place.

"Is it yours?" Simon said.

"That's none of your business, Simon," I said. I couldn't believe my brother would have the guts to say something like that.

"Mine? Ha! Hell no."

I thought about that gun I saw in the glove box, how strange this man was, and I found myself wishing more and more I could have found some way to stop my foolish brother from getting into that Lincoln; and I worried that maybe we were trapped with him now just like Lilly was. Maybe.

And I thought, *Well, I've got a gun, too.*

There was a green flash above us, lighting up all of our faces and casting sudden shadows against the colorless ground.

33

A ball of burning flame tore through the sky. At first, I thought it was a plane crashing down right on top of us.

"Look at that!" I said, pointing.

"A meteor!" Simon turned suddenly, seeing the object, flaring so brightly and shedding little white-hot spores as it fell.

The thing hit the ground so close to us, making a hissing pop as it came to rest in the brush not more than a hundred feet from where we sat at the edge of the well.

Mitch stood up and jogged in the direction of where the rock landed, and we all followed, Simon in the rear, dragging and scooting his noisy feet.

The rock had landed in a cluster of sagebrush, and the splintered twigs and spines smelled like the incense from some ritual. It made an obvious circle in its impact. Mitch leaned over the meteorite glistening in the heap of brush like polished and smoothed metal. The thing was oblong, just the width of his hand, which he passed over the object, and Lilly said, "I don't think you should touch it."

"This is like one of those outer space movies," Simon said.

"It feels warm," Mitch said.

And Simon pushed his way between me and Lilly and bent down and scooped up the rock, hefting it from one hand to another.

"It's heavy," he said. "And it *is* hot."

"Gravity," Mitch said. I could see the white in his eyes as he looked from Simon to me. His mouth was straight, turned down at the edges, like a dog when it growls in the back of its throat. "See what I mean?"

Of course I was thin enough that I could sleep fairly comfortably bent up across the floor in the back of the Lincoln. I had to accept the spot when Simon took over the length of the seat in the night when I climbed out over the trunk to go pee. No one could ever get fat at our house. I stood away from the car, next to the metal man, and faced off into the darkness in the same direction as the black-and-white image that was taped across the statue's face. So when I climbed back in and saw Simon stretched out across the white leather of the backseat, the shining blob of metal from the sky lying next to him and looking so much like one of those Easter Island faces, I thought that I would finally have it out with him and get it over with, shove him back into his place where he belonged, but Mitch and Lilly were sleeping in the front seat, each propped in opposite directions against the doors, and so I gave up the idea, because I didn't want to mess around with waking them up. I squeezed down onto the floor behind the front seats, Simon's feet, still in my socks, dangling just above my face as I shut my eyes and tried to forget about it, thinking, *I know Simon is awake and knows exactly what he's doing.*

I guess I stayed like that for about twenty minutes, thinking about things, unable to sleep. I heard the driver's door open and felt the seat rise as Mitch got out of the car. I kept my eyes shut, in case he looked at me, because I was a little bit scared of him, but mostly because I didn't want to talk to him if he noticed I wasn't sleeping.

Mitch whispered something, but I couldn't make it out. Since my head was so close to the open door, though, I could tell that he began to close the door, then pulled it back open, then pushed it in again, over and over, without actually shutting the door the whole way.

Mitch counted in a raspy whisper, "Nine. Ten. Eleven."

I wondered if Simon heard what was happening, but he didn't move at all, or give any sign that he wasn't asleep. Then Mitch walked around the car twice, came back, and pulled the door all the way open.

He said, "One."

I heard the crunching sound of his feet as he walked away toward the well, still talking to himself.

"I bet you don't recognize him. It's my father. He doesn't even look like a person anymore, does he, Lil?"

Then he said, "Well, he's not." And I heard Lilly shift in her seat a little, like the sound was maybe waking her up, but then she was still again. But I wondered if she'd heard Mitch say her name and was pretending to be asleep, too, just so he'd leave her alone.

"Does he? Oh. It's Jonah. It's that boy named *Jonah*."

I felt my pulse speed up when he said my name, like he was looking at me or something. Like he knew I was awake.

"Mitch, we should stop for those poor boys, she said. She likes poor boys. Poor and stupid."

dumb kids

Poor boys.

Piss.

He pees on the rocks on the side of the well, looks back over his shoulder at the quiet car, the blond head in the front seat, but no heads in the back. *The poor boys must be laying down together. Dumb kids. That Piss-kid should have thought twice before sticking his thumb out while the whore had her eyes on them.*

He walks back to the car, whispers, "Hey, Lilly, wake up."

She stirs and says, "Leave me alone, Mitch."

He glances over the seat behind her. *The dumb kids are asleep.*

"Those stupid kids should have never got in the car with us."

"Go to sleep, Mitch."

He laughs a whispered hiss.

rule

Mitch walked around the car two more times before he got back in. I didn't know what to think about the stuff I'd heard him saying and doing, almost like it was some kind of weird dream. Lilly didn't move at all, or say anything else. Eventually, I heard Mitch begin to snore, and I opened my eyes and stared up at the stars until I finally went to sleep, too.

Everyone woke before I did. I opened my eyes when I heard them at the well filling up the canteen at the end of Mitch's rope. Stiffly, I lifted myself from the floor of the car.

Simon and Mitch were standing there, shirtless, washing themselves with handfuls of water poured from the canteen. Lilly had changed her clothes and her hair was wet, and I wondered, envious, if my brother had been watching her do that.

"Here," Mitch said, pulling the canteen up from the well-bottom again, "we're washing up and then we're going to go get a real breakfast in town."

"Simon and me have ten dollars. I guess that's enough for breakfast," I said, yawning. I took my shirt off, then poured the canteen over my head and bent forward, watching the water run from my hair to splatter as mud at my feet.

"Aw hell!" Mitch said, and jerked. When he untied the rope, it slipped from his hand, and the weight of its length sucked the yellow cord into the shadowed depths of the well.

I dropped to my knees in the mud and caught the snaking end before it disappeared into the black hole.

"Gravity, Mitch," Simon said, grinning, as Mitch, expressionless, without so much as a "thank you" took the yellow rope from my hand and began coiling it around his elbow.

I brushed the mud away from my jeans, rubbed the water into my eyes, and stretched. It felt good, the air dry and warm on that clear morning. I shook my hands and arms off and stood, watching Lilly across the well, brushing her yellow hair, tilting her head from side to side, the contour of her body showing faintly beneath the gauze shirt she wore as the sunlight shone through. And in that light, the sparse trees that sprang up around the creases in the red boulders of the shading hill looked so green behind her.

"Is something wrong?" she said to me, noticing that I was staring.

"No. Sorry." I looked away, reddening. "I'm just groggy, I guess."

"Did you sleep good?" Lilly asked.

"Yeah. I did."

Simon and Mitch lifted the statue back into the car as I buttoned my shirt and tucked it in. Simon's meteorite sat on the backseat behind Don Quixote, and when we had all gotten in and Mitch began to drive back out toward the dirt road to Tucumcari, I asked, "Why is that face taped on the head of the statue?"

"Ha!" Mitch said. "Don't you know who that is, man? That's Henry Kissinger."

Simon leaned over to me and said, "Yeah, dummy. Don't you

know that? Henry something." And then he reached across and touched Lilly on the shoulder and asked, "Are there any more cigarettes left?"

And when she handed Simon a lit cigarette, I pulled him backwards by the stretched-out collar on his tee shirt, pinning his back against the sharp edges on Don Quixote's shield. I pressed my mouth right up into his hair, against his ear, so close that for just an instant I thought I smelled the stink of our home, our sweat-stained pillows on him.

"Why do you think you have to get even with me, Simon? What did I do to you? I been putting up with your crap ever since we've been alone and it's not going to last much longer, so enjoy your smoke."

And Lilly turned and scolded us, "What are you two doing?"

I released my grip on my brother's shirt and said, "Nothing."

"He's just being stupid," Simon said and exhaled a drag of smoke.

Then Simon straightened and turned away, smoking his cigarette as he faced the blur of the landscape rushing past us on that morning. I could tell he was about to start crying, and I couldn't really decide whether I wanted to say I was sorry and hug him, or to punch him in the face, so I said nothing and sank down in my seat, picked up that fallen piece of metallic rock, and rubbed its burned and glassy smoothness in my hands.

"Brothers' Rule Number Three," I said. "We are *not* going to fight."

Simon kept his eyes on the road and said, "Let's see who breaks that one first."

map

Hey Jones,

Sorry I haven't written in a while. And, hey . . . don't look at the pictures in here yet, I need to tell you about them, so hang on. I just finished eating a "lurp." That's dehydrated food. They say it will make me fat in a few months if I keep eating them, but I doubt it. I got so skinny since I came here.

Anyway, the first picture is of my track. That's what we call our Dusters. Tracks. I know you probably think it looks like a tank, but Dusters are so much smaller and faster than a regular tank, which is good because they don't get stuck in mud and can go through just about anything. The picture's not that good cause it was raining pretty hard there. My track is named "Till Death Do Us Part." The arrow that I drew on the picture is where the VC attacked from last week, but our Duster wiped them out. The next pictures are of the bodies after the attack.

Don't think I'm turning into a sadist or anything. I'm just telling you how it is.

My best buddy here, Scotty (he's from Flagstaff, AZ) told me I shouldn't tell you about the shooting around here because it would be bad for you. I think it would be better if you knew where I was at. He *tells his mom we got an easy job and he never hears rifle fire. Now, if something happens to him it would be worse for her. Right?*

Anyway, don't tell Simon or show him the pictures. This is just between you and me since you're the man in the house now.

But, Joneser, I can feel myself slipping a little.

I learned a few Vietnamese words, but most of them are dirty so we can cuss out the Vietnamese. Even though the RVNs are friendly forces, you have to keep your eye on them. A couple of them are pretty nice. A 2nd Lieutenant gave me one of his insignias.

I try to keep away from them, though, because if a Vietnamese officer invites us to eat with them, we're not supposed to turn it down. They feed their guests food which is supposed to be an honor to accept. If you don't accept it, it's an insult, and if you do accept it you'll be sick for two weeks. They serve things like fish heads and chicken heads with the eyes and brains still in them. At least, that's what I heard, so I'm keeping my distance. I prefer dealing with the ones who shoot at me.

Well, I'm going to sleep now.

Say hello to Mom for me.

Bye.

Love,

Matthew

In the early part of the morning.

Before the heat burns the air.

You can see the things that move in the desert.

The dirt road finally gave way to a crusty, paved stretch of utility road that ran south of the interstate, and here we passed among scattered houses, nothing more than scarred and gray plywood shacks with weeds growing up in the middle of their yawning vacant and black doorways.

I stared straight ahead through the windshield, over Mitch's shoulder, my eyes occasionally and helplessly drawn to the girl sitting on the passenger's side. And I wondered about her—she was too pretty, too young, to be riding in that car alone with a guy like Mitch. I wondered if I would ever have the guts to ask.

And I was embarrassed when she caught me staring, again, dazed. She smiled.

"Have you ever been to California, Jonah?" she asked.

I looked down at my feet, feeling the heat rising in my face.

"I've never been anywhere," I said.

"Well, I've never been there, either," Lilly answered. "Maybe you should go. I think you're good-looking enough to be a movie star. Has anyone ever told you that?"

I went red in an instant. I looked at her. She had taken the sunglasses away from those blue eyes. I couldn't speak, felt as though I were choking.

"Oh yeah!" Simon laughed. "All the girls on the beach say that to Jonah when he walks by."

And Simon reached across the metal statue and pinched at my face. I swatted his arm away.

"Simon's an idiot. We've never seen no beach," I said, angry.

"Are you trying to make me jealous, Lil?" Mitch asked. "You going to sit right here and start flirting with that boy in the backseat?"

Mitch smiled, but I could tell there was an edge of annoyance in his tone.

"I'm not flirting, Mitch," she said coldly.

"It sounds like it to me," Simon goaded.

Mitch gripped the wheel tightly with both hands.

"Control yourself, Lilly. The poor boy's only got ten dollars and he wants to eat."

It sounded like Mitch was calling her a whore, and I looked at them both, but I still couldn't tell what was going on between them. And I thought, she probably couldn't tell what was going on between me and Simon, either, or why we ended up together out there on that road.

Simon leaned around Don Quixote and whispered, "See? I told you she's screwing with you."

"So are you, Simon."

Lilly stared at Mitch. It looked like she was about to say something, but she held herself back.

And then she said, sweetly, "I thought *you* were going to pay for breakfast, Mitch."

Lilly smiled and brushed her hand back over the seat and patted me and Simon on our knees.

Simon grinned at me and mouthed, silently, "You're stupid."

I inhaled deeply, turning to look back out over the hood of the Lincoln, thinking about the rule I'd just made, and how hungry I was. "Well, one day we might go to California," I said, "but we've just got to get to Arizona for right now."

"We?" Simon said and laughed. "Can I have another cigarette, Lilly?"

"Sure, sweetie."

Simon leaned forward and smiled at me, half closing his eyes as he mouthed "sweetie," stroking the tin man's leg. I clenched my fists in my lap, digging my nails into the flesh of my palms, trying to make it hurt, trying not to explode.

"And if this was *The Wizard of Oz*," Simon continued, "Jonah would get the part of the flying monkey, anyway."

Mitch laughed.

"I like that," he said. "And who would the rest of us be, Simon?"

Simon scratched his head.

"Lilly would be the good witch . . . the real pretty one. You'd be the wizard, Mitch. We all know who this guy would be," and Simon rang a slap on Don Quixote's flat and hollow chest. "And I'd be the dog. Arf! Arf!"

Mitch and Lilly both laughed.

And just then I saw the pointed ears of a scrawny desert coyote as the animal ignorantly stepped right out onto the road ahead of the car. I leaned forward.

"Look out, Mitch," I said.

The coyote had made it to the midpoint of the road, and Mitch could easily have avoided hitting it, but he pressed his foot into the accelerator. The force pushed me back against the seat.

Mitch said something, mumbling to himself, his eyes focused on the coyote.

The tattered-looking animal pivoted its face around slowly, and Mitch veered the car to the left, so slightly, taking aim just enough to be certain he'd plow the cowering dog over.

Simon looked up. We heard the slap of the hunching coyote when its skull struck metal beneath the Lincoln, and felt the percussive thumping through the floorboards as the tires rolled over the animal's body.

"Well, hello, Mister Coyote," Mitch said, "how nice to run into you this morning!" He exploded in spasms of laughter.

It was horrible. I looked across at Simon, who smiled, his mouth hanging open, eyes wide in amazement and admiration.

"Oh, Mitch!" Lilly said in a tone like she was chiding a mischievous cousin.

"What?" Mitch said, exaggerating his pleading, still laughing. "It wasn't my fault. That thing obviously wanted to commit suicide."

"That was bitchin'!" Simon cheered, turning around to gaze at the butchery in the road behind as Mitch slowed the Lincoln to a stop. He opened his door and stood beside the car, facing back down the road.

"Canine meets V-twelve," he said. "The cruel truth of natural selection."

Simon stood up on the backseat and leapt over the door, not waiting for Lilly to even ask if he wanted to get out.

Mitch and Simon walked back to where the dead animal lay in the road.

I was alone with her in the car.

"He did it on purpose," I said.

"Of course he did," Lilly said, smiling at me. "It's just his way of blowing off some steam. I could tell I made him pretty mad just now."

"You did?"

"Or, maybe you did," she laughed. "I don't know. But when Mitch starts talking to himself like that, something weird always happens."

"I'll remember that," I said.

"Anyway," she said, sliding across the seat to Mitch's side and getting out of the car. "It was just a dog. You coming, Jonah?"

Lilly touched my arm and tilted the seat forward for me. And she held my hand as I stepped out onto the road. Mitch glanced back at us. Simon was already studying the carcass on the asphalt.

I caught Lilly's eye.

"Thank you," I said.

"For what?"

"Helping me out of the car, I guess."

She smiled. "Any time."

"And 'cause no one ever told me that before, either."

"I wasn't fooling, Jonah," she said. "I never really met a boy like you."

"What do you mean?"

She turned away and began walking toward where Simon and Mitch were standing.

I swallowed the lump in my throat and thought about what my brother said about her screwing with me.

The coyote was nearly torn in half at the middle, the two sections turned, ridiculously, in opposite directions, hind paws stretched toward the shining tin statue of Don Quixote, forepaws splayed out on the road, pointing as though offering testimony to which direction the murderer attacked from, the halves connected by a curling pink twist of intestine and nothing more.

"That's bitchin'!" Simon repeated.

Lilly and I stood back.

A spatter of blood on the macadam, every shade of red imaginable from bright crimson at the head to a rusted burnt oxide at the sprayed edges, like a photograph of fireworks against the night sky, starred forward from the dead dog's nose, nearly reaching all the way to where I stood. A curled and jagged rake of candy cane rib bones poked upward from the torn flesh and fur, china white fingers curled around the lifeless guts they no longer fully contained.

"I'm pretty sure he's dead," Mitch said, and laughed.

"Well, he's not wagging his tail, that's for sure," Simon added, leaning over the hind half.

Mitch smiled his big yellow teeth at my brother.

"You guys are morbid," Lilly said.

"Do either of you boys have a knife?" Mitch asked.

My stomach knotted tight.

"No."

"You mean you walked out into the desert all alone and you don't even have a knife with you?" Mitch said.

Well, I have a gun, creep, I thought.

47

"I told you he's stupid," Simon said.

I swallowed. "What do you want a knife for?"

Mitch smiled broadly and held his hands out, explaining the obvious. "To cut his tail off. I want it."

He began walking quickly back toward the car and said, "Lilly's got a nail file."

I felt myself going white.

Mitch worked at sawing the tail with the flimsy metal file for several minutes while Simon watched him. I stood back, nauseated by the grisly sound of the file grinding against the pavement, the dull metal cracking its way between the bones and cartilage and sinew. Mitch's hands went black with the clotted blood and he finally gave up, and, bracing a foot against the dog's rear, tore the length of the tail free with a two-handed tug.

He smiled and held his trophy up for his audience.

"That's nice," he said.

"Cool." Simon added, "Can I hold it?"

Mitch handed the coyote's tail to Simon and then wiped his hands off on what remained of the animal's hind fur.

"Here," he said to Lilly, offering the fouled nail file to her.

"I don't need that thing anymore, Mitch honey," Lilly said. "I've decided to start biting my nails instead."

"Okay, be that way," Mitch said, smiling, and wedged the file down into his back pocket.

Simon fanned the tail back and forth in the hot air rising up from the road.

"What're we going to do with it?" he asked.

"Come on," Mitch said, and led my brother back to the car.

Mitch wedged the stubby and raw end of the coyote's tail down into the top of Don Quixote's helmet so it hung down behind the statue like the cap of a frontiersman.

"Now *that's* pretty cool," Mitch said.

He walked around to the front of the Lincoln and kneeled down so he could see beneath the car.

"It didn't do anything to the car," he said. "Just left some hair on the axle is all."

"That's good," I said.

Mitch looked at me. I guess he could tell I was being sarcastic. He pulled the file from his back pocket and began scratching the point into the black paint behind the front wheel well. He started drawing a stick-figure dog, digging the file's point into the thick metal of the car.

And Simon, Lilly, and I watched him work as he sweat in the growing heat of the day.

"What's that for, Mitch?" Simon asked.

"It's like what they used to paint on planes and tanks in the war. It keeps score of your kills," Mitch explained. "But I can't draw too good."

"Jonah can," Simon said. "He's a real good artist."

Mitch looked at me and held the crusted file up as an offering.

"You want to finish it?"

I was repulsed, and at the same time afraid of setting Mitch off again. So I grimaced and held out my hand.

"Okay, Mitch. Sure."

"Cool," Lilly said, and giggled.

And I didn't even look as I touched the file, I just winced and took it up in my hand, and I drew the likeness of a skinny and tail-less coyote on the side of the black car, the perfect pyramids of its ears pointing upward; and I sat there sweating in the road with my legs cross-folded against the hot and grimy tire, already feeling as though my brother and I had been swallowed up by something we could not escape.

Mitch laughed, admiring my work, and said, "You should have been with us back in Mexico!"

"What else do you want me to draw on there, Mitch?" I asked, wondering what he was talking about.

Mitch laughed. "I'll keep you boys around for a while, just in case we run the score up. There's a war on, you know, and we're fighting against an enemy that looks like regular, plain folk."

"And skinny coyotes," Simon said, and smiled.

"Let's go get some breakfast," Mitch said. "Who's hungry?"

"I'm starved," Simon answered.

I looked at my dirty hand and groaned quietly to myself.

"Hey!" Mitch said.

I could see his eyes in the rearview mirror.

And I was kind of relieved that the dead coyote's tail fluttered away when Mitch sped the Lincoln onto the interstate.

I thought he would stop.

Lilly turned back over her seat.

"Just let it go," she said.

"There goes the tail," Simon said, holding a cigarette, turning around in his seat, watching the warm wind fan the orange fire on the tip.

Lilly smiled at me. I think she knew what I was thinking. I was sorry for that poor animal, that I had helped Mitch in his weird play.

Mitch turned the radio on and sang.

Mitch parked the Lincoln at a place called Flora's Diner and Curios just off Route 66 in Tucumcari. The dirt lot was filled with dusty cars and trucks, and my back was already sweating against the leather of the seat in the gathering heat of the day.

And I thought this was far enough, that Simon and I would be fine from here and we'd be able to get from Tucumcari to Arizona without Mitch and Lilly helping us anymore. I knew that somehow my brother and I would have to change just to get beyond the things we kept building up between us, and I thought I could do that; I believed, hoped, Simon would, too. So I felt pretty confident when I crawled out from the backseat. But it was a stupid thing because that day ended up taking us in directions we'd never imagine.

So I asked Mitch if I could get our pack out of the trunk, and while I dug through it to get my pencil and comp book, I could hear Mitch and Lilly and Simon talking, and laughing about something, but I couldn't tell what it was. I thought they were probably just making fun of me. When I shut the trunk lid down, Simon and Lilly were gone.

"Where'd my brother go?"

"They went in to go to the bathroom," Mitch said. "Come on, let's get a table."

To get to the diner, we first walked through a cluttered and dark room, filled with glass cases and shelves with Kachina dolls and moccasins; scorpions frozen inside epoxy resin; rock collections; sand paintings in sealed shot glasses; a stuffed rattlesnake coiled on a shelf behind a glass counter, its skin cracking open; headdresses and postcards; and signs everywhere that read: IF YOU DROP IT, YOU BOUGHT IT.

Gravity, I thought, holding on to my pencil and book and saying nothing as I followed Mitch through the dark maze of Flora's curios.

"That top shelf," I said, "how many dolls are on it?"

Flick.

I could hear Mitch flicking the cap of his lighter inside his pocket. He looked at the shelf of feathered and painted dolls just once and said, "Thirty-seven."

I stood there and counted, my finger absently tapping at nothing. It seemed impossible, but Mitch was exact. He watched me.

"Well?" he said.

"Thirty-seven."

Mitch laughed. "Now you see? You can always trust what I say, man."

I thought about Mitch talking to himself by the well, when he believed we were all asleep.

"I guess I can, Mitch," I said. I swallowed. I chewed on the inside of my lip. "But I wanted to say thank you for me and Simon. But I don't think you and Lilly want to be stuck with us all the way to Arizona. We'll be fine if you want to just leave us here. And, sorry if we were any bother."

Mitch's face darkened so fast. It looked like he'd been punched or something. Then he smiled, showing those dirty teeth, and said, "Don't be ridiculous, Jonah. It's no problem for us at all. And you weren't any bother. Besides, Lilly's kind of fond of the kid, if you can't tell."

Then he put his arm around my shoulders and said, "So just don't worry about you boys being a bother. I'll have you where you want to go by tomorrow. I promise." He pulled me in tight, and I could smell the reek of his armpit. "Besides, I'll let you know when I want you and Simon to leave."

We emerged from the cave of souvenirs into the light and noise of the diner. I wanted to wash that coyote filth from my hands, and told Mitch I needed to go to the men's room, too. So I turned away from him at the counter where they sold cigarettes and waitresses smiled, chewing gum in their plump aprons.

And I didn't see Simon or Lilly back by the toilets, either, but when I came out, they were both sitting with Mitch in a booth that surrounded them in orange tufted vinyl.

"Where were you, Simon?"

"Nowhere."

I looked around the table at the three of them, and Simon added, "We were sitting here the whole time. What are you talking about?"

A waitress came and brought us glasses of ice water and poured coffee for everyone without even asking if we wanted any. I squeezed into the end of the booth, sitting next to Lilly, across from Mitch.

I wiped my sleeve across the ring of water on the table in front of me and put my book there, starting with just a thin path away from that coffin of a trailer and a sketch of the 1940 Lincoln with its top down, a snake of a line to Drinkwater Flats, Tucumcari, Mitch, Lilly. Then I began writing words on my map.

"What's that you're making, Jonah?" Lilly asked.

"It's his map," Simon said.

"I like that!" She leaned over so her shoulder pressed into mine. "Are you going to draw a picture of me on it, too?"

And she dropped a hand down on my leg and rubbed. It made me so dizzy I had to squeeze my eyes shut.

"This is you right here," I gulped and nodded at the picture. I wanted to take a drink of water but I didn't want to move.

"What happens when we get to the edge of the page there?" she laughed, pointing at the book with her other hand. "Do we just fall off the edge of the world?"

"There's lots of pages," I said. I showed her how behind my drawings I'd scrawled line upon line of my writing.

"Let me see that," Mitch said, and reached across the table and pulled the book right out from under the point of my pencil. I never thought that anyone would do something like that. And I didn't realize how much what I'd written down even mattered.

Lilly beamed a smile at me, and then at Mitch. And I thought she really liked what I'd drawn, that maybe she liked me, too.

I couldn't know. I don't remember ever thinking much about girls at all until that day I saw Lilly driving past us.

But Mitch had a different look on his face as he studied my map. It made me feel sick, like I felt when he was cutting at the coyote's tail. And I figured later, after everything was done, that sitting there in Flora's Diner was when Mitch realized that he could never just let me and my brother walk away from him.

Simon and I ate more food in that one sitting than we had eaten throughout the week of days before, and when we were finished, Mitch left a dollar on the table and told us all he would pay the bill. He pulled a fold of cash from his front pocket and took a five-dollar bill out and handed it to Simon.

"Here," he said. "Go get some change at the register and get a few packs of cigarettes from the machine in there."

Simon said, "Bitchin'."

"You sure have a lot of money there," I said.

"That's why she likes me," Mitch said, and Lilly waved a hand at him and rolled her eyes. She put her sunglasses on and Mitch slid himself out to let Simon go for the cigarettes. When my brother walked away, we could hear the *clop clop* of his loose shoes on the tiles of the floor.

"That boy needs some shoes," Mitch said.

"He's always walked like that," I said.

"That would drive me crazy," Lilly smiled, pushing herself out against my side as I struggled to stand; I was so full of food, so flustered by the girl.

"He does."

Simon stood, waiting for us at the cashier's, clutching four packs of Kool cigarettes and books of matches.

Mitch paid the bill, even though I half expected he would skip out on it. As we made our way out through the cavern of the curio shop, Mitch stopped suddenly, grabbed Simon by the shoulder, and said, "Hey, foot scooter, what size shoe do you wear?"

"Huh?" Simon answered.

"Shoes. What size?" Mitch repeated.

"Whatever size Jonah grows out of," Simon said.

"Ten-and-a-half," I answered.

"Let's get the kid some moccasins," Mitch said. "That way no one will hear you if we have to sneak up on someone and kill them."

Mitch winked at Simon.

"Cool," Simon said.

"Mitch is so nice," Lilly said. I grimaced at that.

"How about you, Jonah?" Mitch asked.

"I don't want any."

"Your shoes look like they're going to fall apart pretty soon," Mitch said. But he sounded so empty when he said it. He watched me, like he was waiting for something to happen.

"I don't care. Really. Thanks anyway," I said. "And thanks for Simon."

So Mitch paid for some moccasins, and he bought a cheap headdress that he tied on top of Don Quixote's helmet while Simon and I climbed into the backseat of the Lincoln, Simon admiring his new quiet shoes, carefully brushing the dirt from them, placing the cigarette packs down in a line beside him as though they were some kind of barrier between us, picking up the meteorite and passing it between his hands like he was playing his own private game.

When we pulled away from Flora's Diner and Curios, Mitch said, "We gotta get some gas." And then, over his shoulder to Simon, he added, "Where are they?"

And Simon answered, "Under your seat, Mitch."

I looked at Simon, who gave no clue to what they were talking about. He just ignored me and focused his attention on unwrapping a pack of cigarettes.

Near Highway 66, Mitch pulled the Lincoln into a service station, and while the attendant there gassed the tank and checked the engine, Mitch got out and walked across the driveway to a truck stop liquor store.

"This sure is a nice car," the attendant said, and grinned at Lilly. He was missing a tooth. "A V-twelve like this one sure wants to burn the oil, though. You're down some."

"Go ahead and put some in," Lilly said.

The attendant wiped his hands on his blue coveralls, two stripes of black grease down his chest and belly on either side of the front buttons with darkened handprints at the bottom of each smear, a red-and-white embroidered patch over his heart that spelled out "Ray" in cursive thread.

As Ray worked at the can of oil from Lilly's side of the propped-up hood, he leered at her and said, "Where are you heading?"

Lilly looked over to the store where Mitch had gone. An Indian sat with his knees bent, leaning his back against the store between the front door and a trash can.

"California," Lilly said.

At the same time, Simon said, "Arizona."

"Well, that's on the way to California," Ray said, smiling at me and my brother in the backseat. He pointed a thumb at Don Quixote. "You boys caught yourself an Indian there?"

"And a meteor." Simon held the glossy black shape up so Ray, uninterested, could look at it.

"It's not an Indian, anyway," I said. "It's Don Quixote."

"Oh."

Ray wiped his hands down his chest again and tossed the empty oilcan away, resting his hands down on the top of Lilly's door.

"Going all the way to California. Nice vacation. I guess you're brothers and sister," Ray said.

"And it's our uncle driving," Simon said. "And if he catches you flirting with our sister while he's gone, he'll probably stab you. Ray."

Ray frowned. "My name's Mike. These aren't my clothes. And you're a little young for cigarettes, aren't you, boy?"

Mitch appeared, walking across the gravel lot, a brown grocery sack held in his arms. Simon dragged from his cigarette and stared at the attendant. Ray watched Mitch as he stepped beneath the shade of the station's awning.

"Nine dollars," Ray said.

Lilly was sick. She needed to get out of the car, so Mitch pulled off into a rest stop outside of Santa Rosa, saying, "I need to take care of some stuff now, anyway. We could all take a break."

There were no other cars at the rest stop, a flattened patch of crumbling asphalt that fronted a flat-roofed men's and women's room, split down the middle; and two picnic tables and galvanized steel trash cans beneath some thin locust trees. As soon as Mitch parked the car, Lilly opened her door and ran out into the dirt and began vomiting, one hand bracing herself on her knee and the other holding her hair back behind her neck.

"What's wrong with her?" Simon asked.

"She's pregnant," Mitch said.

Simon and I got out of the car. Simon scratched his head and admired his moccasins. I looked at Mitch to see if there was some sign in his expression about whether we could do anything for Lilly, but he just lifted the trunk of the car and pulled out a black cloth suitcase, opening it on the ground and gathering up a new set of clothes. I looked back at Lilly. Mitch left the suitcase lying there and then took some things from the grocery sack and went toward the restrooms.

Lilly stayed there in the dirt field, bent over, coughing and spitting.

I brought my canteen to her.

"Here," I said. "Wash your mouth out."

She took the canteen from my hand.

"Are you all right?"

Lilly nodded her head and spit a mouthful of water onto the ground. She was pale and sweating.

"I've been getting like this for a week or so now. I'll be okay."

"You really are pregnant?"

"Yeah."

"Dang." I took the canteen back from her. "How old are you, anyway?"

"Sixteen."

"Dang."

Simon was standing by the open suitcase, smoking, watching us. He flicked away ashes with his middle finger when I looked over at him.

"How long have you been with Mitch?"

"I'm not with him," she said. "Not like you think. I've just been riding with him for . . ." and she stopped. I think she was trying to figure out how long it really had been.

"Since about a week," she said.

"You both from Texas?"

"Yeah."

I wiped the back of my hand across my lips. "What's going on here, Lilly?" My heart was racing so fast, and I thought it was only from what she did to me. But I knew a car like that one carried stories with it.

"You don't want to know, Jonah."

"Okay," I said. "I should change my clothes, too. But I think maybe Simon and me better look for another ride. Or start walking again."

"Maybe you should."

And I walked away from her. I was feeling disgusted, not just from the vinegar smell of her vomit in my nose, but because I thought that she'd tell me the truth about what she was doing in that car. Maybe I was hoping for too much. Maybe I had the wrong feeling about her, anyway. So I told myself it was Simon I had to think about, and as much as neither one of us could give up on picking at each other, we were all we had in the world, besides a ten-dollar bill and a sack full of dirty clothes. So I looked up at Simon standing there, watching me, watching the girl, smoking his cigarette and flicking the ashes.

I stood on the other side of the car from Lilly and Simon and changed my clothes. I didn't really want to be in the small restroom with Mitch, and I wasn't embarrassed to undress outside anyway. But when I pulled my pants off, I saw Lilly was watching me. I looked away, like I didn't notice her. I put on the jeans I had worn when it began raining two days before, tighter and stiffer now, and found some clean socks in the pack, Simon's. Since I didn't have a clean shirt to wear, I took one of Simon's tee shirts and pulled it on, even though it hardly reached to the top of my jeans.

"I took a shirt of yours. And some socks," I said to Simon.

"I don't care."

"Do you want to change your clothes?" I called out across the car, across the width of the crumbling lot.

"Not yet," Simon said.

So I sat down beside the rear wheel, where the others could not see me, my legs folded, and stuffed those dirty clothes back into our pack. I felt my hand down to the bottom, finding the pistol there, wondering if I should try putting it in my pants; and decided not to. But I did pull it out into the light and made certain it was loaded before burying it back beneath the wads of clothes and the letters from my brother. I took the letters out and flipped through them, felt them in my fingers. Then I took my map out, rested it on my lap, and drew a diagram of the rest stop and a likeness of Lilly and the bearded and long-haired Mitch, the string of beads hanging down his chest, his quilted vest unbuttoned.

I put the map back into the pack and closed it up. I put the pack into the trunk and brushed the dirt from the seat of my pants and sat down with Simon and Lilly at one of the rest area's splintered tables.

Mitch came out of the bathroom smiling broadly. He had shaved off his beard and cut his hair; and he was wearing a plaid short-sleeved shirt and powder blue bell-bottom corduroys. He looked like a tourist.

"How do you like me now?" he said.

"Crazy," Lilly, who had recovered and was sitting at a picnic bench having a cigarette, answered.

"It makes you look like a kid," Simon said.

"How old are you anyway, Mitch?" I asked. I thought he had to be in his twenties.

Mitch flashed serious for an instant, and said, "What? Are you going to put that on your map, too?"

"That map's stupid. Jonah said he was making it in case we get killed," Simon added.

Mitch smiled again.

"Hey. I'm just kidding, Jonah," Mitch said. "It doesn't matter, does it?"

"Not really."

Mitch walked over to the car and loaded his suitcase back into

60

the trunk, then he opened the driver's door and dropped down to his knees so he could reach under the seat.

"You feeling better, Lil?" he called out.

"Yeah."

"Then maybe Simon can come help me put these on," and as he stood, I could see Mitch was holding two red-and-yellow New Mexico license plates.

I stared at my brother, who just sat there looking smug, smoking his cigarette. Now I knew what he'd been doing before we sat down at that diner.

"Did you steal those plates?"

"Yep."

I slammed my palm down onto the table. It made Lilly jump. Simon dropped his cigarette.

I was so mad I could feel myself getting dizzy. Everything had piled up so high I just couldn't stand it anymore: our father, Mother, Matthew, and me and Simon being out in the desert, abandoned and lost, swallowed up in the backseat of that black car like we really were swallowed up in the belly of some monster.

We may have had as much of an excuse to as anyone ever did, but Simon and I never stole anything in our lives. And that was all I could stand.

I stood up and walked around the table, and as Simon was attempting to swing his legs out over the bench, I grabbed him. He started squealing and writhing like a pig that was about to get butchered, and I pulled him by the sleeve of his tee shirt and threw him down into the dirt.

"Hey!" Mitch said, jogging over from the car.

"Stop it!" Lilly yelled. But I couldn't hear anything else beyond the pulse in my ears and my gasping breaths, and the sounds of my fists smacking into my brother's chest and face.

"You stupid punk!" I cursed. I sat on top of Simon, pinning his arms down with my knees into the gravel and dust beneath a desiccated locust tree, my hand twisted around in Simon's hair, holding his head steady while my other hand alternately slapped and punched him; Simon, whining with each strike, eyes shut tight, blood spraying out from his nose and mouth.

"You're hurting him! Stop it!" Lilly screamed. "Mitch! Make him stop it!"

Mitch just stood there, where the shade of the tree fell across his eyes.

"He'll stop soon enough," Mitch said. "I seen this coming ever since we caught these two."

I gave Simon's hair a final twist, then launched myself off of him, making a grunting growl as I did, storming away from the others, out past the tree and into the desert, punching my arms in the air and barking curses at no one, barking curses at myself. I tore my shirt off and wiped at the blood from my hands and arms, then balled it up and covered my face as I collapsed to my knees, facing away from all of them, sobbing so hard that I couldn't believe I would ever stop crying.

driver

Joneser,

Hi. What's happening out in the world? That's what GIs over here call home. The world.

I can't sleep. It took me about 10 minutes to write that first sentence because the South Vietnamese are firing their 105s right over my head and I'm starting to get a little worried. The whole place shakes like it's the end of the world.

Last night, two VC were killed at our northern perimeter. You know what the RVNs did? They took what was left of the bodies, because they both got it by claymore mines, and laid them in the road outside the firebase so people can see what happens to VC. One of them was a woman. I don't even want to say what they did to her body.

But the only Army here is a South Vietnamese battery and us, so there's no one to boss us around and we can sleep whenever we want, just not now. But we have a big ice chest filled with beer, and we listen to music a lot.

You know what? My platoon leader was out here to deliver mail, and I got your letter, but some RVN went in his jeep and stole his camera. We reported it to the RVN major and he caught the guy. You know what they did to him? They made him low-crawl in the mud with a mortar round in his arms and while he was doing this, other RVNs were beating him all over with clubs. He was really bloody. Then they threw him naked in a real small cage made from barbed wire. That's what I call a good case of military discipline.

There's a picture in here of me and Scotty in his room. His room is about 9 feet by 5 feet. My room is a little bigger, but they're both like coffins. But they're in bunkers, of course.

I'm watching some rats in here right now, and getting bitten by mosquitoes. Scotty is scared of rats, but he used to have a pet monkey that would chase them away, but I think someone stole the monkey and probably ate it.

On nights like this, sometimes I just watch the rats. Some of them are big enough that they'd kill a small cat or dog. When it's quiet, not like now, you can hear them hissing and screeching all night.

I don't know what I hate worse, the sound of the rats or those 105s.

Tomorrow I might get to go to our home battery, they have showers there. I haven't had a shower in 2 weeks. And I usually have to sleep with my clothes and boots on. I'm dirtier than hell. My sheets have mold on them.

I've been here four months and my nerves are shot. Every time I hear a noise I jump. I'm shaking so bad right now. But the worst thing, I saw a five-year-old boy get killed the other day and then I thought of you and Simon and I thanked God that you aren't in a place like this. I hope you guys aren't fighting all the time, Jonah, you have to be the man.

Scotty just came in right now. He said tell my little brother hi. He can't sleep either, I guess, but I bet there's more rats in my room than his. We're going to have a beer (don't tell Mom and Simon, ha ha) and maybe try to go to sleep. Anyway, I'm getting under the mosquito net cause these things are killing me.

I'll write to you soon.

Love,

Matthew

I don't know how long I sat there.

I felt so tired, like I could just lie down and sleep.

And wait for the buzzards to eat me.

I could hear the motor on the Lincoln starting up.

I took the shirt down from my face, my eyes blind and blurry in the dry light of the desert. My hands were sore and streaked brown with my little brother's blood. I heard someone approaching from behind. I still didn't fully believe what I had done. And I kept hearing myself, on the dirt road from our house, telling Simon how I promised to take care of him. .

"Come on. Get in the car, Jonah."

It was Mitch.

Flick.

I didn't move, didn't look back at him.

"No."

"You sure beat the tar out of that boy."

"I told him I would."

Mitch moved closer. I could feel his footsteps vibrating through the ground.

"Get up now. Let's go." Mitch sounded calm, almost soothing.

"I don't want to go with you."

Flick.

"Then we'll leave without you," Mitch said, his voice closer now.

"And, Jonah? Your little brother will be with us. He's already in the car. And you know what I'm going to do? I bet you know." Mitch paused and cleared his throat, then leaned closer and whispered, "Maybe a mile down the road, maybe a hundred miles down the road. Maybe. I just know I'm going to kill him if you don't get up right now."

I dropped the bloody shirt onto the dirt in front of my knees.

I knew then that all the things I thought about Mitch from the moment I saw him were right; and probably not bad enough. And I knew I'd let Simon down, let myself down, too, and I'd have to do something about it if I could. If I was strong enough, or smart enough.

I put my palms down on the ground and pushed myself up to my feet.

My knees felt like they would buckle.

I looked over at the car.

"There you go, buddy. That's a good boy," Mitch said, smiling, toothy and yellow, as I turned around to face him.

"Can I get a shirt out of my pack, please?" My voice was flat and stoic.

"You can wear that one you left there in the dirt or you can go without," Mitch said.

So I picked up the rumpled and bloodied tee shirt and shook it out. Then, without saying anything else, I pulled it on over my head and began walking back toward the Lincoln. I saw the glinting reflection of Lilly's sunglasses there as she watched me and Mitch, could tell that Simon was sitting in the backseat just on the other side of the metal man, and I felt sick when Mitch put an arm around my shoulders, so fatherly, saying, "Do you know how to drive, boy? I think it's time you take the wheel for a while."

"He's driving," Mitch said. He opened the door on Lilly's side and got into the backseat with Simon.

66

I stood behind the open driver's door, not looking back at Simon. I knew he didn't want me to look at him, and I was afraid of what I might see.

"I'm sorry, Simon. I'm really sorry. Are you okay?" I said, just talking, and not looking back.

Simon didn't say anything.

"I think you broke his nose," Lilly said, and then shifted in the seat to look back at Simon. "Did it stop bleeding?"

While I sat out in the dirt, she had taken Simon to the drinking fountain to wash the blood from his face. There was blood everywhere, in Simon's hair, down his back and chest, drying in black grainy beads, his bottom lip cut between his teeth and my hands, and his left eye was black. She had carefully taken Simon's shirt from him and soaked it in the warm, tin-smelling fountain water and twisted it and bathed Simon with it, wiping it across his skin and wringing it out over and over until the blood was gone.

I turned and looked at my brother.

Simon pressed the wet shirt, now gone completely red, up against his face and let out a muffled "No." Simon turned away so nobody would have to look at him, holding that smooth and shining meteorite tightly in his right hand, flipping it over, tumbling it in his grasp.

"You want a shirt, Simon?" Mitch asked calmly.

"No."

I sighed and sat down. I placed my hands on the steering wheel and just sat there, trying to figure everything out, feeling punished, feeling trapped. I had driven plenty of times in my life, but there was so much in my mind at that moment that I became afraid I'd forgotten anything I might ever have known.

Five miles down the highway, Mitch scratched his fingers through his cropped dark hair and stretched his arms out into the wind over his head and said, "Donny boy, I feel like getting high. What do you say?"

"He says, 'Groovy,'" Lilly beamed.

Mitch patted Don Quixote on the shoulder and said, "He never says no to me."

I was scared. I sat stiff at the wheel, staring down the endless road carved straight from hill to hill, lined with jagged rocks and grasses, following pole after pole stretched with sagging black wire, and I cringed as I heard Mitch digging through his grocery sack and pulling out a six-pack of beer, then popping a ring on the first one, sending a foaming spray of warm yellow beer out like a sneeze against the leather back of the front seats.

I looked at Simon in the rearview mirror.

Simon's nose had stopped bleeding, the bridge swollen smooth from his brow downward, his mouth hanging open to breathe. He sat, eyes pooled and fixed forward.

Mitch twirled the metal ring around on his index finger.

"Do you know what these are good for?" Mitch asked, holding the shining pop top in front of Simon.

"No," Simon said.

"Nothing." Mitch laughed and he tossed the ring over his shoulder, sending it flying back on the wind to tumble downward against the grainy surface of the highway.

And I knew what Mitch was going to do.

"Please don't give him a beer," I said.

"You need to ease up," Mitch said coldly, and I could hear him rustling in the bag again. "Do you want a beer, Simon?"

"Cool."

"That's my man." Mitch laughed. I heard the sound of him opening a second can.

"What if we get pulled over by the police?" I asked.

"We won't," Mitch said, "trust me. Do you trust me, Jonah?"

I didn't say anything. Of course I didn't.

Mitch waited, a silent minute that seemed so long on that highway, and then he said, "Do you trust me, Lilly?"

"Sure." She smiled at me, like she was trying to get me to come along. I wished I could figure her out. She had to know that Mitch was poison, but I got the feeling that she just drank it all in and teased him because she didn't care the least bit about herself.

I looked away from her.

Mitch said, "Do you trust me, Don?"

"Don says, 'Groovy,'" Lilly answered.

"Do you trust me, Simon?"

Simon took a swig from the beer, and then another. And he said, "Yes."

"So there. See? You're outvoted, Jonah. Four to one, baby. And, after all, this is a democracy. The people have spoken. The people trust Mitch."

And Mitch finished his beer and tossed the can out over the back of the Lincoln.

"Hey, Jonah, turn on the radio, man," Mitch said, opening another beer.

I reached for the dashboard, but swerved the Lincoln onto the shoulder and then overcorrected. Mitch and Simon spilled their beers on their laps.

"I'll do it," Lilly said.

I sighed, tightening my grip on the wheel. I felt so lost and out of control. In front of her, I felt like such an idiot.

"It's okay," Lilly said, and rubbed my leg. "It's been a tough day. Let's just forget about it and have a good time."

"Yeah," Mitch said.

Lilly fumbled at the radio's knob until she found a station playing

"Let It Bleed" and stopped it there as soon as Mitch started singing along.

And I tried to stay calm and watch the road and think of a way to save myself and my brother; and maybe Lilly, too.

Mitch ducked behind the seat to get down out of the wind. He began rolling a joint. When he popped back up, he held his arm over the front seat and waved the crooked, stubby cigarette in the air between Lilly and me, saying, "Look what I got."

And I felt my stomach twist and chest tighten. I heard Mitch flicking that lighter. It wasn't because our dad had gotten himself so messed up by drugs, not exactly; and it wasn't that I'd never been around someone who was smoking pot, but it was just something that Simon and I didn't do.

"Not me," I said.

"That's okay, man, that's okay," Mitch said, leaning back. "Just keep driving. And turn up the radio."

"It's up all the way," Lilly said.

"I love this car," Mitch said.

"Where'd you get it?" I asked, shifting and straining to see in the small mirror at the top of the windshield, and the smaller round one on the door, anything that might show me what Simon was doing back there.

"Ask Lilly."

Lilly just turned away, pretending to look out at the passing blur of red and yellow desert.

Even in the open car on that blisteringly hot afternoon, I could smell the ropey smoke from the joint when Mitch finally got it to burn, and dreaded him offering it to Simon. I bit my cheek as hard as I could to not say anything. I felt so terrible for what I had done to my brother, and I wanted so desperately to get him out of there that I felt sick.

So when I heard Simon say, "No thanks, man. But I'll have a cigarette," and Mitch reply, "It's cool, Simon," I felt my shoulders loosen
and I could breathe again.

"I'll have a hit," Lilly said, reaching over to Mitch.

"That's my girl," Mitch said. "Ahh . . . the world is perfect."

"I guess it is," I said.

Mitch lay his head back and stared straight up into the sky. "I'm
floating."

I stared down the road. "Sometimes I dream about floating."

"Can't do nothing about gravity," Mitch said, and laughed as Lilly
handed the joint back over the seat.

The radio played "Run Through the Jungle." I didn't like the
song. It sounded too much like the things I'd read in Matthew's letters, and I was thankful when we lost the signal again and Lilly
couldn't find another station.

Simon drank a second beer.

My hands were sweating, but I couldn't loosen their grip on the
wheel. This was the farthest we'd ever been from home, the fastest
we'd ever gone, and I felt so incredibly small on the road. The desert
seemed so big, and I realized that until we'd gotten in that car with
Mitch and Lilly, there was almost nothing else in our lives or world
besides just me and Simon.

The morning wore on to the afternoon on that lonely and quiet
road, overly decorated with signs hoping to attract carloads of travelers to roadside curio shops selling pecan rolls and Indian souvenirs. Black clouds billowed above the flat heat of the land, the road
sending up blurry snakes in the distance. It looked like rain coming.
I was getting tired at the wheel, and I watched in the rearview mirror as Mitch started to fall asleep, then jerked his head up suddenly,
shook it clear, and unbuttoned his shirt and took it off.

"That air feels good," Mitch said, and fumbled with his pants, removing them and waving them out like a blue flag. He sat there in the backseat completely naked.

"Oh brother," I sighed.

Lilly laughed and slapped her hand down on the top of the seat.

"Don't be a prude, Jonah," she said.

"Let the sunshine in," Mitch chuckled. "Ahh . . ." and he stretched his arms out over the folded top of the cream convertible canvas so that he was hugging Don Quixote.

A truck passed us, honking twice at the foolish Mitch.

Simon was drunk. He could see me watching him in the car's mirror; he held the meteorite up between us to hide his eyes from me. But I saw him bend forward, taking off his moccasins and pants, heard him giggle when he put his bare feet up against the back of my seat, and touched my head with his toes.

"Put your clothes on, Simon," I said. I felt myself getting angry again, tried fighting against it.

"No."

"My brother, Simon!" Mitch shouted and tousled Simon's hair, smiling his big yellow teeth.

"Take your clothes off, Lilly," Mitch said.

Lilly looked at me, gently lifting her blouse, a slight smile on her tight lips, and I just glared at her and quickly turned my attention back to the road. This was ridiculous.

"Jonah doesn't want me to."

"You're no fun, Jonah," Mitch called out.

Lilly turned around and looked at the two of them in the backseat, grinning. Simon made no movement to cover himself. He never was very shy about anything.

"Put your clothes back on, Simon," I repeated.

"They stink. They smell like you," Simon said.

"You're acting like a damned hippie," I said.

"What's wrong with that?" Mitch laughed.

"I like hippies," Lilly said, still turned back, eyes shifting from Mitch to Simon, to the road receding behind them.

"You going to beat me up again, Jonah?" Simon asked.

"No. I said I was sorry."

Simon bent forward and lit another cigarette.

"I have a black eye."

"I know," I said. "You want to hit me back?"

Simon picked up the meteorite, reflecting the sun. "Not right now."

And I pulled my head away when Simon put his foot over the top of the seat and brushed my ear with it.

I scowled. Simon and Mitch began laughing, and I thought, *I've got to find a way to get that gun out of the pack.*

I looked at Lilly and she pulled her glasses down, smiling, and winked at me.

I stared down the road.

"Where are you going?" I said to her.

"I told you. To California."

She was playing with me, I was sure. I glanced back to see if Mitch was listening. His head hung over the side of the car, drugged, tuned out to the blur of the desert.

I whispered, "I'd think there'd be a better way for you to get there."

"Just let me know when you find one, Jonah."

Jonah. She said it like it meant something to her, and it almost sounded good to me. For all I had convinced myself that Lilly didn't seem to care about anything, I found myself hoping that maybe she could.

So we followed the road into the stretching shadows of the afternoon. I thought we were lost. Mitch told me to turn north and off of the main highway, into empty and vast Indian lands, and I was relieved when the first stinging drops of rain fell from the sky. Within moments we were caught in a deluge. Mitch and Simon struggled back into their clothes, Simon leaving the bloody shirt on the seat beside him.

I fumbled to find the controls for the windshield wipers, thinking how ridiculous it was to worry about such a thing in an open convertible. We were all completely soaked in less than a minute.

"Can we put the top up?" I asked.

"Don's too tall," Mitch said.

The water ran in small streams down the metal man, the feathers on his war bonnet flattening and streaking their artificial tinting.

I watched Simon as he wiped the cool rainwater into his face. He looked sober now in the roar of that dark storm.

"We need to find a place to stop," Lilly said.

But I could hardly see the road in front of me, the rain was so thick and the sky had gone so black, and I thought about crashing the car off the road so we could get away, but couldn't make myself do it. Finally, south of Everett, Mitch told me to turn into an isolated spot beneath a giant fiberglass tepee, a motel called the Palms, a gathering of squat stucco cabins made up to look like adobe dwellings, dwarfed by a green neon sign with a palm tree. There were no palms around the place at all. I pulled the car into the muddy parking lot and Mitch asked Simon to come into the office with him, and told us that we would get a room here.

So Lilly and I sat out in the car, in the rain, with the metal man behind us, his mask turning to a gray pulp and oozing down from the hammered tin beard on his chin. Lilly took off her wet glasses and folded them into her purse. I looked at her, and I could see her breasts clearly through the soaked gauze blouse she wore, so I turned away and stared at the motel office.

"Why are you and Mitch doing this, Lilly?" I asked.

"Because Mitch is a nice guy," she said. She said it like she didn't understand what I was talking about.

"That's not what I mean," I said. "Back there. At the rest stop, Mitch told me he would kill my brother if I didn't get back in the car."

"Oh," she said. "Why don't we stand under there?"

And now I could see a more serious look in her eyes. She didn't blink at all. She just looked right into my eyes and I felt like I had to look away, but I couldn't.

She pointed toward the overhanging eaves in the front of the office. I opened my door as a flash of light spit my shadow down across the puddled ground and a thunderous boom sucked the air away.

Under the overhang, Lilly pulled her blouse away from her skin, looking down, and said, "I'm getting fat. Does it show much?"

She pivoted to the side and I looked at her, calmly, seeing the fabric clinging to her, the small bubbles of air trapped between it and her skin.

"No," I said. "Are you going to talk to me?"

"I guess we did some pretty bad things, Jonah. Me and Mitch."

"Worse than stealing that car?"

She tried to giggle, but it just kind of stuck in her throat; then she became suddenly serious. "Yes."

And I didn't know what to think. The rain clapped down like artificial applause from the uneven porch. I stood mystified by the girl, unable to take my eyes from her, watching the droplets of water collect and tumble down from the strands of hair that fell over her shoulders, pasting her transparent blouse against her skin.

Embarrassed, I looked down at my wet feet.

"Have you ever kissed a girl, Jonah?"

I couldn't look at her. I felt like I was stuck on top of the biggest Ferris wheel in the world.

"Why?"

"I bet you never have," Lilly teased.

And I started to say something, but only managed to clear my tightening throat.

Lilly pressed up against me and raised her mouth to mine, lifting my head as she wrapped her arms around me. At first I backed away. It was instinct. Of course I'd never kissed a girl before, and she was so incredibly beautiful that it terrified me and buckled my knees. I put my hands in her hair and pulled her tightly against me.

It was what I wanted to do ever since I saw her floating past me in that car. And at the same time, I felt this tremendous rush of fear because I knew that the only way she'd be doing this right now, right here, had to be that she was going to make me do something bad, something stupid. I tried to think about Simon, but her mouth felt so good that I just wouldn't listen to anything sensible my brain was trying to tell me.

"I bet you never have," Lilly said again.

I let her go. I looked away, toward the door of the office.

I felt her brush up against me from behind. She wrapped her arms around my waist and pressed herself into me. I tried to look away, watching the door across the curtains of rain.

Why was I letting her do this?

I spun around in her grasp and we kissed again, this time harder.

"Mitch is coming. He'll kill us," I said. I pushed her away from me.

"I know," she said.

I pulled the wet locks of hair back from my face and rubbed the back of my neck, still unable to take my eyes from her, watching the door beyond.

"Why did you stop for us?"

"Silly," she smiled. "Your brother had his thumb out. And you're both so pretty and pathetic. I just wouldn't let Mitch drive off. He was going to, you know. Now I guess it doesn't matter, does it? Oooh!" And Lilly pushed her fingers in at her side, just above the waist of her jeans. "Sometimes this thing really hurts me. Do you think that's normal?"

"I don't know," I said.

"Well, when we get to California, that's the first thing I'm going to do. Get rid of it."

"You are?"

"That's the only reason I'd let him drive me there, Jonah."

"Is it his?"

"No."

"Lilly? You wouldn't let him hurt Simon, would you?"

She bit at a strand of her wet hair, then wiped her face with her palm. "I don't think I could stop Mitch from doing what he decides to do."

The clattering of the rain was so loud.

I looked back at the car.

Maybe I had been pretending that things weren't really as bad as they were. But I looked at Lilly and saw that she was scared, and that terrified me.

The door of the office swung open, and they came out, Mitch with his arm around my brother's shoulders, dangling a brass key with an orange plastic fob in the shape of a palm tree hanging from it.

palms

Dear Brother Jones,

  I haven't gotten any mail from you in over three weeks. I know you're writing, but I'm just not getting it. I'm trying to not let it get me down, though.

  The reason I am printing this letter is so it would take up more time. I don't know what else to do anyway.

  You know what happened? Yesterday one of the enlisted men got into a fight with Scotty and he really flipped out. He went and got his .45 and was looking to kill Scotty and he almost shot the platoon leader before he could get the guy to put the gun away. The guy with the gun ended up going behind the supply building and shooting himself. He didn't die, though, they just sent him away to someplace, I don't know.

  If you think I'm going nuts here, you're right. We all do.

  I am trying to arrange my R and R now. I can go to Sydney, Australia, for just a couple hundred bucks. And Jones, Scotty knows people who can get me back to the States from there and I won't have to come back here. Sometimes, honestly, I think I'd rather be shot for deserting than have to spend another minute here. Got to change the subject, man, that's making me want to cry.

When I came here from Phu Bai I rode in a truck and had my gear in the back, and while we were going through Da Nang, a gook teenager jumped in and stole my duffle bag that had all my clothes in it, even the sweatshirts you sent me last Christmas. These people are really starting to get to me. Some of the GIs here will shoot kids for doing that stuff. I think they ought to shoot them more often. Sorry for saying that, 'cause they are just kids and you and Simon just don't know how lucky you are for not being born in a place like this.

I hope you're not fighting all the time with Simon. I'm going to write a letter to Mother and ask her if you are. I guess there are always going to be forces that pull brothers apart that you just can't do anything about, like this war. But the things you can do something about, you shouldn't let them pull us down. Over here, there's nothing you can do about it so you might as well deal with it. I guess in a perfect world, nothing like that ever is going to happen and in a perfect world nothing ever pulls a brother away from his brother. Do you know what I mean? Subject change.

Last night the VC dropped about 20 mortars in on us. I could see the flash where they were coming from, they were so close. Three of our guys got wounded pretty bad, then their position just lit up in a flash, so I think we got the VC who were shooting. Anyway, they stopped.

It's been raining here nonstop for about 2 weeks.

I feel better now.

But my hand hurts from printing.

Good night.

Love,

Matt

Mitch kicked the door.

It stuck, swollen wet, when he turned the key.

The cabin smelled of cigarette smoke and Lysol.

Simon, shirtless and soaked, stood shivering when Lilly turned on the lamp sitting on the scratched table between the two beds. His arms were folded tightly across his sunburned chest.

I glanced at him and looked away.

I felt so sorry for what I'd done; what was happening to us.

The walls in the room came together unevenly, their yellowed paper coverings bubbling and peeling away in spots like dead skin, and the green carpet was frayed and stained with dog urine. Maybe it was dog's. The beds were covered with corded orange spreads, the same dirty-pumpkin color as the fob on the room key, and there was a crooked-hanging painting of a palm tree on the wall by the bathroom; and atop the low, pressed-wood dresser sat a television set with a bent rabbit-ear antenna.

"Can I get into the shower?" Simon asked, slipping the soggy moccasins from his feet. "I'm freezing."

Mitch looked at Lilly.

"I don't mind," she said.

"Can I get our clothes out of the car, Mitch?" I asked.

"Sure." Mitch handed me the Lincoln's keys. "And bring in that black suitcase I had out today, too."

As I took the keys into my hand, he made certain I could see him glance over at Simon. And I knew this was how it was going to be; all of us asking Mitch's permission for everything from now on.

I went for the door. When I passed by Lilly, trying my hardest not to look at her, my knees almost gave out, and I thought Mitch could see it.

Gravity.

"Don't get lost," Mitch warned.

The rain continued to pour down. The dirt lot of the motel was now a windblown sea, and I had to wade out in the muddy water that came over the tops of my ragged shoes. And I didn't know if Mitch had done it purposely, but somehow the cabin he rented was the one farthest from the office. I strained to see if there was anyone inside the office, but it was too far away. And I almost felt that somehow that metal man in the backseat was keeping watch on me for Mitch.

I knew I wouldn't have much time, probably not enough time to make it to the office and back before Mitch came out looking for me, so I had to take the surest choice.

I went right for the Lincoln's trunk and opened it.

It was too dark to see anything. I felt around in the blackness of the trunk for the familiar canvas pack I'd been carrying all that way from Los Rogues. I tugged at its ties and pushed my whole arm down into it, feeling past the balls of clothing, the aligned edges of Matthew's letters, the map—*the stupid map*—I'd been making, until my fingers wrapped around the cool metal of a pistol barrel.

And I was so scared and nervous, I could feel my heart pounding so hard and with each thump came a dizzying pressure in my head. It was like none of this was real, but I felt the rain, could smell the rotting-leaves odor of the old car's trunk. My hand shook, and I pulled the gun from the pack and quickly stuffed its barrel down the front of my jeans, tugging and stretching at Simon's tee shirt to try to make it hide the pistol's bulge.

Trembling and panting, rain streaming from my hair, down my face, I tried to blow the water away from my nose by spouting air up from my mouth. My eyes began to adjust, could discern the shapes of the contents of the trunk. I knocked over Mitch's shoe box, tipping back the lid and the dried masking tape that had once sealed its contents. The shoe box was stuffed with paper money, in bundles separated by paper clips and rubber bands. So I pulled some of the bills out of one of the bundles—I could not tell how many—and stuffed them down the front of my soaked pants, wadding them beside the pistol.

My hands shook. I grabbed the black suitcase Mitch had asked for and slammed the trunk shut. I ran back to the cabin, head down, trying to breathe, as I sloshed through the deepening water and mud.

"That was quick," Mitch said when I slogged into the cabin, leaving dark wet footprints on the carpet. I felt like I had been out there for hours.

"It's coming down so hard," I said, handing Mitch the car keys. "I did it as fast as I could."

The door to the bathroom was shut. I could see the light beneath the crack at the bottom, could hear the sound of the shower running. Lilly had undressed, and was wrapped from her armpits down in a white towel that said "Palms" in blue writing along its border, her blond hair resting in wet strands on her shoulders.

"You're shaking," she said to me.

"I guess I got cold out there," I said. "I'll feel better after a shower."

Mitch twisted at the television's antennas, trying to tune in a station and getting nothing but sandpaper for a picture.

"You need to get out of those clothes," Lilly said.

"I can wait," I said. "It's okay."

The water stopped in the bathroom.

I pushed the door open, and Simon said, "What?"

"Hey. I have our clothes."

Simon pulled the door open and took the pack, then shut the door on me without saying anything. When he came out of the shower, in the light of the room, it was the first time that I had really looked at my brother's face since our fight that morning.

Even though Simon's wet hair hung down in front of him, I could see the lump on his left cheekbone, and the black-green of bruising beneath the eye, the upper lid red and swollen. And there was a cut beneath his mouth, the lip puffed out above a mark where Simon's tooth had come all the way through.

I felt terrible, sick to my stomach, after seeing what I had done to my brother.

And I told myself that it couldn't be helped, that Simon had it coming to him for hitching the ride in the first place, for helping Mitch steal those license plates. And that stealing them only ended up helping Mitch, especially if what he really wanted to do was kill us both.

Lilly went into the bathroom and turned on the shower. Simon sat on the edge of the bed and pulled on some dry socks, dropping our pack open on the floor. I sat on the bed across the strip of worn carpet, watching him, uncomfortable with that gun pushing into my belly, uncomfortable with Mitch sitting there watching us, not really knowing what I would have to do to get Simon out of there. And I wanted to tell Simon I was so sorry, I wanted to hug him and tell him I was scared, but I didn't say anything to him, and Simon never looked at me one time as we sat across from one another.

"Hey, wet dog," Mitch said to me.

It made me jump.

"You two have to share *that* bed," and he pointed to the one farthest from the only door in the cabin, the one by the bathroom.

"Oh. Sorry." I stood up and tossed the pack onto the bed where Simon was sitting.

Mitch changed into some dry clothes as I took what I would be wearing from the pack: my worn red flannel shirt, my only other pair of jeans, and some underwear, and then I had to ask Simon if he minded that I was going to take the only dry pair of socks in there, because they were his.

Simon lay his head down on the pillow, stretching his legs out and shrugging, staring straight above him at the ceiling. "I don't care, Jonah. Do whatever you want."

Mitch gave up trying to tune the television and lay on his bed, silently watching us. I faced the rear wall, quietly filling in details on my map; the stretch of road where I wrote, "I was driving here," a cloud with rain and lightning bolts coming down, and a tepee and palm tree where the line ended.

Outside, the rain continued to pound down, making a constant static-roar, like the rush of asphalt beneath tires.

Lilly came out from the bathroom, still wrapped in a towel. I thought she looked pale and tired. Simon's eyes followed her as she crossed the room.

"We should be in Arizona tomorrow," Mitch said. "Where in Arizona are you boys headed?"

And I thought, *Why does that even matter to you, Mitch?*

"Flagstaff," Simon said.

Lilly slid into clothes she pulled from the black suitcase. She looked at me, loosening the towel beneath her arms, then turned her back as she let it drop away to the stained carpet at her feet and lowered a tie-dyed sweatshirt over her head, shaking her wet hair back as she tugged it down over her body.

I nodded toward the open bathroom door, trying to be casual, and said, "It's your turn, Mitch."

I wanted him to get away from the three of us, but I was afraid Mitch suspected what I was thinking. And I knew then that if he was not going to leave me and Simon alone together, our situation was almost hopeless.

Mitch sat up on the bed, pulling his legs in and crossing them, and said, "I'm good. I had my shower in the backseat, man. You go ahead."

I slumped my shoulders and turned the map book facedown on the bedspread next to Simon, and I covered it and the bundle of Matthew's letters with the clothes I had scattered out of the back-pack, laying out the canteen and the rumpled ten-dollar bill that had been carried with us since we left Los Rogues riding that horse that was going to fall down and die on us.

I wadded the dry clothes into a ball and pressed them against my belly, against the gun that was gouging into my cold wet skin, and, keeping my head down and my back to the others, feeling them watching me, closed the bathroom door behind me and looked for a way to lock it.

There was no lock on the doorknob, just one of those rusted hook-and-eye things that hung weakly from the frame on the doorway. I squeezed it closed and pulled the gun from my pants, placing it down on the chipped porcelain of the sink. I examined the marks the pistol had made in my skin, nearly cutting into the flesh below my belly, a reddened and distorted impression of the hammer and cylinder.

I counted the damp bills I stole from Mitch. There was $360 in wadded twenties, more than enough to get Simon and me to Arizona if we could just get away from Mitch. I put the money into the pocket of the dry jeans and dropped all my wet clothes in a heap at the bottom of the door.

I turned the water on and climbed into the calming heat of the shower.

Somebody in the room tried to open the door, and then there came the pounding against it.

I slapped my hands against the yellowed tiles in the shower stall and dropped my head under the flow of the water, thinking, *What else can possibly go wrong?*

"Jonah! Open the door. I need to pee."

It was Simon.

I stepped out onto the wet linoleum and grabbed the gun. I dropped it down behind the raised edge on the floor of the shower stall. I unlatched the hook on the lock and got back into the shower, shutting the dingy frosted glass door behind me.

"What'd you lock the door for?" Simon growled, standing over the toilet.

"I don't know," I said. "Habit, I guess."

I knew it was a stupid thing to say. It just came out.

"What habit?" Simon said, "We don't have no locks at home."

The toilet flushed and I said, "Simon, I need to talk to you. Alone. It's important. We need . . ."

Then the door swung open as Simon buttoned his pants. With my foot, I pushed the gun up against the yellow edge of the shower floor. I didn't think anyone would notice it. Through the blurry haze of the shower door, I could see Mitch standing in the doorway.

"I think Jonah better leave this door open till he's through."

"Why?" Simon asked.

"The people don't trust Jonah," Mitch laughed, then added, seriously, "we have a pregnant girl here. When she needs the toilet, it better be available."

Simon just shrugged and brushed past Mitch and made his way into the room, out of my view.

I kept my palms against the tiles, letting the water hammer down against the back of my neck, and I could see Mitch standing there, unmoving for the longest time. I knew Mitch was just messing with me, too, and he was probably getting a kick out of it. And I saw the blur of motion as he finally receded back into the room, leaving the bathroom door standing wide open, and Lilly, beyond the doorway, there in the room, just watching me.

We never knew what privacy was in the shack where we grew up, anyway. There was no such thing. And in winter, the only way we'd ever have hot water for a shower was to take one at school with every other boy in our class. That's what we had to do.

But Lilly, that was something different. And I could tell she was looking straight at me, so I kept my face turned to where she was standing and I thought about the rain falling, about us being out there in the dark while Mitch and Simon arranged for the room. And my head nearly howled at me that she was trying to get something, trying to use me, because nothing would ever make me believe any girl, much less one that looked like Lilly, would ever look twice at me.

But I didn't want to listen to that, either.

When I finally came out, dried and dressed, angry, worrying about the gun I left in the bottom of the shower stall, Mitch was sitting on the bed with Simon. The comp book with my map in it was uncovered, turned upward, opened, and Mitch was reading one of Matthew's letters.

I spread my wet clothes out on the dresser table, and hung my pants over the screen of the useless television.

"How many letters in that stack, Mitch?" I asked. I struggled to stay calm, but I wanted to tear Matthew's letter from his dirty hands, and I was so mad at myself for leaving them out, for trusting Mitch.

"Twenty-three," Mitch said.

"Yeah. And they're all addressed to me."

Mitch fired a look at me. I knew he felt challenged by the tone of my words.

I really hated him at that moment, but I was still afraid, too.

Two beer cans sat open on the nightstand next to Simon, and Lilly was already beneath the covers on the other bed.

"You think he made it out of there and is coming to Arizona, like he said?" Mitch asked.

"No," Simon said.

"Yes," I countered. "Can I please have my letters back?"

Simon swigged at his beer and sank lower into the bed.

Mitch just looked at me, bundling up Matthew's letters and placing them on top of my map, handing them over like something exotic on a serving tray.

"And, nice map," Mitch said.

I sighed.

Simon rolled away from Mitch and me and fell to sleep.

Mitch popped open another beer and drank the entire can without stopping. Then he opened another and said, "You want a beer, Prude-boy?"

"No."

Then Mitch stretched his legs out on the bed, kicking our clothes and pack down onto the floor.

I sat down on the bed next to Lilly.

Mitch began snoring beside Simon.

I remember her pressing her lips to my ear, saying, "Jonah, turn out the light."

I did.

And I knew I should have gotten myself up and gone in there and grabbed my pistol right then; should have. And Simon and I could get out of that trap. But I was so tired, and I was shaking.

I listened to the rain, so constant, so loud against the roof.

And, in the dark, she whispered, so faintly, barely a breath, "Jonah. We have to be quiet."

The first gray-yellow light of the morning, the color of Mitch's teeth, fogged its way through the uneven blinds covering the window of the room where we slept at the Palms.

And I don't know if I woke up first, but I know my eyes opened when Mitch was standing over me, bellowing, "Well, isn't this romantic?"

Simon shot up in his bed and looked across at me.

I'd been sleeping, completely naked and uncovered, with my face down in the pillow, and Lilly was lying across me, her bare breasts pressed into my back, her fingers coiled into my hair, the tangled bedsheet wrapped around her hips. Our clothes were scattered everywhere, the orange bedspread thrown down to the floor at the foot of the bed.

I cracked my eyes open at Mitch's hollering, and, realizing where I was, seeing Mitch standing over us, feeling the burn of Simon's stare, reached down, digging between the sheets to the bottom of the bed, and hurriedly, crookedly, pulled my briefs up to cover my nakedness. Lilly sat up and wrapped herself in the dingy sheet, yawning.

She smiled at Mitch.

"Good morning," she said, stretching.

Simon glared at me as Lilly stroked my back so softly with her trailing fingers, drawing slow, small circles between my shoulder blades. I thought about gathering up my cast-off clothes, but I was too afraid to speak or move, afraid to even look at Lilly. And I was terrified of Mitch.

"This is why the people can't trust Jonah," Mitch announced, pacing a tight back-and-forth pathway between the beds. "This is why!"

Simon leaned forward on his bed, the swelling on his face reduced, the flesh around his eye smudged into a darkened purple.

"Now who's acting like a hippie communist, *Jonah?*" Simon blurted.

"Well, at least you don't have to worry about dying a virgin now," Mitch said flatly, and Simon just shook his head in obvious agreement and disgust.

Then Mitch turned to Lilly and said, "And how did you sleep?"

But there was an edge in his voice. He sounded like someone else. I knew he was mad, and I wasn't sure just how mad he was.

Lilly laughed softly and stood, holding the sheet pocked with holes and cigarette burns, letting her other hand brush softly across my bare shoulder. I wondered what Mitch was feeling, watching her touch me like that. But I wouldn't tell her to stop it, even though it terrified me.

"I dug it, Mitch," she said.

I was so scared and sick I just stared at my feet, certain that Mitch was going to kill us all on the spot. I was so stupid. How could I be so stupid? What was I thinking?

I wasn't thinking.

I couldn't stop it.

And I knew that Mitch had a thing for the girl, that he must have been seething inside at the thought of us all tangled up there in that dirty bed just inches away from him while he slept off his booze and pot.

I thought I was going to throw up.

And I wished, hopelessly, that Simon would say something to let me know he was still my brother and that we weren't going to break any more rules and let each other down, but I could see how he'd been looking at Lilly ever since we got into that car, too.

She trailed the stained sheet behind her as she made her way into the bathroom, picking her clothes from the floor as she swept past the stares of Mitch and Simon.

I scrambled to pull my cuffed and twisted jeans up over my legs. I could feel the wad of cash in the pocket, and replayed in my mind what had happened the night before, remembered the gun hidden in the shower stall, Lilly's body pressing madly into mine, completely undressing me as I lay there feeling my heart crawling up through my throat, falling upon me as Mitch and Simon slept soundly just across from us, in the same room as us, her moist lips pressed to my ear, the soundless whispering, "We have to be quiet. We have to be quiet."

And we had fallen to the floor beneath the window when the rain stopped drumming to quiet the creak of our bed, and later, exhausted, we both climbed back up and went to sleep.

It must have been only fifteen minutes before Mitch woke us up with his ranting.

And I never thought at all about getting away, about the gun I'd hidden in the shower, about Mitch, about protecting my brother.

I never thought at all.

I was so stupid.

I stood on shaking legs, trying and failing to get my jeans buttoned up, looking around on the floor for where my shirt and socks had fallen, kicking at the discarded bedcovers and finding nothing.

"And what about you?" Mitch prodded me, poked my chest with a nicotine finger.

I felt the rising heat of redness in my face. I said nothing.

I couldn't make my throat relax.

"Cat got your tongue, man?" Mitch laughed. "Or maybe you left it in Lilly's mouth."

"You're disgusting, Jonah," Simon said, and swung his legs out over the edge of his bed. "I hate you."

And I started to mouth a reply, but stopped myself before anything could come out. I saw my brother looking at me. I must have looked so pitiful. I wished I could tell him I was sorry, that I was crazy, that I wasn't going to do anything bad anymore, and I would take care of him like I promised I would.

Mitch zipped his suitcase shut.

Simon tapped down the pack of cigarettes beside his bed.

Water ran in the bathroom, and all the smells and sounds of that room in the morning made me feel nauseous. And in my swirling confusion, frustrated, silent, I could not find the rest of my clothes, and grabbed my hair in near-panic, already sweating, standing there like an idiot with my fly hanging open in jeans I couldn't steady my hands enough to button. Lilly emerged from the bathroom, her face wet and cleaned, smiling as she bent down and picked up my socks and shirt where she had thrown them, behind a corner chair, the cracks in its vinyl slitting open like sneering smiles.

I inhaled, trying to calm myself down, avoiding Lilly's eyes when she handed the clothes to me, breathing in the smell of Simon's menthol cigarette, and momentarily wondering if I shouldn't smoke one, too.

"You're a pig," Simon said to me.

"Don't be like that, sweetie," Lilly said, pouting her lips at Simon and holding out her hand. "Can I have one?"

I finished dressing, and began gathering the contents of our pack while Simon sat exhaling clouds of smoke in my direction, watching me, watching Lilly light her cigarette.

Mitch opened the door to the room, and, bracing his suitcase along the outside of his leg, stepped out into the light of the morning. He left the door wide open. When I was certain he had gone to the car, I ran for the bathroom.

"Are you okay, Jonah?" Lilly asked.

I quietly pressed the door shut behind me.

"I need to pee."

I flushed the whining toilet.

I reached into the shower stall, lifting the wet pistol nervously, stuffing it down into the front of my jeans, letting the long flannel shirt hang over. I was back in the room before Mitch was.

I finished filling our pack and tied it shut. Lilly watched me without a word. I could tell she wanted me to say something, but I was so confused and tense I didn't want to look at her, even if I couldn't think of anything else without seeing her, feeling her, in my mind.

She put her hand to the side of my face.

"Hey," she said.

I raised my eyes to hers.

Simon stood and went into the bathroom, exhaling an angry

sigh. As he passed by, he pushed me hard on my shoulder and said, "Yeah, I want to hit you back now. It's sickening what you did. In the same room as me. You stay the hell away from her, Jonah."

"It's a little late for that, Simon," Lilly said, and smiled as he turned away from her, taking a last drag from his cigarette, letting it fall from his lips into the toilet with a protesting hiss as he unbuttoned his fly and stood there, peeing with the door wide open.

The room darkened as Mitch's shadow blocked the doorway.

Lilly stood just inches from me, our bodies nearly touching, her hand on my face.

"This," Mitch said, "is likely to become a serious complication." And he laughed, exaggerating his slight Southern accent. "A matter of the utmost gravity."

Then he stepped aside and said, "Come on, let's go."

The toilet flushed.

Today, I thought. It would be today. I promised.

Today.

If things weren't already too complicated.

If it wasn't too late.

river

Dear Jones,

I got your letter today. I'm pretty sure I got all your letters now and so I put them in order and read them.

I don't know what to say, and I don't feel like writing hardly ever except to you. Even my best friends from home stopped writing to me anyway. I'm sorry, cause I'm pretty down today and maybe I won't even get this one into the envelope. I don't know. I did that a couple times, wrote you letters and then threw them away, mostly on days when I felt like this and then didn't want my little brother to worry about it.

We went out in the field to give some guys a break who had been out there for 8 months. Guys who are in the field for that long have a different look on their face, it's hard to explain. The first day we were there one of the guys who lives in the same hooch as me and Scotty got shot by a sniper while he was standing right next to me. He got shot in the neck, and there was nothing I could do about it but lay down with him and try to stop the bleeding but he died. He was just standing about a foot away from me, and he was shorter than me, too. I think that sniper was probably aiming at me and missed.

I get my R and R in June now. I'm going to go to Sydney with

Scotty. Jonah, I think we're going to do what I said, but I don't want to say anything else about it in a letter, so just know that, and trust me.

The pictures in here I took about a week ago. The first one is of me and Scotty outside a bar. Yeah, believe it or not, that shack is a bar. We have our shirts off 'cause we were seeing who was skinnier. Everything we eat here makes me sick. Most of us can't keep any weight on at all. At least they give us free cigarettes. Sorry to say it, but I smoke them. Don't tell Simon or Mother. I'm having one now.

Almost everyone here smokes pot. All the guys who live in our hooch do it, but not me. Whenever I come in it smells like pot and incense. Some of them snort cocaine all day long. That guy who wanted to kill Scotty was shooting coke in his arms.

That second picture is a woman sitting on a box. She was blindfolded because she was a VC spy and got caught. Right after I took that picture the GIs standing around her kicked her face in with their boots and killed her. I took pictures of that too but I'm probably going to throw them away.

So, Dad is supposed to get out of prison this summer? Are you going to try to see him? I would understand if you didn't want to, but if you do see him and I don't get a chance to, tell him I love him. I guess I got to see him around a lot more than you and Simon.

Don't fight with Simon.

You know, of all of us boys Simon is the one who is most likely to turn out like Dad, always getting in trouble and stuff. You know how wild he's always been, so don't fight with him.

See? I said I didn't feel like writing and I ended up writing five pages. I wish I could talk to you, Jones.

Tell Simon I love him.

Take care of him, big brother.

Love,

Matt

I never wanted to say anything again.

I was so tired.

Today I would keep the promise I'd made to Simon.

The floor of the Lincoln was pooled deep with rainwater, Don Quixote slumped over to one side, as though the rain had exhausted him with its weight. His paper mask sloughed down in gray clots of pulp, the electrical tape peeling away in black curls to reveal the metal man's bearded face for the first time, his eyes, deathlike, fixed forward, empty, and round. The Indian headdress had been drained of its hues in the storm, the leather now gone the color of rotted meat, the feathers that had been dyed to look like an eagle's, faded to the dingy white of the turkey they had been pulled from. Mitch pushed the statue upright and tugged the war bonnet away, casting it down into the mud of the Palms lot.

He pushed his seat forward. He looked at Lilly. "Get in the back."

"Is Jonah driving?" she said.

"Get in the back."

She slid in behind the driver's seat.

I watched her, and opened the door on the other side.

"Simon sits up front," Mitch said.

"Don't let him sit back there," Simon said. "After what he did to her?"

"Don't worry about them," Mitch said. "I'm sick of both of them and don't even want to look at them right now."

I felt myself go pale. I climbed into the backseat. It made my pants wet. The dripping statue stood between us.

Simon slammed his door.

Mitch drove the Lincoln away from the place where we'd slept, heading north.

"I'm sorry, Mitch," Lilly said.

"Sure you are. And what are you now, Lilly?" Mitch looked at her in the rearview mirror. I raised my eyes and saw him watching me, too. "Your feelings usually come and go every few seconds. Except maybe with that kid. How you feeling about him now, Lil?"

She didn't answer.

I closed my eyes.

It would have to happen.

Mitch said, "We'll be there today. Arizona. And you can say bye-bye to your boy. That'll be good for us."

I swallowed and looked at Simon. Mitch was going to do something bad, and it seemed like Simon hadn't caught on at all. He just sat there, watching the road, playing with his meteorite. Then he placed it on the dashboard as though it might offer some direction for us, but I thought, the only way it knows to go is down.

Simon trusted Mitch.

I knew there was something about Mitch that attracted Simon. Maybe it was just another way of pushing my buttons, because Simon had to sense I didn't like Mitch from the start. So his emulating Mitch, smoking cigarettes, stealing for him, riding naked in the backseat of the convertible to show off, was all just a way, I think, for him to let me know he was his own boss. And I wasn't his father.

He'd said it once, when we walked on that dusty road away from the trailer on that first morning.

He'd said, "You're not my father, Jonah. So you can stop acting like it."

And I said, "You don't have a father, Simon. You never did. Someone's got to look out for you and make you do what's right."

"Well, not you."

And after what I'd done to him, and what I'd done with Lilly in that room, forgetting all about my promise to take care of him, I knew Simon was probably right.

Mitch filled the Lincoln's tank with gas, grumbling to himself or to anyone who would listen about being gouged the 45-cents-per-gallon price in a do-nothing town full of bums, and how next time it happened he'd just hold the place up as soon as get robbed like that, and then he paid for donuts and coffee that he made Simon retrieve while we waited. Simon and Lilly ate in the car as Mitch drove north on the small road following the Río Cruces, as I silently looked out at the quiet landscape, refusing to eat, refusing to listen to what the others were saying, sometimes closing my eyes and pretending to sleep.

I didn't want to say anything.

It would have to happen today.

And I wanted to hurl that damned metal man as far as I could into the air behind the car and just fall on Lilly, to smother her with my body, and beg her to help us get away from Mitch, to come with me, tell her I was sorry—but I didn't know why—and I couldn't decide on what it was, exactly, that was the worst thing I'd done to feel so sorry for, but I still felt like shooting myself, anyway.

She had to know what she was doing, to Mitch, and Simon. To me.

I thought she must have felt like she was on some out-of-control plane, crashing down toward the earth, and it was like she wanted to keep her eyes open the whole way just so she could see everything right up to the end. And I wasn't going to let her do it.

We had to get away.

It was a perfect day, a terrible morning.

The sky hung so blue with the faintest feather-whisks of clouds above the open car, over the jagged and blood-hued volcanic mountains to the right and the lower, rounded hills dotted with green and rusted popcorn balls of shrubs, the sparse cottonwoods already going yellow on the opposite bank of the narrow river, their trunks shooting straight up among the flaming orange grasses along the rock-strewn banks of the water.

Simon and Mitch smoked cigarettes.

Mitch turned on the radio, but there was nothing to listen to, and he began talking to himself. I couldn't understand what he was saying.

"What?" Simon asked.

"We have to be quiet," Lilly said.

Feeling myself redden, I opened my eyes and looked across at her.

She smiled the faintest smile back at me, and I could tell she winked behind the black of her sunglasses, her brilliant hair tied neatly down to her head beneath the silk of a red scarf.

"What?" Simon repeated.

"When he gets like this," she said, and slid her hand along the seat behind the gleaming Don Quixote, letting it come to rest just before touching me, so I could feel the warmth of her skin, and know she was there, whispering, "We have to be quiet."

I sighed deeply and let my head fall back against the canvas top, closing my eyes, and covered Lilly's hand with mine.

I gave up.

I had to have her.

I wasn't going to listen to Simon. I wasn't going to listen to that voice in my head that kept telling me I'd better look out.

"Oh. Okay," Simon said, and pulled the cigarette away from his lips, blowing smoke into the warm wind.

So Mitch drove on, talking to himself, moving his head and eyes slightly from side to side, offering mumbled questions and answers inside a conversation involving nobody else.

Along the nothingness of the road, Mitch pulled the Lincoln into the driveway of a dark, squat building with a painted sign, the red-and-white lettering peeling in the dry heat of the desert, announcing "Chief's Roadhouse." There were no other cars at the stop, and I wondered how Chief himself ever came there.

Mitch played with the cap of the lighter, back and forth, a ringing metronome.

Flick.

"I need a beer," Mitch grumbled. "Do you want to come with me, Simon?"

"Sure, Mitch."

I looked at Lilly.

"We'll only be a few minutes," Mitch said to us. "Stay with the car. And try to keep your clothes on this time."

Lilly laughed, "That's funny coming from you, Mitch."

Lilly teased too much.

He gave her a look that made her smile vanish immediately. I avoided his eyes entirely, and even though I wished I could somehow stop Simon from going into the bar with Mitch, I was too afraid to say anything.

Maybe all Mitch needed was a beer.

Simon and I had never been apart, not one day in our entire lives. We never even slept one night in different rooms. But our getting into that car with Mitch and Lilly in the first place was what started to drive an unstoppable wedge between us, and I realized we were drifting helplessly apart after that morning when I woke up to Mitch standing over me at the Palms.

Even our story, our map, started going in separate directions on that day. And I never knew the terrible things that happened to my little brother until he'd told me much later.

But I can fill in the map and tell it now.

roadhouse

Mitch pulled the dark green door on the roadhouse open, thick forest-colored curls of lead paint corkscrewing back from the framing beside the panes of dusty glass. A string of tin bells hung from the inside of the doorway, signaling their entrance as Mitch and Simon pushed through strands of green plastic beads that draped from the ceiling.

"Howdy," the man behind the bar said.

At first, they didn't even notice him, he was so short and the barroom so dim. The only light beyond what seeped through the grimy windows came from a flickering yellow fluorescent tube beneath a shelf of bottles lined up neatly behind the bar, and a blue Hamm's Beer sign, a plastic backlit scene of a waterfall in a forest that somehow seemed to move, hanging on the wall near the pool table. The bartender's head, his hair, black and greased flat, barely rose up above the surface of the bar, and until he'd said anything, the man was as inconspicuous as any of the bottles tucked into the shelf behind him.

Simon thought the bartender must have been sitting down, but he was not.

"Hey, Chief," Mitch said, putting his hand on Simon's shoulder and walking him over to a stool at the bar.

Chief climbed up onto a small footstool behind the bar, so he could reach an ashtray and flick his cigarette clean. He slid another ashtray across the bar toward Mitch, who pulled five dollars from his pocket and asked Chief to give quarters to Simon for the cigarette machine.

"Anything to drink?" Chief asked, and Simon just stared at the little man's stubby hands in amazement as he handed the change to him.

"Two beers," Mitch said.

Simon carried his change to the vending machine.

"Two?" Chief asked.

"Yeah." Mitch cleared his throat. "I'm enlisting tomorrow. I'm going to Nam. Maybe this is the only time I'll ever be able to have a beer with my little brother. You understand, man."

Chief just shrugged and began pouring the beers. It was the middle of the week. There was no one in there except for the three of them.

don quixote

I watched the door close behind them.

And I wondered if my brother would ever come out.

I almost wished they'd both just vanish.

So we sat in the back of the Lincoln in silence for the longest time, me just staring at that peeling green door, trying to find what to say first, afraid that as soon as I said anything, Mitch and Simon would come back out again.

"I'm sorry, Lilly."

Lilly leaned forward, so that she could see me there on the other side of the metal man.

"What for?"

"I don't know. For what I did last night, I guess." I sighed. "Simon's right, you know. I am so stupid."

Lilly slid her hand back across the seat and put it on my leg.

"I like you, Jonah. Stop being so hard on yourself. You just make it easier for Simon to pick on you like that."

"Yeah," I said, almost choking on that one syllable. "I need to ask you some things, Lilly, but I don't know how to say it."

"You can ask me anything, Jonah." She smiled. She looked so sincere.

"I'm embarrassed about what I did last night," I said, and looked down at my feet, at the floor still wet with rainwater puddles.

"You don't have to be," she said. "I'm not."

"I thought I was going to pass out from holding my breath so much," I said, and I tried to smile, now turning my eyes to her.

Lilly giggled.

"You were trembling. You were shaking so hard."

"I was scared."

"Are you now?"

"Yes." And I looked away from her for a moment and said, "Who's the father?"

When I asked it, I could feel her tensing up, as though she would pull her hand away. Then I heard her breathe and she said, "Some old man."

"From where you live?"

"Yeah."

"Is he nice?"

"He's not like you."

"Oh." I cleared my throat. "Me and Simon need to get away from Mitch. He's not giving us the chance to. You know we got to get away from him."

"Yeah."

"What did you and Mitch do? Tell me the truth."

Lilly pulled her hand away from my lap and sat back in the seat so that I couldn't see her face. When she spoke, it was almost as though the words she spoke were coming from Don Quixote.

"I known Mitch since I was maybe twelve. He lived by me. He knew I was pregnant, and he wanted to help. I guess in his own way, he always thought there was something between us, but I never liked him back. Maybe I tease too much, I don't know. He wanted some money from his daddy so he could take me to California, you know? I guess he thought he was saving me somehow. In California, a girl can . . . you know. You can get rid of a baby if you need to. Mitch was on speed. He got into a fight with his daddy, and his daddy was going to throw Mitch out of the house. He's nineteen, Mitch is. And he killed his own daddy over it. Then he came and got me, and he told me what he did. I guess we were just bored of Texas, I don't know. That was only about a week ago. No one knows. They lived alone. No one's going to find out for a long time. And I guess I was so desperate that I'd do anything to get away from where I was heading, even if it meant riding along with Mitch and him drooling all over me all the time and trying to get me into bed with him. I guess I was pretty stupid last night, too, 'cause who knows what he's thinking now? But it's my fault, Jonah. I didn't mean to hurt you."

"It's not your fault, Lilly."

I closed my eyes, resting my head back so the sun made me see red through my eyelids.

Lilly said, "And Mitch took everything he could find at the house, and the keys to this Lincoln, and we loaded it up and locked the doors when we left, just like we were leaving on a family trip or something. His daddy kept a lot of money in the house. I seen Mitch counting it once, and he just acted like a dog trying to protect a scrap of meat, so I never said anything about it again. We went to Mexico. I didn't trust the doctors there and I begged Mitch to take me away. And he got mad at me one morning and he stopped at a place and shot a man right in front of me. He made me watch him do it. Then he took this statue from the dead man and we left Mexico. A couple days after that we saw you and Simon on the road and I pleaded with him to stop."

"You saw him kill someone?"

I heard her sigh. "I told you. There's nothing I can do. I got in the car with him, just like you and Simon. I need him to get me to California. Then I can get away from him."

I rubbed my eyes and leaned forward. Then I sat back again and grabbed the statue of Don Quixote and angrily shoved him forward, pushing the front seat into the steering wheel, the metal man falling until his tin plate hat came to rest just in front of the rearview mirror.

We heard what sounded like a door slamming from around the back of Chief's Roadhouse. I had seen an outhouse there when we pulled up.

"Are you just trying to make him jealous? Mitch?" I asked.

"Sometimes. I didn't think he'd care," Lilly said. "It's stupid, really. I never thought about Mitch like that. Ever. I didn't think he'd care what I did."

"It would make me crazy if I was him. Will you help us get away from him?" I asked. "Maybe you could just tell Mitch. I think he'd do what you ask."

"I don't know."

"Will you come with me? With us?"

Lilly trembled. "I'm scared Mitch would kill you."

I said, "Why do you stay with him?"

"I thought he could help me get away. I can't go home, anyway. There's only one direction I can go, even if I don't make it. But every time I turn around, it seems like I haven't gotten anywhere closer to where I want to be. I know I mess with Mitch too much. It's 'cause I'm mad. So he gets mad, too. I know I should stop. And now I'm afraid of him, I guess."

"I want you to come with me, Lilly."

I grabbed Lilly and pulled her over to me, covering her mouth with mine.

The door around back slammed twice more.

I couldn't stop it, even if I knew I had to. She was going to get us killed.

chief

Chief watched them as they smoked and drank their beers, Simon, already beginning to giggle to himself at how froglike the little man seemed, his big dark eyes just clearing the surface of the bar.

"Is he really your brother?" Chief asked.

"Yeah," Mitch said. "Give me some whiskey, too."

Chief spun around and climbed up on the shelf where the bottles were.

"The reason I asked," Chief said, "is 'cause I don't have a problem with a man buying a beer for his own brother. My brother did it for me when I was a kid, too."

"He's hurting today," Mitch said. "He just caught the girl he's in love with in bed with our middle brother."

"Is that how you got that black eye?" the bartender asked.

Simon didn't say anything.

"Brothers shouldn't do that kind of stuff," Chief said, sympathetically, as he climbed down with the whiskey bottle. "You jealous, kid?"

"He's a bastard," Simon said.

Simon began fidgeting on the barstool. He finished his beer and lit another cigarette.

Chief poured out a shot of whiskey for Mitch and another for himself.

"Don't mind if I do," Chief said, and raised his shot glass, "cheers," before tipping his head and pouring the whiskey straight back into his throat.

"Does the kid want another beer?" Chief asked.

Simon fidgeted. "I really need to pee," he said. "But, yeah, I'll have another one."

Chief began refilling Simon's glass, saying, "Go out that back screen door and turn left. The toilet's the first door there. Or you can just piss in the dirt. Not like it hasn't happened already today."

Simon jumped down from the barstool and practically ran for the door, which slammed loudly behind him.

(mitch)

piss-kid

Chief laughs.

He turns around to replace the whiskey bottle.

"Heh heh," he says. "The boy needs a little more drinking practice if he's gotta piss that bad."

He turns around, smiling.

Mitch shoots him in the center of the forehead with the pistol he's been hiding in the Lincoln's glove box.

Smoke and grit spout from the back of Chief's head, through his greasy black hair.

At first, he looks startled, like he's about to bust out laughing when the bullet smashes the same bottle he's just taken his final drink from.

Mitch puts the gun into his jeans and hangs his shirttail over it.

He takes a drag from his cigarette and listens to the sound of the whiskey dripping down onto the floor, the fluttering of Chief's hands on the wet tiles.

He stands so he can look over the bar.

He's a dead fish in the pool of whiskey and blood, the jagged shards of glass that look cool like ice. He moves his mouth just once, and a snotty bubble of blood inflates and pops on his lips.

He dies like that.

Mitch inhales. He likes the smell: whiskey, gunpowder, blood, the cigarette, the way that bars like this always reek of piss no matter how far out they put the toilets.

The door slams again. The little Piss-kid is back.

cool

Simon sat down on the stool beside Mitch and grabbed his beer.

"Do you feel better?" Mitch asked, smiling.

"Yeah."

"So do I, man. A lot better."

Mitch finished his beer. "I just noticed you can't hear your feet in those moccasins."

"Yeah," Simon beamed. "I dig them."

Simon looked around. "Where'd the little guy go?"

"He said he'd be back in a bit," Mitch said calmly. "Are you ready to go?"

Simon drained the last of his beer, and nearly fell down when he stepped off the barstool, laughing, "Yeah."

"Hey. Get a load of this," Mitch whispered, holding an index finger in front of his mouth so Simon would be quiet.

Mitch boosted himself up onto the bar, seated, so he was facing Simon. He reached around the cash register and pressed down the "No Sale" key and the drawer slid open with a bell.

"Shhh . . . Come here," Mitch said, keeping a finger straightened under his nose.

Simon was intrigued. Mitch leaned quietly over the bar and tugged all the bills from the cash drawer. He folded them once, then handed them to Simon.

"Put that in your pocket. And don't say nothing to Jonah or Lilly."

"Jonah's a stupid pig," Simon said.

"Hang on," Mitch said, and scooped a handful of quarters from the till. "Get as many packs of smokes as you can carry."

"Cool!"

"And let's get out of here."

cruces

You feel so nice," she said.

"I never did kiss a girl before yesterday."

"I know that."

"Oh. Sorry," I said.

I pulled Lilly's scarf away and raked my fingers into her hair. She unfastened the top button on my shirt. She slid her hand onto my chest. I thought about her unbuttoning that same shirt as I lay in bed the night before.

"I didn't mean to force you, Jonah. I just wanted to see what it felt like to be the one who was getting what they wanted for a change. I just wanted to see what it would be like to be with someone who was nice to me for a change."

"What did it feel like?"

"A different world," she said. "A perfect world."

I wanted to believe her. I thought I could. But I could almost hear Simon telling me she was just playing, and I didn't want to listen to it. She played with Simon, too; and maybe it was her way of asking one of us to save her. But her voice sounded so nice and I wanted to take her away so bad.

And I put my mouth to her ear and whispered, "We have to be invisible."

Then the dark green door opened and Simon stepped out, squinting in the brightness of the day. Mitch was behind him, with his hand on Simon's shoulder.

"What the hell, Jonah?" Simon said.

But Lilly and I didn't say anything, and we didn't make any attempt to separate as she rested beside me with my arm around her shoulders, her legs stretched out across the white seat of the Lincoln.

"No sale!" Mitch said. "You two need to keep your hands off!"

"You just told us to keep our clothes on, Mitch," Lilly said, pushing away from me. "And we did. This time."

I put my mouth to her ear. I whispered, "Stop it, Lilly."

Mitch put his hands on the top of the driver's door, and stared at the toppled statue leaning down against the dashboard.

I could smell the booze and cigarettes on both of them.

Simon, drunk, took a swing at my head, but I easily got out of the way of the punch, tucking my face against the seat back.

"You stupid bastard!" Simon growled. "I told you to stay away from her."

"Leave us alone, Simon," I said.

"Oh . . . so the mute boy finally speaks," Mitch said.

Simon pushed past Mitch, and, reaching into the car, lifted up the meteorite in his fist as though he were going to crush it against my head.

Lilly put her hand up in front of my brother. "Now just stop it, Simon!"

Simon raised the rock again, then he let his arm fall limp to his side and walked around the back of the car and opened his door.

"That's better, sweetie," Lilly said, and she leaned over the front seat and kissed Simon on the ear and brushed his hair back with her hand. He stunk like beer and sweat.

I guess I never figured we'd eventually have to wash the clothes we left home in.

Mitch started to straighten out the statue, and Lilly said to him, so sweetly, "Mitch, baby, can I trade places with Don so I can sit next to Jonah?"

Mitch looked at her with cold, unblinking eyes and a perfectly straight face, and said, "Don't ever ask me that again, Lilly."

And Lilly gave me a look that told me I was wrong, that Mitch wouldn't do something just because she'd asked for it.

As soon as we were back on the road, Mitch started talking to himself again.

Simon put his head down against the door and went to sleep.

I slid a foot out of one shoe and moved it over and rubbed against Lilly's foot under the seat. I tried to make myself be brave, even if I didn't know what that was.

"Mitch, honey," Lilly finally said. "Don says he thinks you should pull over and smoke a reefer."

Mitch, startled, snapped out of his chat and said, over his shoulder, "Far out."

At a graveled turnout across the opposite lane of the road, Mitch wheeled the Lincoln to a stop alongside a bent and shotgun-peppered green-and-white road sign marked RÍO CRUCES. And I wondered why anyone out here in the middle of absolute nothingness, at least nothing that had any name on it, would care at all what this river was called.

And I had a feeling Mitch decided this would be the place; that he'd try to kill me there by that river today.

Today.

Simon straightened his head up. He may have sensed the car coming to a stop, but I could tell by his eyes he was completely drunk. I'd seen that same look enough times on our father, when he was at home.

I slipped my foot back into my shoe and let go of Lilly's hand where I held it concealed behind the Spanish knight, and the four of us climbed out from the car, Simon practically stumbling. There was a narrow, sloping path down to the river. Small white, bubbling waves streaked over the water's surface where it ran above rocks. To our right, the river bent ahead of us, connecting dirt roads on either side where a sagging wooden bridge stretched. It had been built between crooked telephone poles that jutted up from the banks, drilled through to thread thick and rusted metal cables that shaped the cupping of the bridge's splintered surface.

I stretched my legs out; the gun in my jeans was hurting me again.

"This is a real pretty spot," Lilly said.

"I'm thirsty. Can I have my canteen, please, Mitch?" I asked. I didn't want to set Mitch off, and I knew Lilly couldn't stop herself from pushing at him.

Mitch didn't say anything. He looked at me once, his mouth turned down in a sour grimace. He went to the back of the Lincoln to open the trunk.

A few minutes later, Mitch sat, alone, at the edge of the river and rolled his joint. I watched him from the bank, could hear that lighter opening and shutting. I took out my map and added in the stretch of road we had covered since leaving the Palms, drawing a place I marked "Chief's" and the spot with the sagging bridge crossing the river.

Simon began tripping down the trail toward Mitch.

"Simon!" I called out, already able to smell the oily smoke of the joint from where I sat beside the car.

Simon just kept going until he dropped down beside Mitch.

I could hear them talking, laughing about something. I saw Mitch hand the joint over to Simon, watched as Simon smoked from it.

"I'm not feeling good again," Lilly said. "I need to sit down."

Lilly moved back toward the open door of the car, then stopped and turned around.

"Can I do anything for you?" I asked.

"I'll be fine," she said. "I need some water."

Then she moved over to a clump of sagebrush and dropped to her knees, lowering her head, coughing and spitting. I let the backpack fall beside her in the weeds, the canteen resting on top.

"Here," I said.

She drank. "There. I'm better now." She tried to laugh. "Sometimes it comes and goes so fast."

I helped her to her feet, holding her hand. I looked over my shoulder at Mitch and Simon, both of them facing the river, sitting with their backs to me, and said, "Let's take a walk."

Today. I had to try to get us away. I wasn't such a dumb kid I didn't know what Lilly was trying to do, but I could help her out, anyway.

I led her up the river, toward the narrow and deep bend where the old bridge connected the two sides. The sun, straight overhead, made the water look so dark and blue here.

"We'll need to eat soon," I said. "The next place we get to where there's people around, you and me and Simon are getting away from him. Even if I have to force Simon."

"All right, Jonah."

bridge

Mitch relaxed. He leaned back on his elbows in the dried grass. Simon lit a cigarette and listened to the sound of the water spilling over the rocks.

"Simon," Mitch said, "it's hard to really trust a kid like your brother."

"He's dirty," Simon said.

"What do you say we kick him off our ship, and make him find his own way to Arizona? And you can ride along with me and Lilly. And Don," Mitch laughed.

"That would be fun."

"We'd get you to your daddy. Or your brother. Wherever."

"I like you and Lilly, Mitch," Simon said.

"Maybe you like Lilly too much." Mitch smiled and pushed Simon's shoulder playfully.

"Maybe I do," he said. "I thought she liked me more. It just drives me crazy seeing him all over her like that."

"Yeah."

And Mitch turned and looked at Simon.

Then he saw me and Lilly walking out on the bridge in the distance and said, "See what I mean? You can't take your eyes off Jonah for one minute."

Simon looked to where Mitch was staring and saw me and Lilly holding hands and walking out across the slumping bridge.

And Mitch said, "Know what I'll do? I know what to do."

the fall

"I will go with you, Jonah."

"I guess neither one of us has a home, anyway."

"Will you take care of me?"

We sat down just above the center of the river, dangling our legs over the edge of the old gray wood bridge. I stared down at the blue-black water running like smearing trails away from my feet, and Lilly leaned against my shoulder.

"I'll try," I said. "I will. For all of us. Me and you and Simon. I have to look out for Simon, before he's too far gone. I promised him I would. I promised Matthew."

"I don't think he really hates you."

I sighed. "Simon's confused about things. And he needs to grow up."

"What a pretty picture," Mitch said.

Mitch and Simon had quietly stumbled out onto the bridge. Mitch had pulled his gun from his pants and was holding it alongside his leg, where I couldn't see it. But Simon did. He looked at the pistol, he looked at Mitch, but Mitch was just staring at me.

And I startled and turned my head just as Simon brought his foot up and pushed me from the bridge, into the deep flowing water.

I looked up. It seemed like I was falling forever through that twenty feet of air before I hit the river.

"Jonah!" Lilly cried out, and leaned forward as though to follow me down, but Mitch caught her arm and tugged her away from the edge.

The current sucked me away, the water so cold I couldn't breathe.

My head went under, the weight of my shoes and clothes, the gun in my waist, pulling me down.

rope

Now that's what I call gravity, man!" Mitch said, and slapped Simon on the shoulder.

Simon stood at the edge and watched me being carried away from him in the pull of the current.

"Let's get in the car," Mitch said.

Neither Simon nor Lilly said a word as Mitch drove the Lincoln over the road that twisted its way out of the river gorge. Lilly sat with her head down in the backseat, hiding from the occasional glances Mitch tried giving her in the rearview mirror.

Simon stared ahead, stoned, his blurry eyes transfixed by the rush of the scenery smearing past him.

Mitch turned west onto a flat, straight highway that narrowed to a pinpoint in the distance; the endless sprawl of the desert ahead now gone completely red, dotted with black tufts of scrub weed in the stretching light of evening.

He smiled.

"This is the way I wanted it, just us," he said, brightening when they passed a yellow-and-black hand-painted sign. "Hey, look! 'Friendly Indians Ahead.'"

He pointed at the sign, and Simon smiled and nodded.

"I'm a rat," Simon said.

"This ship is full of rats," Mitch answered, and slapped Simon's arm.

"It serves him right," Simon said, even if he didn't believe it.

"If you didn't do it, I was getting ready to shoot that punk in the back of the head for what he did to our Lilly last night."

"I know," Simon said.

That was when Simon started being afraid of Mitch, too.

"I'm not *your* Lilly," Lilly called out from the backseat.

"Guess what? You're not Saint Jonah's, either, now." Mitch laughed, and added, coldly, "Whore."

Mitch pulled the Lincoln into the empty roadside Indian shop and left Lilly alone in the car while he and Simon negotiated with the couple inside, purchasing armfuls of blankets, sandwiches, and a bottle of vodka.

Simon smoked a cigarette while Mitch carried his goods out to the trunk of the car, and Lilly just sat next to the statue and watched them both in the darkening evening. When he was finished loading the trunk, Mitch told Simon to get back in the car and they continued west.

"We're going to sleep in the desert up here," Mitch said. "I got some food, and I'm going to get drunk as hell tonight."

"Yeah," Simon agreed, forcing a smile.

Mitch smiled back.

A hundred yards from the road, parked in the lightless desert, they ate their sandwiches and smoked cigarettes. Mitch twisted the stamp from the bottle of vodka and began drinking in big gasping gulps. They had spread the blankets on the flat dirt beside the Lincoln and sat there watching the sweep of lights from passing cars that came by so infrequently on the highway.

Mitch, sitting between Simon and the girl, passed the bottle to Lilly, but she gave it back.

"I'll get sick," she said.

He handed the bottle to Simon.

Simon took a swig, but coughed and spit most of the vodka out onto his jeans.

"Drink it," Mitch said sternly. "When I drink, you drink."

Simon took another swallow.

"This is horrible," he said.

"Trust me, man. You'll like it in a couple more swallows."

In minutes, Simon could no longer sit up straight.

He coughed and laughed, "You were right, Mitch. I like it."

Simon fell over to his side, eyes fixed open, watching as the fuzzy cloud of drunkenness distorted the night landscape. It looked as if the ground were breathing, constantly rising up and twisting before his eyes, then sinking back down and rising again.

Mitch pulled him up by the collar of his tee shirt and pressed the mouth of the bottle between his lips.

"Drink again," he said, and tipped the bottle back, spilling its last bits into Simon's mouth.

Simon gagged and rolled away from Mitch, tried to get to his feet, but collapsed. He raised himself onto his hands and knees and crawled headfirst into a mesquite bush and began vomiting.

"Thatta boy!" Mitch said. He stood, wobbling, and hurled the empty bottle out into the darkness, listening for the shattering crash of glass when it struck the ground.

Simon threw up again.

Mitch opened the trunk of the Lincoln and picked up the yellow rope. He formed a slip noose at one end. He stumbled to where Simon had propped himself in the brush and pulled the boy's feet back straight. Simon fell face-first into the brambles and tried to lift himself back up again.

"What're you doin'?" Simon slurred.

Mitch wound the cord around Simon's feet, binding them tightly together and knotting the line snug. Simon was too drunk to resist, and too sick.

"Stop it, Mitch!" Lilly snapped.

Mitch ignored her and dragged Simon from the brush by his feet, Simon's hands grabbing at the dirt and trying to claw away. But Mitch was too strong. He pulled Simon's legs up behind him and stretched the rope up painfully past Simon's crotch.

Simon groaned.

Then Mitch used the line to lace Simon's hands as if he were bound in prayer, his wrists jammed tightly down between his legs, and already numbing from the constriction of the knots.

"What're you doin'?" Simon pleaded, not able to really understand what was happening, because everything seemed like a sick dream, unreal in the vomit stench that burned in his nose; that clung to his face.

"Stop!" Lilly screamed.

"Oh, be quiet, Lilly." Mitch spoke calmly. "Trust me. It's all going to be okay."

Mitch rolled Simon over onto his side and covered him with a blanket.

"That's for your own good. I'll let you loose in the morning. Trust me. You know I'm doing the right thing. I just don't want you getting any ideas like your brother did with the whore tonight. I don't want her getting any ideas about being a slut on you. When you know I'm right, I won't have to do this again. You'll see. I want you to be a good boy, so I got to teach you this lesson. You can trust me, man. You gotta trust someone."

Lilly began crying.

Mitch played with his lighter.

Flick.

Simon closed his eyes.

Mitch took out the scissors he'd bought and began scratching some figures in the paint on the side of the Lincoln next to the image of that tailless dog: a tall and thin boy with long hair, a very short man, a boy curled up and tied with cord.

"Watch this, Simon."

Simon kept his eyes shut. He tried to.

Mitch stood over Lilly, the scissors held pointing down.

"Take your clothes off."

"No!" she said.

"Take them off! You did it for *him!*"

He swiped a hand to grab her, but Lilly rolled away and ran out into the darkness of the brush.

"Lilly!"

He lay down on the blanket beside Simon.

Simon pretended to sleep. He felt the cool of the scissor blades pressed against the side of his throat. Mitch stroked his hair and whispered, "Simon. Simon."

They didn't wake up until late the next afternoon.

Simon's hands and feet were purple and numb, his wrists and ankles crisscrossed with angry red welts. Mitch fumbled with shaking hands at the unmanageable knots he'd tied. Lilly sat emotionless, propped against a tire in the shade of the car.

"I'm sorry, Simon," Mitch said, his voice choked, nearly crying. "I don't know why I did that. I was mad at your brother. I'm sorry, buddy. I won't do it again, I promise. But you know why I did it, okay?"

Simon shook his head. The images from the day before replayed in his head.

"It's okay, Mitch," he said. "Only please hurry up or I'm going to pee in my pants."

"I'm sorry."

And Mitch began crying.

"I like you, Simon. Please don't be mad at me."

"It's okay, Mitch. Come on!"

Mitch freed Simon's feet and, dizzy, Simon stumbled away into the brush.

He could hear Mitch sobbing behind him while he peed.

Miles of empty desert separated us.

Mitch had killed a man in that roadhouse, but Simon wouldn't know it until later the next day.

But, he told me, he did know then he'd have to get away from Mitch.

And he would take her with him, too.

dalton

My brother,
  I'm going to have to write small and on both sides of the paper here because this isn't my paper, and pretty soon I have to ride shotgun out to a position.

Yesterday was some holiday here, I don't know what, and so last night the VC just poured mortars down on us, and a few explosions sounded like rockets.

I guess the war has caught up to me in a big way. One day last week an enemy rocket blew up within spitting distance of me. Then, when I was riding shotgun out to one of our positions in the sticks, and there were a couple trucks in front of me, and the lead truck blew up from a mine. If I would have got to that road five minutes earlier I would have beat the other trucks. I'm not complaining, though, that was the same spot where the sniper killed my buddy.

Tomorrow I'm going to see the medic or doctor because a couple of days ago I hooked up a water trailer to a Chinook helicopter while it was hovering over me and the wind a Chinook makes is two or three hundred MPH and it shot something into my eye. It doesn't hurt but I can feel it in there and last night all kinds of pus came out of my eye.

Two days before that one of our positions lost three guys because their gun blew up on them while they were firing. It just shows that they were a crummy crew that never took care of their guns.

So I guess I've been either getting pretty lucky, or my number's about to come up. I don't know, but either way this place is making me nuts and every day when I wake up, that is, if I actually got to sleep, I wonder if I'm going to ever make it out in one piece.

I know I shouldn't have told you everything that has happened because you'll probably worry more than you should but I want to tell you what's happening with me over here and how sick I am of all of it.

Look for me in August. I'll send you Scotty's address in Arizona to find me.

I know you said not to do it, but I made up my mind.

And remember what I said, you guys are brothers. Don't push Simon around too much, you know he'll go crazy.

Bye.

Love,

Matt

I caught a glimpse of Lilly.

Mitch took her from the bridge.

The water turned me.

I struggled to raise my head above the surface and coughed. Looking downriver, I could see the blurry colors of both banks sweeping past on either side as though I were running on some kind of treadmill, a cartoon character, going nowhere while the world spun beneath me, past me, repetitive and meaningless. And I thought, *Why did Simon do that to me?* And then I cursed myself and thought, *I know why, I know why.*

The river carried me half a mile before I could get any footing near the bank opposite the roadway. I was tired, weak from not eating, and I fell against a rock covered with reeds as I climbed away from the river.

I slipped my shoes off and shook out the rocks and mud before putting them back on my feet. The gun had fallen all the way down into my pants leg, I had to pull them half down to get it, but I was relieved I had not lost the pistol in the water.

That river was moving much faster than it looked from the outside.

I just sat there, dripping, my nose running, and tried to figure out what I would do next. I took off my shirt, almost laughing to myself that in traveling across this empty desert over the past three nights, I had never been covered by so much water, so often nearly drowned, in my entire life.

"Thank God we weren't sailors," I said.

I stood and wrung out the flannel shirt. I slung the pistol inside it and tied it around my waist by its sleeves.

The road we took here stretched along the other side of the river, and I wasn't about to cross it by putting myself back into the current. I knew that if I followed the river north it would take me back to the bridge where my brother had pushed me; Simon's getting even for my taking him away from our shack in Los Rogues, getting even for the beating I gave him, getting even for the girl.

The bank was too steep to walk close to the river, so I had to climb up farther and try to get to the hilltop before I could head back toward the wooden bridge. I made my way through the loose and crumbling dirt and thick brush of the hillside. When I had gotten high enough that there seemed to be some level path along the spine of the hill, I began walking in the direction from which the river had carried me.

Above the river on that hilltop, I could see across to the road and to the dirt turnout with the bent-over sign where Mitch had parked the Lincoln. The car was gone, and I felt so abandoned and alone, afraid for Simon, and angry at him, too, for what he had done on the bridge, for what Simon had been letting Mitch do to him for three days now.

Because I knew there was something in Simon that made him want to be like Mitch, and I was afraid of that.

I'd heard Lilly scream my name when the river swallowed me, but nothing after that beyond the roar of the water, the awkward thrashing of my arms and legs covered in the weight of my wet clothes, my own struggled breathing. I wondered where she was at that moment and wished that she could be with me, too, away from this place, away from Mitch.

Soaked and sore, I finally made it back to the sagging bridge and crossed to the other side of the river where the car had been. My backpack lay in the twisted shrubs where I had dropped it, the canteen still resting upon it in the spot where Lilly had placed it after I offered her a drink. I was relieved in finding my things, in knowing that Matthew's letters—and my map—were still there.

I took the gun from the shirt-sling around my waist and tucked it down into the pack. I didn't change clothes; the only other pants I could wear were still wet from the rainstorm the day before, anyway. But I found a dry tee shirt of Simon's and pulled it on over my head.

It smelled like Simon. It smelled like cigarettes, too.

I ached.

I wanted to cry, to scream, to run down that road as fast as I could, to find Mitch and put a bullet in him, to save Simon, to save Lilly, but I just sat down in the dirt by my pack and rearranged the contents to spare Matthew's letters from the dampness.

Then I took out the map and drew in that short trip I'd taken from the bridge and the walk back on the other side of the river.

I was so tired. For the first time, I realized that I thought we'd never make it to where we wanted to go. I thought I'd never see my brother again.

I decided I'd sat there long enough. As I put my things away and stood up on shaking and tired legs, I heard the sound of a car on the road. So I hurried to sling the pack over my arm and moved quickly out to the roadside, hoping to catch a ride with anyone who might be traveling along that abandoned stretch of highway.

The noise came from a Volkswagen Beetle, painted a dull sand color with rust spots on its skin. It so naturally blended in with the terrain of the desert that it almost disappeared against the background of the river gorge.

The storage rack on the top of the car was loaded with bundles of what looked like canvas and several wooden posts, all lashed down tightly with rust-stained ropes.

It pulled into the same turnout where Mitch had parked the Lincoln earlier.

The driver stuck his arm out the side window and waved.

His face was hidden behind goggles, and he wore a cap the same color as the car he was driving, with what looked like a square towel or rag tucked into it, hanging down over the back of his neck. When I noticed there was no glass where the windshield should have been, I understood why he was wearing those goggles.

So I waved back.

I thought about how Simon had stuck his thumb out to get Mitch and Lilly to stop for us. Dread rose from my stomach.

The driver was alone.

He opened the door and stood beside the idling car. He pulled his goggles and hat away and I could see he was just a boy, probably no older than I was. He smiled. He looked friendly.

"Did you fall out of an airplane or something?" he said. "'Cause I never seen anyone just appear out here all alone."

"I guess I'm lost," I said. "I got stuck out here."

"Are you okay?" Now the boy looked concerned. I noticed he was looking at my wet jeans, and the water dripping from my hair.

I didn't answer. I didn't know if I was okay or not.

"Well, can I help you or something? Do you need a ride?"

"I think I do. Yeah."

"Where to?"

I thought. "I don't know. Arizona."

"Are you high or something?"

"No."

"Well, I can't take you to Arizona right now. I got things to drop off to my dad. And Arizona's a long way. I'd have to ask my mom and dad if it was okay. But I'll give you a ride. Sure. Are you hungry?"

"Yeah."

The boy scratched his head. His hair was very short and dark, and just the way his eyes studied me, so relaxed, almost smiling, made me feel he was honest and sincere.

"I'll take you to my place, if you want. It's a few miles across the river. We can get you something to eat and you can tell them about how you need to get to Arizona. And where you came from. I bet it's a good story."

The boy replaced his cap and goggles and sat down behind the wheel.

I just stood there. I looked back down the road where Mitch would have gone with Simon and Lilly.

"Are you going to stay here or get in? It really doesn't matter to me if you don't want to."

I shrugged and stepped around to the opposite side of the VW. I put the pack down on the floor between my feet and the car took off, heading out across the sagging bridge.

The bridge creaked and swayed as we drove across it. The boy looked at me.

"Scared?"

I guess he noticed I'd tensed up. "Yeah."

I wasn't thinking about the bridge, or the water, though. I was thinking about Simon and Lilly.

And then I said, "I would never think this bridge could hold up a car like this."

"It's never let me down so far. I've driven across this bridge at least a thousand times. Here. Sorry it's such a mess."

He reached behind my seat and pulled another pair of plastic goggles out from the piles of papers and cans, shoes and clothing.

"These will help for the dust. And bugs, too. Only they're not so bad now as they get in spring."

I pulled on the scratched and hazy glasses. I turned around and looked at all the things haphazardly piled in back.

"I'm pretty disorganized," he said. "My dad says I'm a clown. My mom just says I'm a mess. Living out here, I guess neither one is an insult."

The VW lurched and pitched as its wheels hit the dirt road on the opposite side of the river. The boy pushed his foot down and the car sped forward.

"No one ever just *falls* in the river," he said. "And, besides, your pack's dry. Were you trying to kill yourself or something?"

"No," I said. "It was a mistake. I did something stupid."

"Now that sounds like a good story," he said. He shifted gears and stuck a dirty hand out to me. "My name's Dalton."

I shook his hand.

"That's a weird name."

"I know."

"My name's Jonah."

Dalton burst out laughing and slapped his palm down on the steering wheel.

"Now *that's* a weird name, Jonah!"

"I know."

I slipped my wet feet, still wearing Simon's socks, from my shoes. The floorboards of the VW were warm, hot even, and it felt good.

I saw Dalton look down at my muddy feet.

"Man, you are really drenched."

"I don't have anything to put on. All my clothes are wet after last night."

"It really came down last night," Dalton said. "This wash up here must have been under a good seven foot of water. You were outside last night?"

I thought about being in that car, sitting in the muddy lot outside the motel.

"For a while."

"I wasn't at my camp. I just got back from Los Alamos today."

"You live in a camp?"

Dalton shrugged. "Kind of. We own this land, and we plan on building a regular house on it, but for now it's just a camp. There's a few old Indian ruins on it, part of a pueblo, and when my dad found it . . . well, he's kind of obsessed with digging around in it. But he's obsessed with a lot of things. My dad's an artist. He paints."

"What does he paint?"

"You'll see," Dalton said. "Pictures. Crazy stuff, but some people like it, I guess. We lived all over. Mostly in Mexico. You know where the Yucatán is?"

"No."

"Well, we lived there ever since I was about eleven, but about six months ago we all packed up and came up here. Mom, Dad, me, and my sister."

"Oh. It must be nice, living with your whole family together like that. Do you like it where you're at now?"

Dalton bit his lip. "I liked Mexico better, but it's okay living out here, too, I guess. I know you're probably thinking we're hippies or something, but it's not like that at all. That's why I keep my hair so short. So no one will wonder."

"I wasn't thinking that," I said. "And anyway, me and Simon can't afford a haircut. That's why my hair's so long, in case you were wondering if I'm a hippie. 'Cause I'm not."

"Simon?"

"My little brother."

Dalton laughed. "I could give you a haircut."

"Maybe."

"Won't cost you anything."

"What if my brother doesn't recognize me?"

What if I never saw him again, anyway?

"Amazing, isn't it?" Dalton pointed his hand through the open space where the windshield should have been, at a narrow opening in a red slickrock canyon far ahead in the distance. "That's where we're going. Chavez Canyon."

"Thanks," I said.

"For what?"

"For helping me out."

I felt better.

Then I told Dalton our story, as he drove along that rutted and uneven dirt track. I explained everything that had happened to Simon and me since we left Los Rogues; how our horse had fallen dead, the night we spent in the derelict trailer, meeting Mitch and Lilly, the strange old car, and riding across the state in the backseat beside Don Quixote. And I told him about my fight with Simon, and how Mitch threatened to kill him, and that I believed him, that I was scared.

And I even told him how I'd slept with Lilly the night before, and how Mitch and Simon were both so jealous, and that was how I ended up adrift in that river, and soaking wet on the side of the road.

"Damn," Dalton grinned. "You had sex with a girl you just met the day before?"

And then he cleared his throat. "I hope whatever you got rubs off on me. How old are you, anyway?"

I said, "Sixteen."

"Damn. And I'm eighteen and never got nowhere with a girl. Of course, there's no girls besides my sister within a hundred miles of Chavez Canyon."

"I wasn't looking for it," I said. "Like I said, I never even wanted to get into that car in the first place."

"So are you in love with her now? Or just . . . you know . . ."

"I think so. I don't know." I sighed.

"Well, I don't know exactly how you should handle telling my folks this story," Dalton said. "I mean, I never lie to them, and they're really cool. But I don't think my dad would want me to drive you out to Arizona if he thinks we're chasing after some psychopath or something. And you should definitely leave the sex part out when you tell my mom, with my little sister around."

"I'll remember that."

Dalton was calm and confident, skinny like me, with sun-brown skin and a faint black peach fuzz mustache over his lip. He was dressed all in tan, the kind of clothes you'd almost expect an archaeologist to wear, his cotton pants tucked into the tops of dusty, laced-up boots.

And he listened attentively, just saying, "Wow," from time to

139

time, as I told him the whole story, even about Matthew and how I was afraid we wouldn't ever see him again.

"Crazy, man," he said when I finished talking.

And I shifted, uncomfortable in my wet clothes, and saw I'd made a dark spot where I'd soaked the seat.

"Oh. Sorry," I said, seeing that Dalton had noticed, too.

He just laughed. "Oh yeah, this car *never* gets dirty or rained on."

I suddenly felt anxious and guilty for riding along with Dalton, heading in the opposite direction from Simon.

"So that's why I really need to get on the road and try to get my brother back. And Lilly. I think something bad's gonna happen."

"Let's just think about this, Jonah. I mean, I'm all for helping you out. But there's nothing out here, you know? We got no telephone or radio or nothing, so it's not like we can call the state troopers out or something."

"I've got money," I offered. "I can pay you if you take me to get my brother. Please."

"Look," he said, "I really want to help you if I can, believe me. But it's getting late, and my dad's expecting me back today with this stuff."

He pointed a thumb up at the roof. "And it's nice of you to offer money, but if I was going to give you a hand, I wouldn't do it expecting to get paid."

He turned the VW across a creek in a wash, spraying fans of water out from the wheels. I looked across, into the canyon. It really was an incredible place of sheer, slick walls rippled by seasons of weather, cottonwoods and willows springing up from the floor where the water would rush in torrents when the rains came.

"Just come to the camp with me. I mean, there's nothing you can do now, anyway. You got in the car and we're going," he said. "I'll get you something to eat. Then we'll see."

I sighed and rubbed my eyes.

I could tell Dalton sensed my indecision.

"Do you want me to turn around and bring you back to the road, then?" he asked.

I thought about it.

"No."

"Cool," he said. "I know my folks won't mind having a visitor. We don't get a chance to talk to any other people too often. Just remember, you don't have to tell them everything. Okay?"

"Okay. I'll remember."

"You want some of my dry clothes?" He pointed at the stuff in piles behind me.

"Sure."

Dalton stopped the car right in the middle of the road, got out, and pulled his seat back forward. Then he began picking out unsorted articles of clothing from between and beneath the books and papers in the little car.

"Here." And he began handing things over to me. "I think these will fit you okay. I know they make us look like we're Maoists, even though we're Indian."

"You are?"

"Well, my dad's white. But my mom's Indian."

"Does it make a difference?"

"Well, you know how some white guys are. In New Mexico, I mean."

Dalton laughed.

He gave me a set of dry clothes and boots to wear, and it felt so good to get out of my wet things, the clothes I had been carrying around for days, and change into something different. And even though Dalton was just a bit shorter than me, his things fit me better than Matthew's ever did. So when I had finished changing, it almost looked like we were both in the same Army or something; I had on the same loose khaki pants, which I tucked into the tops of the boots he'd given me, and a dry tee shirt that actually fit me and was newer, probably, than anything Simon and I ever owned. He even dug a cap, tan, like his, out from a cardboard box full of canned green beans.

So when I got back into that car, clean and dry, and Dalton started driving again, I tried to tell myself that everything would work out, that things would get better.

But I couldn't stop worrying about Simon.

I couldn't get Lilly off my mind, either.

"Now all you need's the haircut and you'll look like one of us," he said.

I may not have felt sure about what I was doing, but I did get into that car with Dalton, and I was very hungry, so I decided to try to relax and just see where I'd end up from this ride. I sat back in my seat and watched the canyon walls stretching taller as he drove us along the creek toward his camp.

"How far is it?" I asked. I felt myself almost falling to sleep.

"We have a way," Dalton said. "The camp's eighteen miles in from the bridge, and we can't go very fast on this road."

"Eighteen miles," I sighed, calculating the distance between me and my brother drifting away in that Lincoln, and then cursing myself because I thought that counting those miles seemed too much like something Mitch would do. *Anyway,* I thought, trying to erase any numbers from my head, *here I am and there's nothing else I can do about it now.*

"You said it was just a few miles."

Dalton smiled. "Eighteen is a few. To me."

The camp sat in a wide clearing along the creek where a large canvas tent stood beside a truck with a rusting camper shell. There was one table and some chairs sitting beside the tent, a cooking area, and a fire ring with a blackened coffeepot resting atop a rock at its edge. One crooked willow tree extended its branches above the tent, and several yards back, a still, green pool of water formed where the creek backed up against the bend of red rock in the shade of the canyon's sheer face. I could see where there were stones piled, forming walls and storage bins, part of the remains of a ruined pueblo near the bottom of the canyon.

"This is where I live," Dalton said as he opened his door. He peeled off his goggles and cap.

I took my goggles off. I was sweating where they'd been cupped against my skin.

"It's pretty primitive," he said, pointing to the green pond. "There's our bathtub. And up behind those rocks is where our toilet is, currently."

"Where's your parents?"

"They're probably digging around in the caves or working on the house. Or Dad's doing one of his things. We'll go find them in a minute."

I wondered what he meant about his father doing one of his "things."

"You mean there's more to it than this?" I asked. I looked over at the rock walls I had seen when we pulled up, the little black openings on the rounded storage bins at the base of the canyon.

"This is nothing," Dalton said. "You'll see."

pueblo

Jones,

I know I haven't gotten all your letters you wrote to me. They keep moving us around. Don't worry, they'll catch up to me one day.

You know, I never thought a person could get as depressed as I am. I'm always tense and can never seem to relax. You should see me trying to keep my hand steady as I write this letter. It's pretty sad.

Now that the monsoons are over, all kinds of stuff is starting to happen.

About a week ago, one of our positions got a ground attack and the Duster crew there hopped on a truck to take off. A mortar round hit the truck and killed 2. The other 3 are going up for a court-martial for desertion in the face of the enemy. You just can't win at all over here.

A couple nights ago we had a small ground attack. We captured 2 VC and killed a woman, and a sniper killed one of the guys on my crew. The RVNs got the two prisoners and when they were finished with them the prisoners were wishing they were dead, too.

I am at a firebase called Nui Ong. It's really pretty here and there's a river down the hill where we can go swimming or take baths in the daytime. The water feels real nice on days like this.

All I can think about is getting out of here. I miss you and Simon

*so much. Do you think you could send me a picture of you guys? Try
to make it one where you maybe aren't fighting, though, if there is such
a thing (ha ha). I would really like that. I will send you some pictures
in my next letter, like you asked. I haven't been taking many lately.*

*It's about 18:00, so I have about 4 hours till things start happening
again. It's usually quiet in the day, but at night all hell breaks loose.*

*Did I tell you I got a .38 police special and I wear it all the time?
Tonight I'm going to sleep with my pants and boots on so I'll be ready
for them.*

Well, I guess that's all I have to say for now.

Would you believe I still got 7 months to go? God!

Bye for now.

Love,

Matthew

The sun sat low over the rim of the canyon.

It seemed like all the light had turned yellow.

The air cooled, smelled like sage and rusted leaves.

I helped Dalton unlash the ropes binding all the gear that was tied
down on the VW's roof rack. We were sweating, and sat down to
rest on the chairs outside the tent. A breeze whispered out through
the canyon's opening. It felt like the world was breathing on us.

I was so hungry. I felt tired and weak, and I propped my chin up
with both hands as I rested my elbows on the top of the table and
tried to stay awake.

"What is all that stuff?" I asked, and nodded in the direction of
the poles and bundles we unloaded from the VW.

"It's a tepee," Dalton said. "Well, it's going to be after we put it up.
Me and you and my dad can do it. You ever put up a real tepee before?"

"No."

"It's not hard," he said. "I bought it from the hippies in Los Alamos."

"Oh."

"We'll have more living space, then. So I don't have to sleep in the same tent with my sister always. You ever been there? Los Alamos? It's called the Placitas Commune, or something."

"I never been nowhere," I said.

"You been to the bottom of a river," Dalton said. "Come on, let's go find them."

Dalton led me down a trail that followed the shore where the creek twisted away beneath trees and brush. Where the canyon just seemed to tumble open as though spitting out huge red boulders, I saw the rest of the pueblo he'd told me about. It was one of those things you really wouldn't notice at first, because of the way the brush had grown over, but between the spiny brambles of mesquite and yucca, I saw wall upon wall of tightly stacked rocks, flattened and squared, block-shaped rooms with dark doorways and windows tucked back beneath the canyon, and all so perfectly blended in that it took me a while to realize how big this settlement had been, because everywhere I looked, it seemed like something else that proved people had once survived here would just appear from the rock.

Dalton pointed to a spot where the canyon wall arched outward from the bottom, making a sort of cave in the shadows.

"There's some great rock paintings over in there," he said. "That's probably where my folks are. My dad's doing one of his own paintings there."

I suddenly wasn't so tired and hungry.

"This place is amazing," I said.

"Yeah."

I followed Dalton as he led me through the brush along the trail toward the spot he'd pointed out.

"And, Jonah? I forgot to mention something you should know. My dad is kind of peculiar."

I wondered what he meant by that, but I figured you'd kind of have to be different to want to live out here, the way that they were living.

Dalton went on, "So don't mind him if he says or does anything weird. He's just, well, you'll see."

The thing that struck me most about his parents was their difference in age. His mother was so pretty and young, she could have passed for being in her twenties, even if Dalton *was* eighteen. And Dalton's dad had the stubble of a gray-white beard and the white nubs of a military-style haircut showing where the hat didn't cover his scalp. He was short and very strong, and had gleaming eyes that looked like they were frozen in constant amusement. Dalton's sister, who eyed me with unblinking curiosity—maybe because of my hair, I thought—looked to be about ten years old.

We all stood in the cool shade of the cavern, just a shallow mouth, really, beneath a huge overhanging lip of red stone.

It was like being in another world.

At one edge of the cave, the rock face had been splotched with white, splattering around the negative impressions of hands, vacant silhouettes, open palms of the Indians who'd lived there centuries before. Next to the panel of hands, I saw a large set of concentric circles surrounded by black-silhouetted figures: more handprints, and animals that looked like snakes and bulls, a rider on horseback carrying a weapon, and something that looked like a giant man with spines coming from his legs, his arm outstretched, a tree springing up from his hand.

But the strangest thing in that cave was the painting at the opposite end of the back wall, the one that Dalton's father had been working on. It was a mural, brightly colored, of an open-topped black convertible driving on a crowded street. I recognized the scene. It was a picture of the assassination of President Kennedy.

Dalton's father held a reddened brush in one hand. He looked at me, and then at his son.

"Who's this, Dalt?"

"He's a friend," Dalton said. "His name's Jonah."

And his father said, "Nice to meet you, Jonah."

He stuck his hand out for me.

I shook his paint-smeared hand as he continued, "Just call me Arno."

I looked at Dalton, who just shrugged as if to say weird names ran in the family. But then Arno told me his wife's name was Bev, and their little girl's was Shelly.

"I like the painting," I said.

"Well, only this part's my work." Arno waved his hand across the Dallas scene. "This happened seven years ago. These others probably happened seven hundred years ago. Heck! I just thought of that. I gotta paint a seven up there somewhere. Balance it out."

He scooped up a cup of blue paint and stirred his brush around in it.

"See what I mean?" Dalton whispered, shrugging. "He gets weird when he paints."

I felt better because it sounded so normal to me, the way his dad's voice echoed in that cave, the way he smiled at the little girl, Shelly, and they all had such pleasant-looking faces, even if they were all dressed in the same kind of clothes that Dalton wore—that I was now wearing—which made us look like some kind of desert cult or something.

I tilted my cap back on my head so they could see my face, and I thought about what Lilly had said about me being handsome, hoped

I looked nice enough to Dalton's family. I tried to smile, but I knew I looked nervous.

While we walked back to the camp, Dalton's father told stories about the Kennedy assassination: how he'd been there on the street when it happened, and then went home and took Dalton and the rest of the family to Mexico the next day. And he pointed out another wall he'd painted, called 1968, and he said, "That was the year I thought the world was going to come to an end."

"Why would you paint out here if nobody will ever see it?" I asked.

"Maybe they will," he said. "In seven hundred years or so."

And Arno smiled at me, turned to his son, and said, "I'm glad you brought a friend home, Dalton. I hope you know you can stay as long as you like, Jonah."

I bit my lip and looked at Dalton.

My stomach growled as we pushed our way through the brush.

"Sounds like the boy needs to eat," his mother said.

I helped Dalton and his father build their tepee while Bev and Shelly cooked.

I was tired, but also kind of rejuvenated from spending time with Dalton and his family. I especially liked Dalton's mom, and I envied him, wondering what it must be like to live with parents who obviously cared about you, loved you, even if they did live like Indians.

We had to take off our shirts. It was so hot, working in the late afternoon, and I was soaked in sweat.

I apologized to Dalton about the shirt.

"Don't worry about it," he said. "You can keep it, anyway. We have tons of clothes from the surplus. Didn't you see it all in the car?"

"It was kind of buried," I said.

His father carefully placed round stones from the riverbank in a circle at one side of the tepee.

"Dalton's never been exactly organized," he said.

I pulled my wet hair back behind my neck and held it away from my skin.

"He said I could give him a haircut." Dalton looked at me, like he was testing me.

"I did?"

"I was wondering if you were a hippie or something," Arno said.

I felt cornered. I didn't really want my hair cut. I felt like somehow it would make me that much farther away from Simon. But I gave up.

"I just . . ." I began. "I haven't gotten it cut in too long, I guess."

"After, you can wash up in the pool before dinner if you want," Dalton said. "Sorry there's not much privacy living like this."

"I wouldn't know what privacy is, anyway," I said.

Dalton tied the last strap from the outer covering onto one of the posts. "Me and Jonah will sleep out here tonight, Dad."

Arno brushed his hands on his legs and looked up at where the twelve poles lashed together at the apex of the structure, staring out at the sky through the circular opening of the tepee.

"Looks like a pretty good job," he said. "I think we're about finished here."

The tepee was much bigger than I'd imagined those things to be, from only seeing them in old Western movies. There was even a place where you could make a fire inside it, and once we'd gotten all the rocks for the fireplace positioned, we spread canvas tarps and blankets out to cover the dirt floor.

The little girl just sat and watched us, unblinking, staring at me while Dalton cut my hair. I sat as still as I possibly could, shirtless and scared, trying not to think about the long straight razor Dalton flashed in his hand. That and a comb were the only things he used. And he moved so quickly, but the razor made no sound as it swiped across the teeth of the comb, sending soft clumps of my hair down, tickling my shoulders, tumbling down my bare chest into the dirt.

Shelly picked up strands of my hair and she held them up in front of me and lined them up with one of her eyes as though she were animating some before-and-after cartoon of me.

She laughed.

She teased me in a singsong voice, "Jonah, Jonah . . ." And when I'd move my eyes to look at her, she'd drop a strand of hair to the ground and smile at me.

Bev stood cooking by the fire they'd started. It smelled so good, and I didn't know if my eyes were watering from the smoke, the thought of finally eating, or because I was holding back tears because it felt like Dalton was cutting off all my hair.

"Put your chin down," he said.

I felt the razor scraping my neck.

Arno sat back on the bench, resting his elbows on the tabletop, one leg crossed over at the knee, watching us as the sun dipped beneath the canyon's edge, dimming the light.

"The boy is real good with that razor," he said.

I realized my lower lip was sticking out, like I was pouting. I guess I looked like I was acting like a little kid about that haircut, but I knew it wasn't really about that at all. I couldn't stop thinking about Lilly and Simon, and I felt almost guilty because I had landed in such a good place with Dalton's family. I tried to forget about it and let it go.

"Relax," Dalton said, and I felt him push the top of my head down firmly, so I was looking straight at my lap, and all that hair piled on it. "I never cut anyone yet. At least, not by accident."

"I think he looks a lot better," Shelly said. "You did a good job, Dalt. Now he doesn't look like a girl anymore."

"They call you Dalt?" I said, trying to get my mind off my situation, my teeth clenched together.

Dalton made one final, upward scrape against the back of my neck. "Yep."

I felt naked. I couldn't feel any hair at all around my ears or neck. I felt like a dog whose ears had been clothespinned behind his skull.

Dalton stood back.

"There," he said.

He was finished. Finally.

"Now remember, Jonah," Dalton said. "Don't be mad. You told me I could do it. We're friends, right?"

I swallowed, and fought the urge to bring both my hands up and feel if anything was left there.

"Right."

Bev turned away from their camp stove. I could see her in the orange light of the fire.

"Let me see," she said.

Dalton folded the razor and slid it into his back pocket. Bev came over and stood next to me, turning her head so she could see Dalton's work. Then she brushed the hair away from my shoulder. And her hand felt so nice on me, the hand of a mother.

"You are very handsome, Jonah," she said. "You look five years younger. You're just a little boy. And good God! You're so skinny, you look like you haven't eaten in days."

She brushed her hand down my cheek.

"I don't think I have," I said.

"Well, go wash this hair off. We have more food than we can eat, and it's waiting for you," Bev said.

"Thank you," I said. I didn't want to move.

"Well, hurry up, boys," Arno said. "I'm starving."

I washed all that itchy hair off in the wide part of the creek Dalton called their bathtub. As I sat there in the cool water, rubbing my hands over my scalp, feeling the bristles of my hair that was now so short I couldn't even pull it, I worried about getting out of there, and at the same time it felt so good to be with Dalton and his family, like I almost belonged, even if I couldn't get Simon and Lilly—and Mitch—out of my mind.

The sun had gone down. The sky faintly glowed in the west, and in the darkness above me the first fiery stars in the evening showed themselves.

My head was strangely light. I rubbed the smoothness of the razor-bared skin at the nape of my neck. I felt smaller.

Dalton had already gotten out of the water and was drying himself off on the shore.

"I never had hair this short," I said.

"It'll grow back," Dalton said. "Come on, get out and dry off. Time to eat."

I cupped another handful of water over my head, pushed myself up, and waded over to where Dalton stood on the shore.

He held out a towel.

I wiped it over my head and dressed quickly. "What are we going to tell your dad, Dalton?"

"Tell him about what?"

"I need to leave. I *have* to." I sighed. "I think I'm a bad person, that I messed up things, and being here isn't right. I just can't forget about how bad I hurt my own brother. And I can't stop thinking about the girl. Lilly. Even out here, being where everything seems so normal and comfortable with your family. It should be easy enough for me to just relax, but I can't stop thinking about it all."

I dropped onto a knee so I could lace up the boots he'd given me.

"Do you love her?" Dalton asked.

"Yes. I know I'm just being stupid, but I do."

He looked out across the water.

"We'll leave in the morning, okay? I can make it work with my dad. Trust me."

I guess I'd heard that enough in the last couple days. *Trust me.* But I did trust Dalton. I stood up and brushed the dirt from my knee.

"And thanks again for the clothes. I like them."

"Let's go eat."

I draped my towel on the limb of the willow tree, tucked in my tee shirt, and followed Dalton toward the light of the campfire.

And somewhere at that moment, out in the abandoned desert, my brother was being bound up like an animal.

We all sat at the long table—boards of redwood nailed together—Dalton, his dad, and I, wearing the same clothing, crowded together with his mother and sister, touching each other, unable to avoid it on the short splintering benches. As soon as we seated ourselves, Bev put a plate down on the table in front of me: something that looked like cooked spinach, beans, tortillas she'd made by hand, and some strips of pale meat that looked like chicken. And they all looked at me when she put that plate down, and I looked at it, then back at their faces, but I didn't know what I was supposed to do or say and felt myself reddening, unable to hide behind the drape of my hair, so I just swallowed and whispered, "Thank you."

And I think it was the best food I'd ever eaten. I must have told her that five times before I finished the first plateful.

"You like it?" Arno said. "That's snake meat."

It didn't matter to me. He could have told me it was anything at that moment and I'd still have eaten it.

154

"Tell us about yourself, Jonah," Bev said. She smiled at me and I could see the little orange reflections of the fire in her eyes.

"What about?"

"Where are you from? How old are you?" she asked.

Suddenly, I dreaded talking about myself.

"We came from a place called Los Rogues. It's by the Texas border. And I'll be seventeen next March."

"We?"

"My little brother and me. Simon's fourteen."

"Where's Simon now?" she asked. I thought she was being cautious, like she was afraid something terrible may have happened to him, to us. But maybe it was just my imagination.

"We split up. Made a mistake. It was an accident."

"How'd you get here?" Arno asked.

I looked at Dalton, but I couldn't tell from his expression whether or not I was supposed to say anything that even came close to the truth.

I took another bite of food and chewed it a while so I could think.

"I fell in the river. When I got out, Dalton was there and he offered to help me."

"And how'd you get all the way from Los Rogues to the river, just so you could fall into it?" Arno asked. He was smiling, but his eyes were intent and I knew he was curious about what I'd left out of my explanation.

"It's a long story," I said.

"Good." He took a bite of snake meat. "Tell it."

"Dad," Dalton said, and swallowed. "His brother might be in trouble. He's heading to Arizona by himself. Jonah asked me if I'd help him, if I'd take him to Arizona, but I told him I had to come home first."

155

Arno looked at his son, then me, and then turned to his wife.

"Where are your parents?" Bev asked.

I looked right at her, so she'd know I was telling the truth, and said, "We're all alone. They left us. It's just me and Simon, and I promised I'd take care of him."

"Everyone's got parents," Shelly protested.

"Not me. Not Simon," I said.

"It's not far, Dad," Dalton said. "Heck, we could get there and back by the day after tomorrow."

I could see Arno thinking about it, and then he said, "You can take the camper truck. I don't like that windshield missing on the Bug if you boys run into rainstorms. You're old enough, and I trust you'll be careful, Dalt."

I felt so relieved when he said that. I think he must have heard me let out the big breath of air I was holding.

"Thanks, Dad," Dalton said. "We'll leave in the morning."

"Are you and your brother going to come back here?" Arno asked.

I thought about Matthew. About our father.

I thought about how stupid I had been, dragging Simon away from home, away from that dead horse.

And I needed to see her again, too.

"I don't know."

"You're both welcome to, I want you to know it. If you're Dalton's friend, that's good enough for us. We have space, we could use some extra hands sometimes, especially building that cabin."

"I don't know if we can come back," I said.

"One thing," Arno said. "If you do, you have to tell me the whole story."

"Okay. I promise."

And he left it at that.

Dalton burned a candle upon the rocks inside the tepee. We had just stretched out on the floor to sleep, and it felt so good to be there; but not only because my belly was full. The canvas skin of the tepee glowed in pulsing amber from the fire outside. I pulled my boots off and stretched my legs across the blankets.

I began pulling the contents from the pack and laying them out on the mats that covered the floor. I made a small pile of the clothes I had, Simon's and mine, wadded and wrinkled. The gun was there, I could feel it at the bottom of the pack. But I didn't want to tell Dalton it was there.

I opened my comp book.

I began to draw, thinking as I traced a line onto a clean page how nobody had fallen from the edge of the world yet, at least not really. I drew the Lincoln, Lilly, Simon, and Mitch, going off in one direction, the line fading away from where the sagging bridge was placed.

I scraped tiny bits of wood away from the pencil's point with my thumbnail and began to draw. I sketched in the winding creek we'd followed to Chavez Canyon, the ruins of the pueblo, Dalton's camp, and his family. Finally, I drew a small image of myself, standing beside the bathtub pool, and I drew an arrow toward my head and labeled it "haircut."

Dalton glanced down at what I was doing.

"Cool," he said.

On the same page, I had drawn a VW, an unmarked road stretching before it, a boy wearing goggles and a cap with a tail hanging from it, the name "Dalton" written beneath.

"Is that how you spell your name?" I asked.

"Yeah. Nice. What is that?"

"It's a map," I said. "I guess it's more like a diary. So I won't forget what happened to us. Even if it's not going to matter to anyone."

"Can I look at it?"

"Sure."

I sat up, cross-legged beside the candle, as Dalton turned around in his blankets so his head was near my knee.

He propped himself up on his elbows and looked down at the pages.

I spun the book around so it would be right side up for him, and he turned back through the pages of map and writing.

"Can I read the part about the girl, too? Do you mind?" he asked.

"I don't care."

I watched him while he read my journal. He didn't say anything, but sometimes he'd stop and turn a page or two so he could look at the map before going back to reading. When he finished, he opened the book to the map of the pueblo and turned the book toward me.

"What are you going to write about me?"

"I don't know yet."

Dalton put his head down and rolled over onto his back and closed his eyes.

"Say it was a good haircut."

"Okay."

He fell asleep almost as soon as I began writing.

I took Matthew's letters out of the pack and thumbed through them. I wondered what Dalton thought when he read my journal. I told the truth about Lilly, and I wasn't embarrassed for him to know it, either. And I wondered if he thought I was crazy for ever starting off with Simon on such a pointless journey. I knew we'd never find Matthew. I knew we'd never see our father.

Simon knew it, too, and we still left Los Rogues on that horse.

But it was too late now.

Brother Jones,

Well, as of today I am officially no longer a teenager. Now that I think about it, 20 seems like being real old, but still not old enough. It seems like I'm older than most of the guys at my base here. It's funny to me 'cause this war was started by a bunch of old guys but there's not one old guy anywhere around here who's fighting it.

There's one old guy who I saw just show up at our firebase named Hungry Jack. He's a GI who went AWOL and he just roams around and picks up with whatever crew he can find. He's only staying here because of how cheap heroin is, and nobody cares about it at all. They should have sent Dad to fight the war, he would like it here, ha ha ha, don't tell anyone I said that. But, you know.

A couple nights ago we killed a lot of people. There were 4 sampans on the river that were full of VC and we fired direct fire right into them. I guess some other VC carried all the bodies away so we wouldn't get the credit, but there was blood and stuff all over the place.

To tell you the truth, I don't envy anyone for being on the receiving end of our 40 mm's. We can put 300 rounds into a group of them in less than a minute. We're right on the Laos border, and it's really getting to be a mess around here. The NVA are using heavy tanks and heavy artillery against us and a lot of GIs are getting zapped.

Last night I got drunk. Don't tell Simon or Mother, though. We celebrated because one of my crew has less than 90 days to do over here, and 'cause of my birthday.

You might have heard about firebase Mary Ann getting wiped out. Don't worry, they were 30 clicks from here. But there are a lot of VC villages around us, only we can't do anything to them until we catch them at it. One of my buddies from NCO school got messed up the other day. He lost a leg and an eye, but he gets to go home. When I get back, I'm going to come see him. I'm going to see my other buddy in Leavenworth, too.

I wrote Scotty's address in Arizona on the inside of the envelope.
Save it. I am going there.
   Take care of yourself and Simon.
   Love,
   Matthew

I held the dry, stained paper of Matthew's letter between my fingers, feeling the small dents on the pages where my brother's hand had pressed a point to form the words I saw there. The clothes I piled from the pack were all dry now, and I bundled the letters up inside them and pulled one of Simon's tee shirts out and held it to my face and smelled it before folding it up and placing it around the letters. Then I tucked the map away with the rest of our clothes and blew out the candle flame and lay down.

I bundled myself in blankets on the floor of the tepee, the smoke from the candle and campfire hanging like gauze in the apex of the shelter. In my dream, I was floating above the earth, and I looked down upon a ceaseless and unnamed void of desert, could see Simon standing shirtless beside the girl, Don Quixote watching over them, his face, uncovered, showing a toothy yellow smile. And the tin man was a burning rocket fired in a decaying arc toward them, his body blackening and crumpling in upon itself, calcifying, turning to stone, screaming with speed through the lightless sky, tumbling and plummeting downward as Simon and Lilly looked up to watch the falling, while Mitch's disembodied voice shouted wildly above it all, over and over again, "This is why the people can't trust Jonah. This is why the people can't trust Jonah."

trust

Simon lit another cigarette as Mitch sped the Lincoln westward along the narrow road toward Farmington. Lilly sat beside Don Quixote in the backseat, her scarf pulled tight against her head, the glasses hiding her eyes. He leaned over the door from time to time so he could see the blackness around his eye in the side mirror, to catch a glimpse of the girl in the backseat, to convince himself, maybe, that everything would be okay.

He tumbled the meteorite around between his hands, and studied the streaked, red welts from the rope where it had cut into his wrists. Simon had seen the figures Mitch scratched in the side of the car. Simon knew one was supposed to be him. He knew what it meant.

Simon knew he had to get away.

Mitch turned on the radio, then turned it off and began humming. He sounded happy.

Simon finally got up the nerve. He bit his lip and said, "I want to go back for Jonah."

Mitch stopped his humming. "You waited all this time to decide *that?* You were the one who kicked him off the bridge, man."

Mitch twisted his hands, the knuckles whitening, around the steering wheel.

"I was drunk," Simon said. "And I shouldn't have done that."

"He's gone," Mitch said. "Trust me. He's gone by now."

"Mitch," Lilly said softly.

"No," Mitch said. "We'll be in Arizona while it's still light. Let's stop and get some dinner at the next town up here. I'm hungry. The punk can find his own way, if he didn't drown."

"Don't call him that," Lilly said.

Mitch tipped his head so he could see her in the mirror. "What?"

"*Punk*," Lilly said flatly. "Like he's nothing. He didn't do anything to you."

"Lilly needs to shut up," Mitch answered. "Lilly can't have him. Ever."

Simon and Lilly sat silent.

Then Mitch tapped Simon on the shoulder. "Do you want me to drop you off on the side of the road? 'Cause I will."

Simon thought. He thought the only things Mitch ever dropped off got hurt first.

"No."

"That's my man," Mitch said, smiling. "And anyway, I have no doubt that *the punk* made it out okay and probably already has a new girlfriend by now. And I bet he's forgotten all about our sweet Lilly, too. So, relax. It's going to be a perfect day. It is a perfect day."

They stopped for hamburgers at a cafeteria in a small settlement on their way toward Ship Rock. The few other diners stared at them as they walked in, because that old Lincoln and the shining metal man were plainly visible in the bright late afternoon sun, sitting in the lot outside the diner's front wall of windows.

"Thirty-six," Mitch said as they sat down at a table near the door. His voice sounded relaxed, like he was playing a game.

"Thirty-six what?" Simon asked.

"Place mats on all the tables," Mitch replied.

Simon looked down at the paper mats on their table, yellow and red, with maps of New Mexico on each one.

A stocky, dark-skinned waitress sighed and scowled as Simon quickly balled the mat at their table's vacant seat in his hand and dropped it onto the floor between his feet.

"Wrong," Simon said. "Thirty-five."

Simon smiled across the table at Lilly.

"You like to push buttons, don't you, Simon?" Mitch said. "That's okay. I like that about you. I like to push them, too."

Mitch chuckled.

"I think he's cute," Lilly said, and brushed her fingers along Simon's arm.

Simon grinned at her.

Mitch's smile vanished.

"Oh, come on, Mitch," Lilly said. "Why don't you lighten up? You know I'm just teasing. We're just having fun."

"I guess we all are, then," Mitch said, forcing a smile again.

Before she finished eating, Lilly stood up to go to the bathroom, leaving Mitch and Simon, ketchup smeared in a line from both sides of his mouth, alone at the table.

"You like Lilly, don't you?" Mitch said, watching her wind her way through the cafeteria, away from them.

"I don't know," Simon said, swallowing, not really paying attention. "Yeah. I guess. Don't you?"

Mitch smiled. "Who wouldn't?"

"Yeah." Simon drew a line with a fry through the ketchup on his plate.

Mitch pushed a plate forward on the table until it clinked against his sweating glass of ice water and Simon looked up at him. He flicked the cap of his lighter, under the table.

Flick.

163

"You know that little guy back there at Chief's? Where we had those beers yesterday?"

Simon thought about the money in his pocket, about the cigarettes he stored in the glove box in the Lincoln.

"Yeah."

Mitch stared intently at Simon, watching him finish his burger.

"I killed him when you went to pee."

Flick.

He said it just as plainly as if he were ordering dessert.

"Remember how you asked where he was when you came back from your piss? He was about a foot away from your feet, on the floor behind the bar, lying in his own brains."

Simon swallowed the last bite and looked at Mitch, his eyes wide, trying to figure out if Mitch was playing a trick or not. Simon pulled the ashtray across the table and slid another cigarette from his pack and lit it.

"I shot him. Right through his head."

Simon reached for his Coke and drank until the straw sucked empty.

"You did?"

"Yeah." Mitch wiped his mouth with his napkin.

Simon rubbed his palms on his pants, the cigarette dangling from his lips.

"What's it feel like?"

"What? To kill someone?" Mitch spoke quietly, leaning toward Simon.

The waitress plodded back and placed their bill down on the table, then promptly ignored them.

"It feels like being stuck at the top of a Ferris wheel."

Flick.

Simon had only been on a Ferris wheel one time in his life. But he

164

remembered that feeling, being up there and swinging in that seat, squeamish and tense, everything so silent and vivid. And he liked the way that felt, so Simon was confused about what Mitch was trying to say to him.

"Why are you telling me now, Mitch?"

"'Cause you helped me rob the place. 'Cause you stole those plates for me. 'Cause I was mean to you last night and I want you to be my friend. My best friend. I guess that makes us partners. All three of us now." Mitch put his hands out on the table in front of Simon. "What do you think about that?"

Simon bit the inside of his lip. He held his breath.

"All *four* of us, if you count Don," Simon said, squinting and grinning with his mouth closed, hoping it was what Mitch would want him to say.

It was.

Mitch laughed and said, "That's the second time today you caught me being off by one, Simon."

"I like to push buttons, Mitch. You said."

They watched Lilly walk back, making her way through the maze of tables, moving so gracefully and light. She radiated a cautious smile to both of them from across the room.

"Are you going to finish that, Lilly?" Mitch asked, pointing to her half-eaten food. She squeezed down on the seat beside Simon.

"Do you want the rest, Simon?" she asked.

"No, thanks."

"Well, you've got the money, Simon," Mitch said. "Why don't you take this up and pay it?"

And he pushed the check across the table in the direction of Simon.

Simon thought about the money in his pocket he'd taken from Chief's. He felt sick.

✦ ✦ ✦

Before they left the township, Mitch filled the Lincoln's gas tank and bought some food and drinks from a liquor store. He asked Simon and Lilly to come inside with him, and Simon dreaded that he might have to watch Mitch kill someone just because Mitch thought it felt like a carnival ride. Simon was relieved that the only thing he had to put up with was Mitch tearing a page from a magazine and asking Simon to hide it under his shirt. The page turned out to be a black-and-white photograph of a soldier's face, and large enough that when Mitch, Lilly, and Simon returned to the Lincoln, Mitch fixed the picture with black electrical tape right over the face of Don Quixote, saying, "Now that looks good. He looks real mean."

Mitch drove into Arizona, through a forgotten area east of Kayenta, where the road cut straight through a desert unmarked by any signs of men. The highway stretched like an asphalt streambed following an upward-sloping ridge of huge and seamless mountains that turned from gold to red in the light of the evening, the stone gapping unevenly, like Mitch's teeth. The Lincoln began to wheeze and sputter.

The car was dying.

"Damn!" Mitch slapped the steering wheel.

"What's wrong?" Lilly said.

"I don't know," Mitch answered. "I don't know anything about cars."

Simon fumbled with that meteorite in his lap.

It was just like a horse falling dead beneath them.

He didn't say anything. He didn't know if the car's dying was a good or bad thing.

The Lincoln jerked and seized as Mitch guided it off the road and onto the moonlike surface of the desert. When the Lincoln finally expired, wheels half-buried in the dry soil, smoke billowing out from both sides of the undercarriage, it ended up wedged inside a small stand of hopseed brush that swallowed them up, making the car nearly invisible from the road.

Mitch hammered his fist into the steering wheel again, and just sat there as white steaming clouds coughed skyward from the Lincoln's engine. Simon looked back at Lilly. He wanted to tell her this was it, but he said nothing, and he followed the white puffs upward with his eyes into the dimming sky. It looked like they were sending smoke signals into the quiet evening.

Simon lit a cigarette.

"Looks like we're spending the night in the desert again," Mitch said.

"It's cool," Simon said, swinging his door open. "But, Mitch . . ."

"You don't have to ask me, Simon. I won't do it. I promised."

The Lincoln's engine began ticking and cracking.

"Let's unload," Mitch said. "This thing smells like it might burn."

Lilly was sick again. She sat down, away from the smoking car, as Mitch and Simon began unpacking it. Simon put his black rock in his pocket and helped Mitch lift Don Quixote from the backseat. They stood him beside Lilly, Mitch's bags of groceries at his feet, turned so that he was almost watching them.

The sun had vanished behind the western mountains; there were no sounds from the highway. Simon knew they were completely alone. The Lincoln began sighing, then belching blackening smoke up into the dimming sky from its engine compartment. Mitch pulled the trunk open and grabbed the black suitcase, slinging it away. Simon peered into the trunk, his neck craning so that he could see everything that was there.

"The pack!" he said. "I think we left my pack back at the bridge."

Mitch froze at the edge of the bumper, his head swallowed in the awful-smelling cloud. And Mitch found the shoe box; the tape torn away from its seal. The rope was still coiled at the bottom of the trunk.

Mitch pulled the box out and took two steps away from the burning car.

"That stinking punk!" Mitch said, growling at Simon. "Your brother stole money from me!"

Simon swallowed. He could hear Lilly vomiting behind them.

Simon reached into the trunk and pulled out their loosely piled wad of blankets and threw them onto the suitcase, hoping his helping would satisfy Mitch. He left the yellow rope in the trunk. He wanted it to burn. Mitch stood away, his back turned, staring down into his opened shoe box. Simon knew what he was doing.

Counting.

Adding.

All those numbers always in Mitch's head.

Orange flames began snaking upward from beneath the front wheel wells, the smoke thickening above Simon's head against a darkening sky. Nobody would see it. The Lincoln popped and hissed a futile protest, but the flames were going to win out.

Simon quickly slammed the trunk lid down. He dragged the blankets and suitcase away through the dirt toward Lilly. Mitch followed, walking backwards and watching the expanding fire, cradling his box in his arms.

Standing thirty feet off from the Lincoln, the three of them had to back farther away, the heat from the fire becoming so intense, blazing away so brightly in the middle of that dark and empty land.

They left all of their belongings at the feet of Don Quixote, encircling the metal man like offerings at a shrine.

"Maybe it's a good thing," Mitch said, watching the flames as they swallowed the old Lincoln, shooting up into the sky. "I needed to get rid of that thing, anyway."

Lilly sat down behind them, leaning over her knees.

"We're in the middle of the desert," Simon said.

"Everything'll work out," Mitch said. "Don't you trust me?"

"I trust you, Mitch," Simon answered, carefully.

A small explosion flared from beneath the pyre of the Lincoln, sending bits of metal and glass spraying out into the night. Simon jerked and twisted just as a piece of glass caught him on the right side of his neck. He slapped his palm across the wound to cover it. The glass had cut him, a deep gash as long as his finger.

"Ow!" Simon blurted, looking at the blood on his hand and then turning away from the fire and running back out into the darkness.

Mitch and Lilly backed away, too, afraid that the car might explode a second time. They stood in the dark and watched the fire grow high. They watched the Lincoln wither away to nothing more than smoldering, steaming, stinking debris.

Simon stood at the edge of the dark.

"Are you okay?" Lilly put her hand on Simon's shoulder. He pressed his fingers against the cut on his neck. The blood had dried between them, and ran in thick black lines down the back of his hand, all the way to his forearm.

"I don't know," he said. Simon moved his hand down and tilted his chin so Lilly could see the cut. It opened again. The blood snaked down toward his collarbone.

"Is it very big?"

Lilly leaned close to Simon. She was so close he felt her breath cooling the blood.

"Oh. It's deep. I don't think it's too bad," she said. "Let me wipe it off with something."

Mitch watched them. He was mumbling again. Talking to himself.

"There's a bottle of whiskey in one of those bags," Mitch said.

Lilly opened the bottle and Simon pulled off his tee shirt, blood-stained for the second time in those past few, blurry days. Lilly dampened a clean corner of the shirt with whiskey and wiped the blood away from Simon's neck and shoulder. Then she pressed the cloth against the wound and held it there tight.

Simon grimaced from the stinging. But it felt so nice the way Lilly's hands pressed against his skin.

Mitch came over and took the bottle of whiskey from Lilly. It sloshed when Mitch tipped it back, and Simon could hear the gasping breath after his swallow.

"That got you pretty good," Lilly said, lifting the other hand to touch the hair behind his neck, like she was hugging him, or like they were getting ready to kiss.

"I'm a mess," Simon said, opening his eyes. "Whatever that was that hit me could've killed me. If it was bigger, it would've."

Mitch stumbled away, carrying the tattered shoe box off into the darkness of the desert.

"It probably could have," Lilly agreed. "Do you want me to find you a shirt?"

"No."

Without the pack, any shirt she found would have been one of Mitch's.

Simon put his hand over Lilly's and looked straight at her and whispered, "Lilly, we got to get away from Mitch."

"I know," she said.

"Jonah's going to come."

"He will?"

"I know it," Simon said. "We've never been apart. Not one day in my entire life until just now. I know he's coming. He promised."

Lilly wiped the bloodstain away from Simon's skin. They heard Mitch rustling around in the brush.

"Do you love him?" Simon asked. "Jonah?"

Lilly sighed, "Yeah."

Simon looked down at his moccasins. Lilly dropped her hands away from him.

"He's your brother," she said, her voice so hushed. "Why do you hate him so much?"

"I don't," Simon admitted. "I don't."

Mitch came back, dangling the bottle of whiskey at his side, his eyes already glazed over.

"Well, it looks like we're going to all sleep here tonight," he said. Then he looked at Simon and Lilly, how they were standing so closely. "And you two just better not get any ideas, Lilly. Simon. I mean it."

"He got cut pretty bad, Mitch. And he's just a boy."

"You think I don't see how he looks at you?" Mitch said. "He's not looking at you like he wants to play hopscotch."

"I guess you just didn't notice how his brother looked at me, then."

Simon started to say something, but thought better of it.

"It's a good thing for all of us that the other one is gone," Mitch said.

Lilly looked at Simon. And Simon put his hands down into both pockets and emptied them, pulling out his meteorite and the crumpled wad of money he had taken from Chief's bar. He held the money out to Mitch.

"Here. I'm not going to do anything bad anymore. I'm not going to smoke or steal or nothing, so just take this money."

Mitch grabbed the money, looking at it, looking at Simon.

Simon's hand trembled and Mitch stared at him, unblinking. He felt like that scrawny coyote in the road, and he knew Mitch wasn't going to stop.

"Yes, you are," Mitch said. "You're going to do whatever I tell you to do, Simon."

Mitch pocketed the money and snapped the cap of his lighter.
Flick.

"No," Simon said. His voice quaked and his eyes welled. "Please, Mitch. I don't want to do any more bad things. Please."

Mitch just looked at Simon, his face blank. Simon thought he looked like he did when they sat alone in that cafeteria, when Mitch told him about killing Chief. He opened the bottle of whiskey and took another swallow and then held it out toward the boy, the reflection of the flame from the Lincoln's tire dancing inside the bottle like some trapped ghost.

"Drink some whiskey, Simon."

Simon felt a tear run down his face. He grunted, trying to force himself not to cry in front of Mitch.

Mitch held the bottle up in front of Simon's face.

"Drink some whiskey, Simon, or Mitch is going to do something really, really bad."

Simon looked at Lilly.

He wondered if Mitch was picturing himself on top of a Ferris wheel.

Simon raised his bloodstained hand, grasped the bottle around its neck, and shuddered as he took it from Mitch.

"Hello there!" a man's voice called out from beyond the edge of the fire's light.

Mitch, startled, jerked around.

Simon let the bottle fall into the dirt.

"Is everyone okay here?" the voice from the dark came back again.

walker

My brother,

I know it's been a while since I've written, but I have a hard time thinking what I should say to you. I'm putting some pictures in this letter, and like you can see, you're right about me losing weight since I got here. I think I've lost about 30 pounds and I hardly ever get to eat any hot meals. And I smoke about two packs a day. I think Simon could kick my butt now. You know. Don't say nothing.

A couple guys in my crew should have been home a month ago, but because of all these firebases getting wiped out, they're not letting anyone go. They probably think they'll do the same thing to me when my time is up, but I got news for them if they do.

The real reason I'm not writing is that it's hard for me to think of anything normal anymore. I sometimes can't remember what you look like, or what things smell like at home. When I got that picture of you and Simon, I just cried like an old woman or something. I had to keep telling guys that these are my brothers, like I couldn't even really believe that you are, you both look so much bigger now.

Remember how I told you my buddy Scotty is terrified of rats? Well, the other day a couple guys in my crew caught a rat that was about as big as a small dog and they let it go in Scotty's hooch while he was asleep. Anyway, the rat woke him up and Scotty pulled out his .45 and started trying to shoot it, but he just ended up shooting up about everything he owns. We thought it was pretty funny, but Scotty is still mad about it.

I listened to the liftoff of Apollo the other day.

I hear it's hard to find a job back home, and a lot of guys are going to reenlist because of it.

I think I'd rather be a bum than reenlist.

Sometime next month they're going to send us out to a place called Hill 270. Sounds like a vacation, doesn't it? The only way to get there is by helicopter, so I don't really have to worry much about the brass in the rear. They don't like to get their boots too dusty or their starched jungle fatigues too wrinkly. I don't hate them or anything, but the way this war is run is pretty ridiculous.

I heard about a guy who went missing after he crossed a river. I heard he fell into the water and just swam away. They found his dog tags along the shore downstream, but no sign of him. Some guys here say he just walked right out of the war, and I believe them.

Scotty said to say hi. He's still a little bit mad at me, but not as much as the other guys 'cause all I did was laugh about it, and try to stay out of the firing.

Tell Simon happy birthday for me. Now he's fourteen and I bet he's a real ladies' man like his two older brothers . . . ha ha.

I love you guys.

Bye.

Matt

Simon watched as the bottle coughed out its contents, lying sideways in the dirt, exchanging gulps of whiskey for gulps of air in the flickering and tawny light of the fire.

The man who had called out to them was standing in the dark beyond the rim of light spreading away from the dead Lincoln.

"Hello!" Mitch called back. "We're okay!"

Mitch, Simon, and Lilly all stood with their backs to the fire, straining to see out into the darkness. There. Simon caught the orange reflection of the man's eyes, and then movement in the brush.

Simon thought he was going to see Mitch kill someone now, for sure. He looked out to where the man's voice sounded, trying to figure out if they were surrounded. And he wondered what *anyone* would be doing out here, anyway.

Then the gray figure pushed its way into the light.

He wore an old cowboy hat and walked very stiffly in beaten and dusty boots, his right leg straight, unbending, as though it were something dead propped under him to hold him up. And Simon thought he looked like he belonged in the desert, his skin was so tight and brown, like leather, eyes fixed in a permanent squint against the sun, wearing a long-sleeved green shirt tucked into tattered jeans held up by suspenders. A long sheath knife was strapped across his left suspender, hanging diagonally across his chest, and Simon guessed from the man's long black hair and faintest, stubborn stubble of beard that he was probably an Indian.

"I could see the fire from my house," the man said, "so I took off when I seen it. That was maybe an hour ago. I walk slow, you know. I thought it was a plane crash, there was so much black smoke coming up. I thought it might be something real bad."

He studied the three of them, one by one, almost as though just looking at the silent refugees from the burning car would tell him enough of a story about what was happening there.

"Everyone's okay," Mitch said again.

"How the hell'd you get so far off the road?" The man eyed the burning car in wonder and then, lifting his hat and pushing his long hair back, looked at Mitch again.

Mitch smiled that grin of his and gave his most reassuring look. "I'm not going to lie. I've been drinking."

"Hell!" the man said, and chuckled, but he watched Simon and Lilly all the while to see if they gave any indication of the truth.

"Can you help us?" Lilly asked. "Do you have a car?"

Mitch jerked his face toward Lilly. Simon could see by the way Mitch clenched his jaw that he didn't want them talking to the man.

"Aw hell," the man said. "I don't drive nowhere. I'm Walker. That's my honest-to-God name, and I walk everywhere. Even to town. That's twelve miles from here. Most people think they call me Walker 'cause I only walk everywhere, but it's my real name."

"Twelve miles," Mitch said. "Then I guess we should start walking in the morning."

"If I was going to walk to town," Walker said, "which I've done enough to know, I wouldn't wait until daytime, unless you want to die of heat."

"That's probably a good idea, Walker," Mitch said. "We should just start walking now, then. Let's pack up. We could probably thumb a ride if we're lucky. Thanks, man."

Mitch's tone implied he was giving Walker permission to leave.

"I thought there were four of you," Walker said. "It looked like four of you in the firelight. Then when I got close I seen that one there is just a statue. And I thought, what the hell? At first it scared the bejesus out of me, and I'm not fooling, I thought I was seeing a spaceman. Like you all came from outer space or somewheres. That's about the strangest thing I've ever seen just standing out in the desert at night. Well, that, and this old car. What kind of car is that? I never seen a car like that. Or a metal man like that, neither one."

"It was a Lincoln," Simon said. He glanced at Mitch.

"Hell," Walker said. He turned his head, lizardlike, eyeing Simon up and down. He looked from Lilly to Simon, Mitch, then back at Simon again. "You two are just kids. What are you doing out here? Are you hippies or something?"

"Yeah," Simon said. "Hippies, man." And he looked over at Lilly and tried to wink at her, his eyes reflecting shrunken images of the fire that continued to burn.

"Well, I don't mind hippies so much, I guess," Walker said. "I've never really talked to any before today, though. You seem okay, though. Sure you don't need any help or nothing?"

Mitch faked a grin with clenched teeth. "We're okay. Really. But thanks anyway."

Simon was afraid that Mitch was going to kill the man if he didn't leave soon.

"Well, okay then," Walker decided, and began to limp away from the light of the fire. Before he had faded away entirely, he stopped and looked back at the three lost travelers and said, "You know which way you're going, then?"

Mitch made a move toward the blankets and their other belongings, pretending to pack up, trying to ignore the strange man.

And Simon called out, "We're going to town. West."

"Okay, then."

And Walker vanished into the dark of night.

Mitch picked up the empty bottle of whiskey, its mouth crusted with sand and ash, and glared at Simon.

"That guy scared me," Simon lied, making an excuse for letting that bottle fall.

"It's okay, Mitch," Lilly said. "Let's just relax now."

Mitch threw the empty bottle into the blackened wreckage of the Lincoln, and Simon tensed when he heard it shatter, half expecting a second shard to come firing back at him through the night.

Mitch lifted his shirt and grabbed at his pistol, waving it before him so that it caught the light from the fire.

Simon froze. Mitch pointed the gun directly at his belly, so casually, and Simon could see the one empty chamber in its wheel that had held the bullet Mitch used to kill Chief.

Simon looked at Lilly.

"Oh, come on, Mitch," she said, carefully.

Mitch exhaled, and nodded at Simon.

"You really think I'd get mad enough to shoot the kid?" he said. He began walking past them, following the shuffling tracks in the sand made by the limping man who had walked into the dark.

When Mitch got to the same place where they had last seen Walker, Simon said, "Please, Mitch. Don't kill that man."

Mitch stopped, his back turned to Simon and Lilly.

"Please?" Simon asked.

Mitch turned around and looked at them both, the fire now just an annoying stink, small fingerlike flames fluttering up unevenly from beneath the carcass of the car.

"I'll do whatever you want," Simon said. "I'm sorry if I made you mad."

Mitch smiled at Simon, his teeth glowing.

"I knew you were with me all along, Simon."

And Mitch walked back into the dim light from the dying fire and tucked his gun into his pants.

Simon stared up at the stars from where he lay in the blankets that had been scattered on the ground. The night, moonless, seemed so incredibly bright, so empty. Occasionally, he could hear the whooshing sound of a car on the rough macadam of the distant highway, and he'd tried counting them but had given up after three because it took so long.

He passed his first two fingers over the cut on his neck, still gapped and swollen, aching, and he thought about dying and wondered what that would be like.

He heard Lilly yawn, her body rustling the blankets where she lay.

Mitch sat between them, drinking a Coke and just staring straight ahead at the flat stretch of desert and the black silhouette of the mesa that erased the light of stars that should be there.

"I'm tired," Lilly said. "I'm going to try to go to sleep."

"The kid's asleep," Mitch said.

Simon almost reacted the way he usually would, by saying, "No I'm not," but kept his mouth still and remained motionless, listening, closing his eyes. He could hear her stretching out on the blankets, trying to find a comfortable spot.

"Are there any cigarettes?" Mitch asked.

"I think they burned in the car," Lilly said. She grunted, "Oh, God, this thing hurts."

Simon felt Mitch moving, standing; could hear his feet against the ground as he walked to the suitcase. He heard Mitch opening the buckles on the bag, the sound of his hands rustling through the contents, and then Mitch came back and sat down between them.

Mitch flicked his lighter. Simon could see the orange flash through his eyelids, then could smell the sweet burning of the joint.

"No, thanks. I don't feel good," he heard Lilly say after a moment.

Mitch exhaled.

"Would you really have hurt him?" Lilly asked.

"Who?" Mitch said. "The Indian? Yeah."

"No. Simon."

"I almost did. I felt like it," Mitch said. "I don't anymore. I like the kid, but he's pushing it. If it was his brother doing this crap, I'd have killed him a long time ago."

Simon felt his heart pounding, afraid that it might be visible on his chest. He struggled to control his breathing, to pretend to sleep. The air was cooling, and he wanted a shirt, but his was thrown out, soaked with whiskey and blood, and he couldn't ask for one from Mitch. He rolled over, turning away from Mitch and Lilly, curling his knees up toward his chest, his face down in the blankets.

He started to cry. He thought about that horse that had died when he left home, and it seemed now like it was all such a long time ago.

Lilly stirred and moved over to where Simon lay.

"He's cold," Lilly said. She put her hand down onto Simon's ribs, and she could tell that he was crying.

"Well, get him a blanket, then. And stay away from him." Mitch's voice was a cold warning.

Lilly rubbed Simon's skin, but he maintained his stillness, stubbornly pretending to sleep, trying to ignore her, trying to ignore Mitch. She got up and went to grab another blanket, saying, "What do you think I am, anyway, Mitch?"

"A whore," he said plainly. "That's what you are, aren't you?"

Lilly didn't say anything. She draped a blanket over Simon and kneeled down, tucking it snugly around his folded arms. Then she lifted the corner of the blanket and wiped the tears from Simon's face and stroked his hair once. She left him and went back to her place on the other side of Mitch.

"I remember when I was just a kid in Fort Stockton. It seemed like every time I turned around, I'd see you watching me, or just hanging out, following me," she said. "Even when I was twelve years old I knew I'd always be able to get anything I wanted from you."

"So, what do you want now, Lilly?"

"I want to get out of here," she said.

"You got a thumb. The road's that way."

"You'd just let me go?"

"You know better than that," Mitch said. His voice was a gravelly whisper. "Not after what we did in Texas. Not after what we did in Mexico. And not after what you did in that bed with that kid. You know better than that, Lil. So you might as well get used to it and start liking me. 'Cause you're stuck, as far as I can see."

"Leave me alone."

Mitch laughed and blew a cloud of smoke. "I'll leave you. I'll leave you on the corner and drive around the block with a five-dollar bill in my hand and you'll think I'm someone new."

"I don't know why you have to be so nasty," she said. "You weren't like this before."

"Before what?"

"I don't know," Lilly said. "Before you saw me and Jonah in the room that morning? Before we picked up the boys?"

"You tell me."

"I just did, Mitch."

"Groovy, Lilly."

The Lincoln ticked and hissed as it cooled in the night. Simon lay under his blanket, his eyes open and staring straight forward along the flat of the ground, looking at nothing, only listening, thinking.

He waited.

Later, he pushed the blanket away and quietly sat up. Mitch and Lilly were sleeping, three empty beer cans tipped over between them on their blankets. Simon walked off into the bushes to pee. He could see Walker's tracks. He stood still, just watching and making sure

181

Mitch was still asleep, just watching. He pulled his meteorite from his pocket and looked at it, then put it away. He went over to the piles of debris they'd salvaged from the Lincoln.

Simon held his breath while he moved.

Those moccasins made his feet so quiet.

He took a can of Coke that was lying in the dirt beside Mitch's grocery sacks and put it in his back pocket, then he circled around on the outside of the brush to where Lilly was sleeping.

He crouched to his hands and knees beside her.

He looked at her, just waiting to see if she might wake up. Simon hooked her blond hair in his fingers and pulled it back away from her face and curled it behind her ear.

Lilly opened her eyes, but did not move.

Simon put his mouth down against her ear. He stayed there frozen, because she smelled so good to him, felt so warm.

His heart pounded.

He whispered, "Let's leave."

She turned her face and looked up at him. For a moment, he thought she looked terrified. He could tell she was calculating, adding things up, but not how Mitch did. No one did things like that.

Then she sat up, so quietly, and looked once at Mitch, and then back at Simon, and nodded her head.

Lilly followed Simon through the brush past the sentinel-statue of Don Quixote, his face masked behind the grainy photograph of a soldier. She followed him away from the place where Mitch lay sleeping beside the ruins of the Lincoln. Neither one of them spoke as they crept farther into the night.

Simon watched the ground, following Walker's tracks, assuming that the man had made his way back to the road, but when he realized that Walker had not gone toward the highway, he knew they were lost.

He felt panic rising.

In the distance, off in the dark, a dog began barking.

Lilly froze and clutched Simon's arm.

"It's a coyote," Simon said. "Don't be scared."

"Okay."

"I don't know where we're going," Simon said. "I was following Walker, but he didn't go back to the road, so I don't know where we are. I can't see his tracks anymore."

Simon rubbed his hair and looked around, no longer able to see any sign of where they had been; everything blended into a dark sameness in the warm and moonless night.

"Do you think we're far enough away from Mitch?"

"Far enough for what?"

"Maybe we could just wait here until morning. Then we might be able to see something. To see where we are," Lilly said.

Simon kept moving forward. "I don't know."

"Maybe we should just go back, then."

"I thought about that, too," Simon said. "But I don't know which way back is. And Mitch would be so mad at us now."

"Yeah."

Simon stopped walking, his foot pressed down onto a twig of sage.

"Do you think he'll come after us?"

Lilly laughed softly. "Mitch? I never know what he'll do. But he's so jealous of his stuff. I don't think he'd leave all those things of his just sitting there in the desert. He goes crazy if someone takes something of his. Crazy."

"Like me taking you away right now? Like what you and Jonah did?"

"Let's not talk about that, Simon."

"Okay."

"And I don't belong to Mitch."

"He thinks you do, Lilly."

They began walking again. Lilly just kept her head down and watched Simon's feet, following his path as he made his way farther and farther into the dark nowhere.

"Do you have any idea where we're going?" Lilly asked.

"No," Simon said. "I'm not the one with the map."

"What if we get lost?"

"We already are."

"I mean, what if we get stuck out here or something?" Lilly continued.

"I have a can of Coke," Simon said.

"Groovy."

"And my meteor."

Lilly sighed. "Can we sit down?"

There was no hint of the dawn anywhere around the horizon. Coyotes yelped like panicked ghosts, invisible in the distance.

"Sure," Simon said. "You want to split my Coke?"

"Yeah."

Simon pulled the Coke from his back pocket and they sat facing each other on the red, dry dirt. When he pulled the tab from the can, the warm soda spit geysers of sticky foam at them. He threw the ring away and held the can out to Lilly. She drank and handed it back and he held it to his tongue for the longest time, not drinking, just tasting the spot where her mouth had been.

"I'm sorry I got you and Jonah into all this," Lilly said. "I should've just let Mitch keep driving by you that day. He wanted to."

"He did?"

"I got mad at him for driving by," she said. "He said the last thing we need is a couple of hippie freeloaders. And I told him that's exactly what I didn't like about him, that he wasn't nice. So he stopped the car."

"I had my thumb out," Simon said. "I was asking for it."

He handed the can back to Lilly.

"Yeah, but there was something else," she said. "I can't really explain it. I just had to stop. I couldn't do anything about it."

"It was Jonah," Simon sighed. "I saw you looking at him the moment you got out of the car. I saw you take your sunglasses off and smile at him."

"You did?"

"Yeah."

Lilly drank. "Well, I'm sorry for all this."

"I had my thumb out."

Simon folded his legs and brushed the sand and dirt away from his moccasins.

"Why were you crying, Simon? When I covered you with the blanket?"

Simon shifted uncomfortably and took a swallow of Coke, then cleared his throat.

"I don't know. I guess I was thinking about sad stuff."

"Like what?"

"Nothing."

Simon drew a circle with his finger in the dirt.

"My brother never had a girlfriend," he said.

"How do you know?" Lilly asked. "He could have. Maybe he just never told you."

"No," he said. "I know everything about Jonah. Everything. We've never even been apart one day since I was born until yesterday. We even sleep in the same bed, most of the times. It's the only bed we got, the only one we ever had. When Matthew was home, we'd all three sleep in the same bed, or he'd kick us out and me and Jonah would sleep on the floor. And when we were little, we'd get so cold sometimes we just had to hold on to each other."

"Matthew's your other brother?"

"Yeah. The one in Vietnam."

"Well, you and Jonah should try to get along better."

"He thinks I hate him."

"You told him you do."

"Yeah." Simon cleared his throat. "It's not about you, though. It's about him turning his back on me. I don't have anyone else. There's no one."

"Then why'd you knock him off the bridge?"

Simon almost started to cry. He put his face down so she wouldn't see.

"I'll tell you the truth. I wanted to knock him so far. Just 'cause I hate seeing him all over you like he doesn't care about anything else. And 'cause he beat the crap out of me and I needed to get even. But I wouldn't have the guts to do it. Then I saw Mitch had a gun out. And Mitch was going to shoot him. And as mad as I ever was at Jonah, I had to help him."

"Your eye looks better now," Lilly said.

"How can you tell? It's dark."

"I can tell," she said. She reached across to Simon and lightly touched his collarbone. "And your neck?"

Simon slightly recoiled at Lilly's hand on his bare skin, and then he relaxed and took a breath, lifted his chin, and said, "How's that look?"

"I think it'll be okay. A doctor might put some stitches in it."

"Oh." Simon swallowed. "Lilly?"

"What?"

"Mitch keeps calling you a dirty word. I don't care about it, if it's true or anything."

She sat for a minute, not saying anything.

"It was true. Not anymore. Sometimes the truth is a dirty word, I guess."

"Oh."

"Will you tell it to your brother?"

"Do you want me to?"

"I don't know."

"I won't say it again."

She pulled her hand away and Simon let his chin drop, just staring down at the diamond of dirt formed inside his crossed legs.

"But, Lilly?" he said. "If we get out of this, you're not going to hurt Jonah, are you? You're not lying to him, are you?"

She didn't say anything. Simon watched her.

Something moved, and Simon jolted.

"This is a hell of a way to get to town." Walker stood about five feet from where they were resting. "A hell of a way. Unless you were planning on walking all the way around the world first! Unless you were planning on killing yourselves out here in the desert. Hell! Damn hippies."

Walker moved stiffly out from the darkness, staring at them and shaking his head as though scolding reckless children.

black simon

Hey Jones,
   I'm in the hospital. It's hard to write because my arms are stitched up. I thought I might get to come home, but it's not too bad and they're only going to keep me here for a couple days, so don't worry. It was a stupid thing, anyway. I cut myself with a machete and then the cuts got really infected 'cause I was embarrassed about seeing a medic about it, and I was drunk anyway, so don't tell Mother or Simon. I was stupid, but it's not like that was the first stupid thing I ever did.

   I didn't even tell you but I got a tattoo before I left Fort Bliss. That was stupid. "Bliss" . . . that's a great name for a place they send boys to before they go off to die. Sounds more like a whorehouse than death row.

   I got a tattoo of the Pink Panther on my arm from a Mexican. I always liked that cartoon. He's cool and things always luck out for him, even when he's stupid. But I don't think he ever cut his wrists with a machete either.

   The cuts don't hurt anymore. It just feels tight. The tattoo hurt for a few days, though.

   Most guys here spend their money on drugs and prostitutes and stuff. I'm not that stupid, though. I've been saving all my money so when I get home I'm going to buy a car. Then I'm going to take you

and Simon on a road trip across the country. That would be cool.
Maybe we'd never come back to Los Rogues. We could go see Dad.
Do you write letters to him like the ones you write to me? If you do, I
bet that makes him feel really good. I know, because I'm in the same
kind of situation he's in. And I love the way you say things when you
write. Sometimes they probably make him cry, too.

Anyway, I'm not going to say anything else right now. The way
my arm is I can't fold this letter up and put it in the envelope so I have
to give it to someone else and trust them to do it. I'm practically hand-
cuffed. I'll be all right, trust me. We'll all see each other soon.

Love,
Matt

Piss.
Piss.
Piss.

A tickle of sweat in his hair wakes him. He needs to piss so bad
that he clamps a hand over his crotch, but that makes it hurt worse.

A blanket is wrapped around his head and he trips getting up
and almost pisses on himself when he stumbles. The sun beats down
so hot.

He yawns and stretches, and the blanket hangs around his head
in sweat-filthy drapes and he fumbles with his pants, peeing without
looking, and he hopes he's pissing on Piss-kid and that whore.

The blanket stinks like burnt rubber.

Everything does.

Feeling sick, Mitch pulls it away from his face, lets it drop to his
splattered feet.

"You should have woke me up," he says to the blankets where the
others should have been sleeping, too.

189

Lilly's gone.

He spins around, thinking he might catch her being a slut with Piss-kid, but Simon's not there, either.

"Hey!"

"Hey!"

The tide of his blood makes his head darken in waves of dizziness.

"What is this?"

He pivots wildly. Frantic pirouette. Scans emptiness here in this piss-puddle-center of hell.

"What is this?"

The Lincoln sits on blackened wheel hubs. Tires split and uncoiled like dried black snakes, crooked and charred fingers all point at him like he's the object of the joke at the moment.

Mitch pushes his way through the brush at the head of their dirt beds, tramples in uncoordinated steps. He trips, catches himself. Arms scrape and bleed against the brambles that hid them from the highway.

"Simon? Lilly!"

Sweating and panting, he runs a circle around the scattered wreckage, the flotsam of the Lincoln adrift on a sea of dead piss-reeked desert.

He calls them again and again, counts the times, the names, the letters, the breaths.

Nothing.

A crow hops along the ground, flapping its wings.

Mitch swings his arms in the air, punches at nothing, whimpers.

"Hey!"

He crumples to the ground, sits, legs out on the flat, rocky dirt. He hammers a fist down into the grit until his knuckles bleed and he sobs.

Numbers pour into his head: spines on the brush-weed between his feet, vertical lines on the mesa, stacking, multiplying in rows, tables, orange stitches down the inseam of his jeans, all numbers, whirling, expanding, and condensing again into endless single-digit reductions piling number upon number inside his howling brain.

"Hey! I'm calling you!"

He hugs his knees, rocks back, forth, counts the rocking, a metronome, everything is a number. Everything. He shakes, mumbles to himself, quieter, softer now.

"That whore. That whore."

He wipes a bloodied hand across the sweat on his face, smears snot and tears toward his ear.

"They're dead. They're dead. That whore."

Ten. Ten. Nine.

Twenty-nine.

Eleven.

Two.

Numbers.

He slams his palms into his temples.

Endless tabulations.

"What am I going to DO?"

Mitch stands, crying again. He walks a tight circle, eyes fixed on the ground at the center, the midpoint of its diameter, counts the steps, calculates circumference, then area. It is a prison circle, and the numbers hold him there.

He pulls the gun from his pants, presses the barrel up inside a nostril until it hurts, begins to tear the flesh. He smells the powder, the residue of the gunshot in the bar. Small bits of Chief's brain and skull adhere to the thick metal.

It smells good.

He waves the gun in front of him until the Lincoln sits black in the grooves of the site, and fires.

"Simon? Buddy? Are you there?"

He is calm now. It is a joke.

Piss-kid.

He turns, sees Don Quixote standing off in the distance, and fires another shot at the metal man. A small piece of tin rips away from the statue's head.

Running as quickly as he can, he follows the course of the bullet, pleading. He stumbles over the brush and rocks.

"I'm sorry, Don. I'm sorry. Look what they did! Look what they made me do!"

He puts his face on the tin, rubs a thumb on the jagged hole torn open at the back of the statue's head.

"It's not that bad," he says. "I can fix you. I'm sorry."

The gun slides back into the waist of his pants and Mitch marches over the flat ground where the whore and the Piss-kid had slept last night, walks across their blankets, thinks, takes stock of what had been salvaged from the burning Lincoln. Back and forth. He makes piles of boxes and bags, neat around the foot of the statue. He wedges the box of money under some sagebrush, then moves it, and puts it back again.

Everything sits perfectly now.

He kneels in the low shade and drinks a warm beer, looks at the metal man.

He expects him to answer.

Mitch opens another beer.

"Why did they do it? Why did they leave? It had to be that punk Simon. Piss-kid. Whore. After all I did for him. He's dead, that's it. I should have never listened to her, never picked them up. But Lilly always gets what she asks for, whatever she wants. Doesn't she? Well, we left that one drowning back in a river in New Mexico, and we'll leave the other out here in the desert with a bullet in his face. Whore."

Sixteen swallows drain the can.

He drinks four beers and counts the steps he takes to the Lincoln. The paint on the door peels away from his touch in dry blistering flakes. Greasy soot blackens his open palms. He rubs his hands on his face, blacks them against the car, and smears the black on his skin again.

He wipes the side mirror, spiderweb cracked, with the tail of his shirt, rubs more and more of the ash-soot grime until his face is completely blacked. The mirror shows Mitch, smiling behind a drape of lightning bolt fractures, the colors, pink lips, yellow teeth, crooked teeth. He soot-smears his forearms, tears the shirt away from his body, and paints himself, the skin on his chest, his belly, his back, all black.

"Bullets," he says. "Need bullets."

Mitch returns to his pile of possessions and opens the suitcase. He touches Don Quixote on the knee and offers him another "I'm sorry." Black hands snake through the womb of the case. He dangles Lilly's purple shirt, pendulumlike, between two fingers, stares at it, disgusted.

Mitch spits on the blouse and tosses it away.

"Whore."

The bullets to the .357 sit at the bottom of the small bag containing the razor and scissors he used to shave his beard and cut his hair. He looks at his hands. He doesn't want the black to rub away.

He stands and walks back to the Lincoln, wipes more ash-grime on his body, goes back to the open satchel and places the bullets out straight on the ground. He builds an altar there: the gun, the row of bullets that point up from the dirt, a silver rood formed there by the crossing of the scissors and the razor.

He paces back and forth between the wreckage and the thing he is building, until it is all so perfect in his mind.

Mitch lifts the razor. The handle twists, makes the faintest sighing sound. The guards across the flat blade yawn open, a mouth. He looks at the paper-thin blade there; its edges are dotted with dried soap and the black specks of hair, dots, like the scabbed bits of Chief's brain on the snout of his pistol barrel. He pinches the blade between his finger and thumb, lifts it from the cradle of the razor and turns it over, examining both sides. He holds the blade flat against his palm, studies the contrast—the black of his skin and the gray reflection of the metal, the uneven lines of the hand and the perfect and flawless edge at the lip of the blade.

He carries the blade back to the broken mirror on the Lincoln and lifts his chin, stretches out the skin of his neck, watches all the Mitches in the jagged bits of mirror. He cuts a line on his neck with the corner of the blade. It is in the same spot where Simon had been hit by the shard of glass. Dark cherry blood spills from the gap and he pulls the lips of the wound apart between his fingers, smiles, lets the blood run over his nails, and says, "I am Black Simon."

He goes back to the objects arranged in the dirt, kneels there.

The first cuts are straight, slashing lines, horizontal strokes across his chest that make the pattern of his rib cage. A sternum, the collarbones, the lines of his arm, the arc of the ulna, the radius, all etched in bloody swipes of the blade across his skin. His hand pulses as it tracks the pattern, slowly and carefully, the blade not stinging at all, just cutting so smoothly and lightly, and Mitch's blood pools and bubbles over the black of his skin, drips down to the black-smeared waist of his jeans. Counting the lines, feeling nothing but the rush, the Ferris wheel spinning, he watches the red and black mix on his skin, watching it flow, whispers, "Gravity."

He seats the blade back in the maw of the razor, twists it closed; reassembles the cross with the scissors.

Mitch loads the gun, pictures each bullet a gaudily painted bucket seat on a Ferris wheel as he spins it around.

When he stands, he feels the burn of the cuts. Arching his back, he stretches the skin tight on his chest and belly, feels the heat of the sun as the congealing wounds spring open with bright slivers of blood.

He tucks the gun into the back of his pants and rubs his grimy palms over his skin. His blood becomes a sooty paste mixing with the ash from the car, and he smears it smooth, covers his body, his face, watching the crooked bits of his reflection in the car's mirror.

Mitch walks away from the car, past Don Quixote, out into the desert to find Lilly and Simon.

Quietly, tunelessly, he sings, "We're off to see the wizard . . ."

drum

Hey Joneser,

It's night and for the first time it seems like it's quiet. I can't remember it ever being this quiet here. It's creepy, and I can't sleep. Usually, you can hear the sounds of the rats, or bugs crawling across the floor, or the bugs outside in the jungle, but tonight it's like all the sound just got sucked right out of the air.

I was laying there on my bed, just staring up at nothing. There's a bit of light coming in and it just catches the gloss on that picture of you and Simon and I was staring at it, but it made you look like ghosts, like you were disappearing, and I couldn't see it clearly and then I couldn't even hear myself breathing, and I started to think that this must be what it's like to be dead. I guess I got myself pretty scared over nothing because I ended up turning a light on and decided to write you a letter, even if I don't have anything to talk about besides being scared and wondering if I'm even still alive, or maybe if I'm just out of my mind. I was looking at that picture of you guys. You both look so good. I bet all the girls are after you. Oh, I forgot, there are only two girls in Los Rogues and the younger one is about a hundred (ha ha).

There are lots of girls here. To me, they all seem to think that the GIs are like knights or something, that we're here to save them and take them away. But if you ask me, there's not a single one of us here who's interested in rescue or salvation. I'm not going to lie, I have paid for women more than a few times here. It's real nice when you've been out in the bush for a while and you come back and they'll give you a bath and whatever a guy wants. And that's just brother talk, Joneser, between you and me. But you have to be careful, too. Anyway, if they won't send you home for cutting your wrists, I guess they won't send you home for getting the clap, either.

But you and Simon be careful around the girls.

I bought a tape recorder from a guy who's getting sent home soon. I've never actually used one before, but it's pretty cool how you can record stuff off the radio and then play it back over and over. I recorded my voice talking on it, but I don't think it sounds like me. It sounds pretty stupid, actually. I'm going to send my tape recorder home for you and Simon, and then when you listen to my voice you can tell me if it really sounds like me. I don't think it does, though. When you get it, don't fight over it. Or if you do fight over it, record yourself and you guys can hear how stupid it makes you sound, too (ha ha).

Today a general came out here and visited us. All he did was walk around for about 10 minutes, all clean, and then he got in his chopper and left. He said we needed to keep our rifles locked up. How stupid is that? I guess he doesn't think we need them or something, when all he probably does is watch his color television all day long. So we locked them up, and about 10 minutes after he was gone, we got them back out, too. Then a bunch of us got into a card game and we all got pretty drunk. I know I shouldn't do that, but I did anyway. I know what you'd say about that. My eating is even worse. When I got sent into the rear outside of Da Nang, they had a mess hall there and it gave about 100 guys food poisoning, so I stopped eating. Now all I eat is the peanut butter out of C-rations because everything else tastes like dog food, and looks like it, too. I bet Dad gets better treatment in prison

than we do out here, and we're supposedly the ones serving our coun-
try instead of serving time for our country (ha ha).

I guess I'm getting crazy from not sleeping, but I just can't keep
my eyes shut.

We put up some Christmas lights on the ceiling of our hooch and
when we went to sleep a few nights ago, they caught on fire and bro-
ken glass and pieces of burning stuff started falling on us. That's how
it is over here, everything is crazy and the weirdest things are always
happening, like how quiet it is right now.

Well, I'm going to try to get some sleep, even if I have to drink two
more cans of beer.

Good night.

Love,

Matthew

We left in the morning.

It was still dark when we got in that noisy camper truck.

His mother and sister gave me a hug.

Dalton stopped the pickup just across the bridge—I asked him to—
and we got out and walked back onto that sagging wooden span.

His father had told him to be careful, saying that he knew we'd both
come back, and I offered to pay him for letting us use the truck but
he just smiled and waved it away. I could tell that Arno knew there
was more going on than either of us admitted, but I think, too, that
he was letting his son grow up and he respected Dalton enough to
let him help me out.

"When we lived in Mexico, an American man saw my paintings
on the street," Arno had said. "It was in Mérida. I painted scenes of
the people in the town, how they would all come out to dance in the

plaza on Sundays. The American wanted to buy them. Every one of my paintings. I realized, then, that I didn't even *want* to sell them. It seemed almost dirty to me, and after all that time I'd been trying to sell them, but I realized that I was afraid to. But my family needed to eat, so I asked him for a bag of rice. He ended up giving me more money than I'd ever seen in my life. I would have taken the rice."

We all sat at the table and ate breakfast in the cool of the morning, tortillas with jelly on them and black coffee.

"Did you buy rice with the money?" I asked.

"I couldn't bring myself to spend it. I felt so bad about what I'd done. I felt like I sold my own children, or worse. It was pretty naïve, I suppose, but I'd spent all this time wrapped up in the idea of being an artist and I never faced the fact that surviving meant I would have to actually exchange my art for other things. I almost felt like I didn't have the right. We probably would have starved to death, and Bev talked me into coming here."

"And that's how you got here?" I asked.

"Yes," Arno said. "Now, Jonah, when you come back, you can tell me how you got here, too."

"Okay. I will."

In the dark, I opened my comp book and began to draw in it. Dalton's sister leaned over me, resting against my shoulder, watching.

"That's Dalt," she said, putting a finger on the picture I'd drawn of him.

"Yeah. It's my map."

"Are you going to draw me, too?" Shelly asked.

Arno lifted his eyes over the top of his coffee cup so he could see the page I was open to.

"I like that," he said.

"Thanks. It's a kind of map, a diary."

"It's all a map," Arno said. "That's all we do. The same as those hands painted on the cave wall. Those people so long ago wanted to leave a map, showing where they had come from, showing us where they were. It's what we do, Jonah. We all make maps."

"His is a story, too," Dalton said. "A good one. About him and his brother. And a girl. He let me read it."

"Then that proves he thinks you're his friend," Arno said. "Maybe he'll let me see it when he comes back. When it's finished. I'd like that."

I was embarrassed.

"I promise I'll draw you, too, Shelly," I said, and I closed my book.

I wore the clothes and boots Dalton gave me. The backpack sat between Dalton and me. I kept my map book and pencil out, open to the last pages I'd drawn.

I walked out onto the bridge and stopped at the same place where Simon had pushed me down into the water below. The sun wasn't up yet, but the sky was light and cool, the river polished mirror smooth and glassy, like the surface of the meteorite Simon found.

I stood at the edge of the bridge, almost wishing something would push me back into the water, wanting to jump, to fall, to be rescued again, to strip myself out of my strangling skin that smelled like the road, like cigarettes, to go back to the camp where Dalton's father painted and worked on the ruins of that pueblo and forget everything else.

Dalton stood behind me.

I knew he was waiting.

"In some way, I don't want to go," I said. "I'm just tired. But I promised Simon I'd take care of him."

"Come on," Dalton said. "Let's go."

I looked once back down the road, almost expecting to see the Lincoln. I was scared for Simon and Lilly.

We walked back to the truck and Dalton drove out onto the road.

"Don't crumple up any more place mats," the waitress scowled at me and clanked our drinks down on the table in front of us.

Dalton gave me a confused look, but I had no more idea what was going on than he did.

"You cut your hair off," she said. "So you got a haircut and now you think I don't remember you?"

How could she know I cut my hair?

"What?"

It was night, and we had stopped for a Coke. Dalton nearly fell asleep on the road, and so we ended up at the same café outside of Farmington where Mitch had told Simon about what it felt like to kill a person.

"Don't think I don't remember you," she warned. "You were here earlier with those other two, smoking your cigarettes and making a mess like you owned the place. You threw the place mat on the floor and got ashes all over the place. You were wearing blue jeans and moccasins." She looked at Dalton, and then she waved her hand in front of me as though she were painting a picture of me. "So you went home and got a haircut and put on some clean clothes. Well, you better behave this time. And don't even try smoking in here again, a kid your age."

I scratched my head and smiled at Dalton.

"That was my little brother."

The waitress leaned forward and looked closely at my face. I could feel her breath.

"Well. He did have a black eye," she conceded.

"I know."

The waitress shrugged, an unapologetic dismissal of her mistake.

"What time were they here?" I asked. "We're trying to find him."

The waitress looked around as though scanning the room for customers needing her attention, but the place was abandoned except for Dalton and me.

"A few hours ago."

I swallowed.

"Did he look all right?"

"What do you mean?" she said. "Except for his hair, he looked exactly like you. Just like you. Is something wrong? Did he run away or something?"

"Yeah," I said.

"Well, I thought so. I thought something was up with all three of them." The waitress put her notepad down on our table and leaned her weight against the edge.

"Do you want me to call the police?" she whispered.

I thought. I could feel Dalton looking at me, waiting to see what I would do.

"No. He's done this before," I lied.

"Well, maybe he's old enough to let him go, then," she said. "It's a different world nowadays." She looked at Dalton and asked, "Are you going to get anything to eat, honey?"

She stood, straightened, as if to leave.

Dalton shook his head. "If I eat now, I'll have to take a nap. And we've got to drive."

The waitress looked at me.

"Just the Coke," I said. "What about the girl? How did she look?"

The waitress looked impatient and bothered, but I could tell she wanted to talk. "She looked like a girl. What do you want me to say? Not one of them looked very happy to be here, if that's what you want to know. That one guy gave me the creeps. And a dirty look, too. The girl? She spent most of her time in the bathroom, then they left in some old black convertible with a big piece of metal junk

202

sticking up out of the backseat. That's all I know about that, but you can trust me on it."

"Okay."

"Well, I am over thirty, honey, so you might not want to." She started walking away from us, toward the counter where she had left a cigarette burning, and said, over her shoulder, "But I guess you got no choice."

"I could drive if you want me to."

I could see that Dalton was fighting off sleep.

"You ever drive before?"

I thought about being on the road to the Palms, Simon and Mitch stripped naked in the backseat of the Lincoln, how it rained so hard on me and Lilly, standing under the eaves of the motel, when she put her mouth on mine.

"A couple times."

"I'll be okay," Dalton said. "But I was thinking. What, exactly, are you going to do when we find your brother and your girlfriend?"

The road was so dark now.

"I'm going to take them away."

"And what if Mitch doesn't want that to happen? You said he has a gun."

We passed the sign that said ARIZONA STATE LINE.

"So do I."

"I thought so," Dalton said, and sighed.

"I'm not going to shoot no one."

"Okay."

"I promise."

"We'll find them, Jonah."

"Arizona," I said. "I never been here before. I think you should pull off the road and park it."

203

✦ ✦ ✦

Dalton turned the truck's headlights off and parked behind a rock berm along the darkest stretch of roadway, so no one would see us there.

I was afraid we might miss something if we kept driving at night, maybe miss some sign of Simon and Lilly swallowed up by the dark, a sign gone silent now in our search. And I tried to tell myself that it was enough to know that they had come this way, had been on this same stretch of highway just hours before, but that was such a long time and things kept moving no matter what. I knew I had a long and troubled night ahead before the first streaks of light would spill across the rust of the desert and set me into motion again.

"Let's just sleep for a bit," I said.

We were both tired.

"That sounds really good," Dalton said.

I carried my pack and comp book with me and we climbed into the camper in the truck's bed. It reminded me of being in that trailer the first day Simon and I left home, the day when it rained so hard on us.

Dalton found a flashlight and turned it on. He laid it down on a small table just inside the door. We stood hunched over in the confinement of the camper. At the front end, two narrow bunk beds stretched across the width of the shell, one set back over the cab of the truck. Dalton pulled back a thin white curtain that hung across a fogged and slotted window. He propped the window outward with a broken wooden spoon and dust wafted in, blown on a faint warm breeze.

"It's gonna be too hot in here tonight," he said.

And through the window I could see the dark outline of a mesa rising, towering up, between us and the stars that hung so thick, like a cloud, in the night sky.

Dalton took off his cap and shirt, then kicked his feet out of his boots and sat down on the lower bunk.

"Man, I am so tired," he said.

I sat down on a wooden bench beside the table. I didn't say anything, and I guess I must have looked bothered or something, because Dalton said, "Don't worry, Jonah, we'll find them tomorrow. I have a feeling it's all going to be okay."

"I like your family, Dalton," I said. "Do you ever get tired of living like that?"

"As opposed to living like what?"

I thought about it. I thought how lucky he was.

"I wouldn't know," I said.

"I bet you're pretty mad at your mom and dad, huh?"

"I gave up being mad at them a long time ago. Simon's the one who's still mad. That's why he fights me all the time. There's no one else for him to blame, I guess."

"You and your brother can come back and stay with us. You can help me and my dad build our cabin."

"Okay."

"You really think you're going to find your dad when he gets out of jail?"

"No."

"You think you're going to find your brother?"

"Which one?"

"At that soldier's house? In Flagstaff?"

"No."

"It'll be okay, Jonah."

"Okay."

"Jonah?"

"What?"

"I always wished I had a brother."

"Why?"

"I don't know. Turn the light off when you get in bed," he said, and he stretched out on the bunk and threw his pants down onto the floor.

"I'm just going to write down some things," I said. "I'll turn it out in a few minutes."

"Stay up as long as you want. I'm going to sleep. Good night."

"'Night, Dalton. And thanks again."

"Yeah."

"We should have eaten something back there."

"Yeah."

Dalton rolled over and covered his head with the bedsheet.

I put my pack down on the floor, took off my boots and shirt, and stepped over Dalton to climb up onto the upper bunk. I sat up, resting my bare back against the wood-paneled wall of the camper, and stretched my legs across the bed, my bare feet pushing down into the sheets.

It felt good. I swung my arm over the side and pulled the pack up onto my lap and opened it. I snaked a hand down through the tangles of dirty clothes to feel for the pistol, knowing it would still be there, but wanting to touch it anyway, if nothing else to convince myself that all the things that had happened since Simon and I left Los Rogues really did happen.

I spun the cylinder with my thumb, checking that each bullet was still in its proper place, then I popped the wheel open and telescoped an eye down the barrel and blew a short blast of breath through the opening when I saw some lint in there.

"I can hear what you're doing," Dalton said. "I know what that sound is."

"Sorry."

"Just be careful."

"I will."

And even though I forgot to bring enough of my own clothes when we left Los Rogues, I did remember to bring some extra bullets—a small handful that were loosely scattered at the bottom of the pack. I put the gun back inside, and left Simon's and my clothes scattered out on my bed with the pack lying open so I could get the gun quickly if I needed to.

I knew Mitch was out there somewhere. I could feel it.

I stretched across and pivoted the flashlight so its beam was aimed at my bunk. I opened my comp book and bit away small splinters at the pencil tip and spit them into my hand.

What was the name of that town back there? I wrote beside the small block-image of the café, *They were here just a couple hours before me. I will have to find out the name of that town. I should pay better attention, which is why I'm not going to drive at night. Here's where me and Dalton sleep.*

I drew the truck, hidden behind the hill of rock and dirt, beneath the shadow of a monstrous black mesa.

I traced my fingers back along the line of our journey, feeling the grooves I'd made in drawing my map, some of them deep when I was excited or angry, some just the faintest indentations when I was tired or sad. I rubbed a finger over the pueblo-image of the Palms motel.

Was it only two nights ago when I was with Lilly?

Sometimes I'd think about how time was like standing in a room and I could see everything so clearly as long as I faced back. And why couldn't I just turn the other way and see what would happen tomorrow?

I ached to see her again, to touch her again, and completely disregard the rest of the world, the ones who slept beside us, brothers, the obligations I carried with me that were heavier than anything dragged along on that insane journey in the black convertible. I wished, if there ever were such things, willing to put up with the hatred and jealousy Simon spewed at me, and the lunatic ravings of Mitch proclaiming this is why the people can't trust Jonah.

That's what set him off, I knew. Mitch realized that Lilly was not his and would not be his.

I rubbed my fingers over the Palms and followed the line to where I had drawn the roadhouse where we'd stopped. I closed my eyes, trying to relive the feeling of Lilly's hand in mine, sweating, her fingers unfastening the buttons on my shirt and her smooth hand sliding in to stroke my chest, covering my heart, her hand curved back like the spine on that sagging bridge.

I opened my eyes and stretched my legs. It felt good, wearing those clothes Dalton gave me. Spending that day at the pueblo with his family made me feel like I could almost forget everything, like I had washed away something that stubbornly clung to me for so long when I bathed in the stream in the evening.

I knew I would go back there.

After.

I kicked my legs out of my pants and dropped my clothes down onto the floor. I reached over and switched off the flashlight and put my head down onto the pillow.

I had a dream about my mother.

She sat on the porch of the shack in Los Rogues in autumn. The dirt of the ground, the dark-dry grasses were covered in splotches, the yellow scales of cottonwood leaves cast down on the gray wind. I could see the black pane of the window behind her, taped over with cardboard in the corner where Simon had thrown a rock and received a beating. She held a narrow whip of a stick and made me come to her and kneel and she thrashed me for my failure to keep an eye on "the younger one." And when I turned away so she wouldn't see me crying, so my tears wouldn't make her angrier, so she wouldn't win, watching the blurry scattering of the yellow against the dull dust color of the sky, I felt the other mother's hand brushing the hair from my skin, and Bev said:

"Mapmaker, what do you imagine is on the other side of the black mesa?"

And then I was looking at the map I'd drawn: Dalton's truck, the mesa beyond it, and suddenly I was outside in the desert in the night, seeing where the stars came down and vanished behind the cloak of the table rock, a shroud of earth the blackest of blacks.

I imagine a great pueblo-city of people that we have never seen. They float above the ground, unchained by gravity, released from the earth, but not departed from it.

I saw Dalton standing there, laughing beside a stone house, and his hands were white with paint; the house all dotted over with the outlines of Dalton's open palms, like ancient cave paintings, the fingers splayed like those drawings of turkeys we'd do in grade school; and I was sitting in the cooling water, ladling handfuls over my head, rubbing at my short hair, watching my friend on the shore, seeing the handprints he'd left all over the walls as the city of stone expanded behind him.

And, now in the light, the city became a cluster of buildings towered over by swaying palms and I could hear the insectlike rustle of their leaves in the wind, warm against my naked skin. I looked up, feeling the water, drowning in the rain, to see the one palm tree—a buzzing green neon sign—as I squinted against the rain and turned my eyes so I wouldn't catch myself looking at how the gauze of her clothing became transparent under the storm.

"Have you ever kissed a girl, Jonah?"

And I could see myself driving the Lincoln; driving so fast, unable to stop or slow, the road turning and coiling before me. And I knew they were all there, could see them in the mirrors: Mitch, Lilly, Simon, the metal man, his paper face a monochrome blur, a picture of a dead horse abandoned beside a streambed. And I was saying, *I can't stop, I can't stop*; and I felt her breath against me, her lips just touching my ear as she whispered *we have to be quiet we have to be quiet*, her chanted line becoming a sound like drumming in the hot nowhere of the desert, drumming and drumming, the sound echoing through my skull with each strike of Simon's hand, rising and lowering, clutching the bloodied meteorite, bashing it into my skull, *drum, drum*, and Simon saying I can't trust you, Jonah. *Drum drum.*

Drum drum.

I opened my eyes.

It was light.

Drum drum.

I turned my stiff neck and looked over at the slot of the window. A crow was perched crookedly on the bed rail of the truck, tapping its beak against the glass of the window, just inches away from my head.

Drum drum.

I just watched for a few minutes, lying there in that half-awake state where everything that had happened just crawled slowly back to me in bits.

The black bird continued hammering at its own reflection. Blood had been spraying out from the crow's nib in a mist of fine red droplets against the glass, but the bird would not stop. I tried to shoo it away by flailing my hand at the glass, but the bird could not see beyond his own reflection, continuing its futile ritual, pecking and bleeding.

"What's that?"

Dalton woke up.

"A stupid crow at the window."

I heard Dalton sit up. I climbed down from my bed and pushed open the door to the camper. Dalton followed me out. As I came around the side of the truck, I began waving my arms over my head, yelling, "Get out of here!"

The big crow kangaroo-hopped a few feet from the truck, like he was just waiting for us to leave, still watching the window, lured by the reflection. I pulled at the waist of my underwear where the elastic had sagged past my hip and hobbled, barefoot in the rocks and gravel of the desert, and bent down to grab a rock. I raised my arm to throw, and the crow just cocked its head and watched me.

It was already so hot, so late.

"Hey," Dalton said. "It doesn't matter, Jonah."

I dropped the rock and climbed back inside the camper to get the rest of my clothes.

Ahead, out there in the desert, Mitch was cutting himself with a razor blade.

"I should've let you kill that crow," Dalton said. "We could eat it."

"I'm really hungry, too."

We had eaten all the food his mother packed for us the day before. Dalton drove, and we listened to the drone of the highway, both of us shirtless in the dry heat, the wind rushing in through the lowered windows, my fingers curled around the top of the door and my elbow out so I could feel the hot air blowing through the hair of my armpit. And sometimes, out of habit, I'd bring a hand up to brush my hair back, only to realize I was practically bald.

The highway was empty except for us two boys in that truck.

The road was without shoulders on either side, nothing more than grainy gray asphalt rolled flat across the rusted gravel of the

Arizona desert, fading white lines at its borders, broken yellow dashes along the center. To the left, I saw the desert spread out, flat and endless, tufted with green-gray brush, and to the right of us, the jagged mesas rose from soft pillows of sandstone, streaked across, red near their bottoms and ash-white near the tops, all painted across evenly as though they had been stenciled hastily like that. I imagined the vast sea that once ran over them, the eyeless creatures that must have floated and swam and died, without a mark, in the lightless and cold depths just at the same place where we were driving.

And then I saw a wink of light off in the desert to my right.

We drove on for a hundred or more yards before I said, "Hey, Dalton, I saw something back there. I think."

"What was it?"

Dalton stepped on the brake.

"I don't know."

And Dalton turned the truck around in the middle of the highway.

He drove down and back three times until I saw the flash again, and then he saw it, too.

He parked, and we climbed from the truck and boosted ourselves onto the back wheels so we could see above the stands of dark brush between the highway and the source of the light.

And I realized that we were looking out across the desert at the metal statue of Don Quixote.

"What is it?" Dalton asked.

"He's gotta be there," I said. "That's the tin man."

I squinted, trying to scan with my road-blurred eyes as much of the land as I could, but there was no movement, no people, no sound. Dalton noticed the tracks where the Lincoln had veered off the road, the flattened brush lying broken between the snaking tire lines.

"It's them," I said.

212

And I believed they would all be there, and I knew what I would have to do.

We got back in the truck. I took a drink from the canteen and handed it to Dalton.

He didn't say anything when I pulled my pistol from the pack and laid it between us on the seat. He just looked at me once and then started the truck.

"I don't know how far in we can go. I don't want to get it stuck out there," he said.

"You don't have to come."

"I told you I'd help you," he said. "I guess I didn't know it would be like this."

I felt myself getting mad, but then I thought, maybe I'm scared, too.

"I told you the truth," I said. "You read everything I wrote there. I wasn't making it up."

"Let's just be careful, okay?"

"Okay."

So Dalton pulled the truck off the highway in the direction of the fading tracks that had been left behind the day before by the Lincoln. But we had only gone a few feet when he decided we'd be better off walking into the stand of brush where we'd seen the metal man. Dalton parked between thick palo verde trees where we hoped the truck couldn't be seen from the highway.

I looked at him once. I wanted to see if I could tell whether he really wanted to come with me to get Simon.

Dalton opened his door and stood outside.

"Let's go get your brother."

And Lilly, I thought.

I spilled the contents of my pack onto the floor of the truck: all of

Simon's and my wadded and dirty clothes, my money and map, some loose bullets, all of Matthew's letters. Since I knew we'd be walking in, I put the canteen and pistol into the pack, leaving it yawning open, and slung it over one shoulder. It sagged heavily with the weight of the water and the gun, against the back of my rib cage.

Dalton silently pressed his door shut, and I did the same.

We both knew it was time to be quiet.

We set off through the brush, out across the desert.

Dalton moved like a hunter, noiseless, staying low behind the lines of brush that made uneven screens across the distance between the metal man and us.

In the silent stillness of the desert, hunched down behind a black-brown clump of brush, trying to hide from whatever might be there, I could see Don Quixote standing militarylike, as though the statue was somehow keeping guard. And I could also see just the faintest outline of the trunk of the Lincoln parked behind a stand of hopseed brush.

Dalton stood so close behind me I could feel the heat radiating from his body.

"It looks like they scattered stuff all over the place," he whispered. "Like they unpacked everything they had."

I noticed it, too, and I wondered what it meant.

I could see the grainy image of a face taped across those hollow eyes of the statue, the corners of the photograph curled at the bottom in the draining and arid heat. We both just stood there breathing so faintly, listening for sounds that never came.

My hands were shaking.

I tried to swallow, but I didn't have any spit.

I lowered the pack to the ground and left it at my feet. I clutched the pistol, thumbing the hammer back so it could fire quickly. I didn't want to look at Dalton now; I was afraid he might be ready to back out. So I swiped a hand across my eyes and stood, holding the gun before me and rounding into the clear.

I felt, somehow, that they were gone, but I didn't trust the feeling. I looked just once across my shoulder at the metal man, caught a glimpse of the arrangement of objects at his pedestal, as I quietly made my way to the stand of weeds where the Lincoln rested.

Dalton followed behind me.

I heard him gasp.

We both realized the car had been burned.

I wanted to scream out for Simon and Lilly, but I was afraid.

I waited.

Nothing.

"They're gone," Dalton said, his voice little more than a breath.

"Yeah. All of them."

I tried to erase the terrible image I expected to see inside the destroyed car. I imagined Simon and Lilly in there, huddled together, dead. What made it worse were those swiping handprints I saw in the ash and soot all along the Lincoln's charred body. They reminded me of those mythical stories I'd heard about wrongfully buried victims who clawed away futilely at their casket timbers.

And they looked like the ancient handprints on the stones at the pueblo, the handprints I'd dreamed about the night before.

I remembered how the three of us—Matthew, me, and Simon—would follow the creek bed to get to school; and one morning we came upon a cattle truck that left the highway, lying nearly upside down in the shallow water. Cows had been pinned under the crumpled side of the truck's bed. Matthew made me and Simon stay back, and he climbed up on the fender and saw the driver. He said he looked like rags knotted around the big steering wheel. I remember Matthew saying, *I wonder who he was.* And I remember wondering, too, if any of the cows got away.

We stayed there and watched, with the other kids from Los Rogues. What else would you do there, anyway? We watched as they pulled the truck back up onto its wheels and cows spilled out, rolling onto their backs, their heads flopping on broken necks. They hung a blanket over the windows to stop us from seeing what Matthew had found inside the cab.

But this was different.

The smell was awful; things that should never burn were rendered putrid in the hot summer air above the carcass of that car.

Dalton stepped in front of me. He knew I was afraid to look.

I forced myself to take the last few dreadful steps toward the car.

The seats had been cooked away. The leather was gone, revealing a tangled and blackened mash of twisted coils and ash, the skeleton of what carried my little brother and me so far away from what we had called home. I exhaled in relief at finding no charred and mummified leavings, dead relics of the people I had come to take away.

And I could sense Dalton was relieved, too.

Then we both saw Mitch's petroglyphic drawings, etched and burned into the skin of the Lincoln. The coyote that I had drawn there was now followed by three other symbols: the first was supposed to be me, a long-haired boy carrying a map; then there was a small and stout man I didn't recognize, and a scratched image of a child that was curled as though awaiting birth, a rope or cord wound around its hands and feet.

I felt like I couldn't breathe, like the ground was rushing up around me.

"What's that supposed to be?" Dalton asked.

"The things Mitch kills," I said. "That one's me. Mitch must think I drowned."

I began to panic. Was that last image supposed to be Lilly's baby?

I spun around to look behind me.

It felt as though someone had been watching.

Nothing.

"This car hasn't been here long," Dalton said. "They must be close."

"If they're alive," I said.

My throat had gone dry. I breathed, trying to force myself calm, to think, to calculate and add up the meaning of what I saw there scattered like dry and pocked bones in the desert.

Dalton followed me with his eyes as I walked a circle around the Lincoln. I didn't touch the car, but I could feel it had gone cool. I noticed where the broken side mirror had been wiped clean, the ash there had been turned to dried mud by something wet; spit, sweat, maybe blood, I thought. I looked down at the ground.

"All these footprints are the same," I said. "Mitch's. Simon was wearing moccasins."

He's okay, he has to be okay. I promised I would take care of him.

There's no prison worse than "I promise."

Dalton walked to the edge of the brush and kneeled down to look over the scattered objects that had been tossed to the ground.

I sat in the dirt beside the empty hub of a wheel, cradling the pistol in my lap.

I needed to think. It felt like anything I'd do now would be stupid and wrong.

"There's three blankets laid out next to each other over here in the shade," Dalton said. "Beds. They all rested here after the fire. And someone took a piss over here, too. Not too long ago."

I stood and walked across the open dirt to the scattered beds. I kneeled at the first blanket and put my face onto it. It smelled like Simon.

Over to one side we found a cross that had been formed from scissors and a razor, with three bullets left standing in a fragmented line. There was dried blood on the razor.

I saw Lilly's blouse hanging in the brush, the suitcase lying open beside some paper bags and empty beer cans.

Dalton pushed his hand through the contents of one of the bags and pulled out an unopened can of peanuts.

"Hey! We got something to eat, Jonah."

I laid the gun down and sat in the dirt beside Dalton. We were both so hungry. We each filled our hands with the nuts and slapped them into our mouths, and then once again before emptying the can.

Then I picked up my gun and tucked it down into the waist of my pants.

We drank cans of warm Coke and I filled the pack with some white bread and peanut butter that had been left behind in Mitch's bags and slung it over my shoulder.

"That's the weirdest thing I've ever seen." Dalton was staring at the paper mask taped onto the statue of Don Quixote. "You drove all the way across New Mexico sitting in the backseat next to that?"

I didn't answer him.

I placed the lid from the can of peanuts in line with Mitch's bullets. Then I put the empty Coke can at the apex of the cross and straightened up. I walked through the brush to where Dalton stood beside the statue and I peeled the picture-mask away from Don Quixote's face.

"Moving things around like this would drive Mitch crazy," I said. "If he comes back here."

"He already sounds pretty crazy to me."

I wadded the magazine picture into a ball and threw it.

"Which way do you suppose they went?" I said.

"If they left all together, they would have taken some of this stuff with them, don't you think?"

"I think Simon and Lilly ran away," I said. "Mitch went after them."

And we left the metal man and burned-out car behind, and began walking out deeper into the desert.

meteor

Dear Jonah,

Sorry I called you Jonah, but my hand just wrote that without me even thinking about it. Seems like everything I do now is somebody else doing it and the person that I was has just shrunken away to nothing. I don't think about anything anymore, I just do it, and things just happen. Whether I like it or not, there's nothing I can do anymore that isn't automatic, just trying to stay alive, just trying to keep out of the way of everything that's coming down on me.

You know how when things get bad you can just say I wish someone would kill me? Well, I feel that way all the time, but when someone really starts shooting at me I get so scared and something takes over like I'm terrified of dying, but right now I wish I was dead.

This has been the worst week for me since I got here. I honestly don't think I can handle it anymore. I can't even tell you what happened, just know that I'm OK and in a couple weeks I'll be going to Sydney. Then, you know.

I can't write anymore. I'll try to write you before I go. I hope this isn't my last letter. But no more pictures. I'm not taking them anymore. It's too hard to get rid of the pictures in my head.

Tell Simon I love him.

Love,
Matthew

Simon just stared at the limping man.

"We weren't planning on killing ourselves," he said. "Me and Lilly are trying to get away from that guy you found us with back there."

"You in some kind of trouble?" Walker said.

"I think he wanted to kill us. I'm pretty sure he was going to," Simon said. "He was getting ready to shoot you when you came up on us."

Walker shook his head and wiped a hand across his mouth. He looked at Lilly, not saying anything.

"I think he was going to," Lilly said. She nodded. "He was."

"Hell," Walker said. "I could tell something was off with that guy. With that whole situation."

Walker leaned closer to Simon, looked at the boy's cut neck and bruised face.

"He beat up on you?"

"No."

"Who did that, then?"

"My brother."

"Your brother?" Walker bit the inside of his lip. "Where's your brother now?"

"I don't know."

"He took off back in New Mexico," Lilly said. "He got smart. He knew what was going on."

Simon stood and pulled Lilly to her feet.

"My brother's looking for me, though," Simon said. "I know it. We just got lost. He'll probably never find us now. Or, he won't before Mitch does."

"Hell, boy. You two ain't lost if I could find you. Anyway, what do you want to find your brother for? To beat up on him, I bet," Walker said.

Simon looked down at his moccasins. "I already got even with him."

"I guess brothers'll do that. I should know. I beat the tar out of mine more times than I can count. He did the same for me, too." Walker looked at Simon, then Lilly, and said, "I don't have a phone or nothing at my place, but at least it's a place, and it's not too far from here, so you can come with me. At least until daylight. Then we'll see what we can do."

Lilly began sweating. She was sick again.

Walker's homestead was less than a mile from where he'd found them. It was built, he explained, at a crack in the bottom of the mesa, the only place around with water, and he promised, too, that he would lead them out of the desert when they were ready to leave.

"What if Mitch comes and finds us here when he wakes up?" Simon asked.

"He'd be crazy if he tried that," Walker said.

"Well, he is crazy," Simon answered.

Walker limped along, with Simon following, as Lilly struggled. She had a fever and was beginning to shake.

"My side hurts," she said. "Can we stop for a minute?"

"We're almost there," Walker said. "See that yellow light up there? That's a candle burning on my front porch. I lit it when my dog started barking, and I came out looking for you."

"She's pregnant," Simon said.

"Oh," Walker swallowed. "Well, I won't ask you to tell me nothing else. Please. Every time either one of you opens your mouth, the truth gets worse and worse."

They made their way across a gutted streambed and up the slight

222

slope to where the light from Walker's candle flickered in the dark. Lilly suffered the walk, breathing in sharp and abbreviated gasps.

"Are you okay?" Simon asked.

"Yeah. You know."

"You look different," he said. "This is different than those other times you got sick."

"Yeah."

As they came trudging up the small rise before Walker's home, panicked, yelping barks called their warned welcome, and, somewhere ahead in the dark, Simon could hear the clanking of a dog chain sweeping against the rocky ground there at the bottom of the towering mesa.

"Shut up, Lady!" Walker shouted, and the dog immediately stopped barking, whimpering its joy at the man's return.

In the dark, Walker's home looked like a sort of spaceship to Simon. The candle burned on a slat-wood porch built out from the door of a gleaming metal trailer that was surrounded by stacked rocks on the bottom. The trailer sat just at the base of the giant towering mesa, a frozen explosion of red boulder. Simon could see a small, windowless mud hut with an open doorway covered only by a fraying blanket, a narrow black stovepipe coming up from the rounded adobe roof. And he could make out the dark form of another hut, built in the same manner, farther down along the dry rocky bed.

Walker bent down and unhooked a stocky and tailless merle-colored dog that yelped with excitement and huddled down at Simon's feet, shuddering its rump and urinating all over the ground.

"She's going to pee on me," Simon said, backing away from the frenzied dog.

"He always gets that way when he sees someone new," Walker explained.

"He?" Simon asked. "I thought you said his name was Lady."

"That *is* his name," Walker said.

"Oh. Okay."

Lilly slumped down on the railing along the steps up to the trailer's porch.

"I don't feel good," she said.

She dropped to her knees on the lower step. The dog, still whimpering and dripping piss, sniffed at her feet.

Simon put his arm around Lilly's shoulders. He sat beside her on the steps, pressing his bare chest against her.

"You'll be okay now, Lilly," he whispered.

"You're so sweet," she said. "I just need to lay down."

"Is there somewhere she can lay down?" Simon called back.

"Let's get her inside," Walker said, kicking at the dog. "Lady! Get the hell out of the way!"

Simon pulled Lilly to her feet and helped her up the creaking stairs as Walker fumbled past them, placing both feet on each step as he did. He opened his door.

"There's no electricity here, so be careful," he said.

Walker swiped a wood match against the doorjamb and lit an oil lamp dangling from the ceiling.

"Put her on the cot," he said, pointing to a low metal bed strewn with dark wool Army surplus blankets.

The trailer was small, twenty feet long, barely bigger than the one Simon had slept in the first night away from home, hiding from the monsoon storm, but it was very clean and orderly. Simon could see in the yellow light cast from the lamp that everything Walker owned was perfectly arranged, dustless and straight. Lilly sat on the edge of the bed, curled tightly forward, and pulled her legs up onto the blankets so she could rest on her side.

Simon stroked her hair away from her face. She was sweating and pale.

"I'll be okay," she repeated.

Simon tugged a blanket over her.

"Just rest," he said.

The dog sat outside, with his ears up, his begging nose just inside the open doorway.

"Are you going to throw up?" Walker asked. "Do you want some water?"

"No," Lilly said, and closed her eyes.

Walker sat on a wood and canvas chair, his hands folded between his legs, watching his visitors.

The floor was completely covered by Indian rugs, but there were none of the "Friendly Indian" trinkets that were so common in the places Simon had traveled through. He sat down on a rug beside Lilly's cot. At one end of the trailer, there was a shining chrome sink, a hand pump jutting up behind the faucet, which stood between carefully stacked shelves that were filled with canned food, all the labels aligned and facing outward. There was a four-burner propane stove with a coffeepot in the corner, and the walls were smooth and glossy polished wood. The windows had been screened with curtains made of flags, an American one and some sort of military flag. A black-and-white picture of soldiers hung, framed, on the wood-paneled wall, and beside it, another frame with some sort of official-looking certificate behind the glass.

"What about you?" Walker asked.

"What?"

"Are you thirsty?"

"No thanks. I had a Coke."

Walker rubbed his leg and winced.

"Well, you can sleep in here with your girlfriend, I guess," he said. "I don't mind sleeping in the hut, anyway."

"She's not my girlfriend," Simon said. "She's my brother's girlfriend."

"Oh," Walker said. "If she's your brother's girlfriend, then why'd he take off?"

"It was my fault."

"Oh. Hell. Brothers fighting over a girl."

"I guess so. More than that, maybe."

"Is it his baby she's carrying?"

"Yes."

"Oh."

Simon didn't think it was so much a lie as a protection of the girl. Lilly slept.

Simon looked around the small room.

"Were you in the Army or something?" Simon asked.

"Yeah."

"I have a brother in Vietnam. He's missing, though."

"I'm sorry to hear that," Walker said. "It's how I did this."

Walker pulled up his pants leg to show Simon the scuffed mannequin leg he limped on.

"You were in Vietnam?" Simon asked.

"I'm not that young," Walker laughed. "Korea."

"It's pretty funny," Simon yawned, "a guy named Walker who's missing a leg with a dog named Lady who's a boy dog."

"You think that's funny?"

Simon thought.

"Yeah."

"Well, you're the first one who ever got the joke," Walker said. "I think it's pretty funny, too. Almost everything out here is like that. A contradiction, I guess."

226

"What else?"

"I got a drum of gasoline outside, but no car to put it in. I got a gun, but I don't have any bullets for it."

"That's not good," Simon said.

Guns scared Simon, anyway. But he was more afraid of Mitch finding them there than he was afraid of guns.

Simon looked toward the end of the trailer, at the rows of all those cans, the red curtain with a black hourglass shape on it covering what had to be a window on the other side.

"You got a can opener?" Simon asked.

Walker erupted in laughter.

"You like to mess with people, don't you, kid?" he said. "Why? Are you hungry?"

Simon was hungry, but he didn't want to ask for food.

"No. No thanks." He stifled another yawn. "Are you an Indian?"

"Yes. Why?"

"I don't know. I was just wondering. Some people talk bad about Indians in New Mexico, where I come from."

"Do you?"

"I never knew any Indians. Not really."

"Well, I heard it all before."

"Did you make those huts out there?"

"Yes."

"I think they're bitchin'. If I had a hut like that, I'd live in it."

"Well, you got the shoes for it. You'd do okay, I bet."

Walker smiled at the boy.

Simon raised a foot up from the floor and turned it in the air.

"Yeah."

Simon stretched out on the rug and put his head down on his arm. Uncomfortable, he twisted around and pulled the meteorite out from his pocket and put it down on the floor beside him.

"What you got there? A rock?" the man asked.

"A meteor," Simon said. "I saw it hit the ground the other night. It was still hot when I picked it up. Everyone else was scared."

"Let me see that."

Walker leaned forward in his chair and took the shiny black rock from Simon's hand. He turned it over, examining the features on the heavy stone.

"It kind of looks like a face," Walker said.

"That's what I thought, too."

"Well, it's a real lucky thing, finding one of those."

Walker handed the meteorite back to Simon.

"How do you know it's a lucky thing?"

Walker thought.

"Well, I guess I don't know," he said. "I've seen plenty of them fall, but I've never actually touched one, so it must be lucky. Just think of how far that thing came to end up in some boy's pocket."

"Yeah."

"So it's gotta be lucky. You should hang on to that."

"Do you believe in good luck?" Simon asked.

"If you didn't believe in luck, life would be pretty sad, and pretty boring, too. So, yes. Of course I believe in luck."

"Thank you for helping us, Walker."

Walker looked disappointed.

"I don't even know your name, boy."

"Simon." Simon pointed his thumb at the girl in the bed. "Lilly."

"You told me her name once. And you're welcome, Simon," Walker said. "You'll be okay. But you shouldn't go to sleep on the floor half-naked like that. You'll get stung by a scorpion."

Simon's eyes widened, suddenly not as sleepy as he was a minute earlier.

"I'll get you some blankets to wrap up in," Walker said.

By the time Walker had pulled some fresh blankets from the cabinet under the picture, Simon was asleep on the floor. The man covered the boy and tucked the blanket around him, saying a prayer as he did. He lifted Simon's head and slipped a folded blanket under him, and said, "C'mon, Lady," as he turned out the lamp. Then he shut the door and climbed down the stairs to the cool of the mud hut.

At the bottom of the stairs, the man paused and said to the door, "I really hope your brother's okay, boy. Both of them. Hell."

"Walker. Hey, Walker!" Simon pulled the tattered cloth back from the doorway on the hut. Walker was covered with blankets, sleeping on the straw mats, the dog curled up beside him. The man's plastic lower leg stood, detached, along the wall like some incomplete effigy. The dog perked its head up, and Simon prepared to get out of the way when it started peeing again, but the man under the blankets did not move.

It was morning. Enough light spilled in from the hut's wood-posted doorway that Simon could see a crude stove made from a black oil drum sitting in the middle of the flat dirt floor, a rectangular opening cut near the bottom, and a wide pipe leading up through a hole in the hut's timbered ceiling.

The air inside the hut felt cool and clean.

"Walker!"

Finally the man moved, pulling the blanket down from his face and squinting at the boy, a paper-shadow silhouette in the doorway. Walker sat, bracing himself upright with his arms locked straight.

"Something's really wrong with Lilly," Simon said. "She's really sick."

Walker took a moment to let it sink in, recalling the events of the long night, the talk he'd had with the boy.

"Give me a minute, okay?" Walker said and grabbed at the leg, knocking it over as he did.

"Okay."

Simon was embarrassed. He let the blanket fall back across the doorway and looked out at the desert. He didn't want to watch the man attaching that lifeless thing to himself just so he could stand up. He rubbed the crust of sleep away from his eyes and combed his hair straight with his fingers. He held his open hands before his face, studying the bruised welts across the soft undersides of his wrists where Mitch had bound him with the yellow rope.

The dog came out of the hut and immediately began peeing, scooting itself clockwise in a tight circle at Simon's feet, and Simon danced backwards to avoid the spray. Walker pushed the blanket aside and limped out into the light.

"Sorry. I don't usually sleep that late," he said, looking at the sun behind Simon, pulling the hat down on his head. "But it was four o'clock by the time you fell asleep. What's the matter?"

"I don't know," Simon said. "She's really hurting. She says she can't move and she's sweating. Burning up."

"I don't know anything about women, especially pregnant ones," he said.

"I don't know anything about anything," Simon said.

The boy was scared; Walker could see that.

When they got inside the trailer, Walker saw the grayness of Lilly's skin, how her mouth was drawn back in a tight grimace. It was real, something was very wrong with her.

He asked her if she was bleeding, and she said no, but her side hurt so badly. She lay on her back, her eyes shut tight. Her skin was damp, her hair pasted to her neck.

Simon dropped to his knees at the edge of the bed and held

Lilly's hand while Walker hovered over the boy and looked down at the girl.

Neither one of them had any idea what they could do to help her.

"You'll be okay," Simon said. He touched her white fingers. "Put your hand where it hurts the most."

Lilly moved her fingers to her belly and placed them just inside her hip.

"I'm going to look, okay?" Simon asked.

Lilly didn't say anything.

Simon lifted her shirt and pulled the waist of her pants down.

"Does this hurt?" Simon asked. He pressed his fingers into Lilly's skin, just below her navel.

"Yes," she said. Her eyes remained shut.

"It feels tight," Simon said. He placed the flat of his palm across her belly and pressed so lightly against her smooth and perfect skin. Lilly jolted in pain.

"I'm sorry, Lilly," Simon said. "It feels like a rock in there."

He lowered her shirt back over her belly and pulled the blanket up around her.

Walker just watched.

"What should we do?" Simon pleaded.

"It could be just a normal thing," Walker said. "I don't know. It could be she's bleeding inside, or losing the child. I don't know."

"She's going to need a doctor, isn't she?" Simon said.

"I think so."

Walker turned and went to the door, thinking. Simon squeezed Lilly's hand again and followed the man out onto the porch.

Walker stared out across the desert.

"I don't know what to do to help you two, Simon. I'm sorry," he said.

231

"Show me the fastest way to the highway and I'm going to run and get help," Simon said. "I have to try."

Walker looked at Simon, and then up at the sky.

"You can get to the highway in less than an hour," he said. "Here. Come over here."

He led Simon to the side of the trailer and opened a spigot, splashing water down over the red rocks at the bottom, raining across the sand of the desert, up onto the boy's moccasins.

"Drink some water first."

Simon bent forward and began gulping the cool water. He held his head under the flow and let the water run through his hair, down his body.

"What if he's out there?" Walker said.

"He is," Simon answered.

"Well, I have that gun," Walker said. "But no bullets. Stupid. I meant to get some, but I never did. That was stupid. You should take it anyway."

Simon had always been afraid of guns.

"No. I'll keep away from him. I can handle that guy," he said.

He thought he could figure out what Mitch wanted to hear, if it came to that.

"Don't you have no shirt?" Walker asked.

"No."

"I'll get one."

"No."

"Then take this," the man said, and put his wide hat down onto the boy's head.

"Okay."

Simon drank again. "I had enough."

Walker turned the spigot shut.

"I need to go now," Simon said.

"You left that rock in there."

"I'll come back."

"Okay."

"Just give me a minute before I go."

Simon launched himself up the steps to the door and looked in at Lilly, her body motionless beneath the cover of blankets. He held Walker's hat in his hand and kneeled at the side of the bed and stroked her hair.

"I'm going to go get help, Lilly," he said. "You'll be okay."

Then Simon swallowed hard, his throat constricting. "I love you, Lilly, and I love Jonah, too. I do. I'm sorry for everything I did. I'm going to stop being bad. I'm going to stop doing bad things. I promise."

"You're a good person, Simon." Lilly's voice surprised him. "I'll be fine."

And Simon picked up his meteorite from the floor where he'd slept and placed it on the bed beside her.

Then Simon kissed her cheek and whirled around and ran down the stairs.

Walker led Simon from the shade of the trailer and into the blaring sun.

"See that notch right out there?" he said.

Walker extended his arm straight out, pointing at a gap between two rounded boulders of naked hills.

"Yeah."

"Keep going straight that way. It's the fastest way, you'll cut the bend out of the road. When you come out across the dirt road that circles around to my place, follow it to the right and it will take you to the highway."

Simon studied the line.

"Okay."

"Watch out, Simon."

"Okay."

Simon pulled the old hat down tight on his head and began running straight out across the desert toward the gap between the hills in the distance.

homestead

Blood and ashes sprinkled on the bodies of unclean people make their bodies holy and pure. He remembers the verse from Hebrews. Something like that.

He's caked and cracking all over with the paste of his own blood. Black Simon.

His armpits reek. His sweat softens the cardboard and tape on the tattered shoe box he carries. His shins are raked raw with cholla spines that rip through his pants.

Mitch stops and watches. He keeps perfectly still. Counts, can't help it.

There is a shining metal trailer sitting out there in the piss-middle of hell. It sits atop a spreading mound of red lava rocks beside two Navajo mud huts.

He knows this is where they came.

"Bitchin'," he says.

He smiles.

paths

Brother Jones,
    It's now about 2 or 3 in the morning. I'm not on guard, I just can't get to sleep. In case you were wondering, my arms are getting better. In case you were wondering, my head is getting worse (ha ha). I've seriously thought about doing drugs. Seriously, but I don't want to end up like our old man.

    You know all those stories you hear about marijuana over here? Well, they're true. About 8 of 10 enlisted men I've met here smoke or use cocaine, or do both. Marijuana, I don't care about, but if I catch my men using coke, I'll bust their butts for it. The only reason I don't care if they smoke marijuana is because if something happens, they straighten up right away.

    This letter is for you and me only, Joneser. I don't want you letting Simon or Mother read it or tell them anything about it, OK? Just tell them I'm OK.

    I killed someone yesterday. It was a kid, about 16 years old. He threw something at me, which I thought was a grenade, and I shot him in the belly. It turned out it was just a bottle. He fell down in the mud and rolled around for a minute. It looked like it hurt so bad I thought about shooting him again. I didn't know what to do. And then he just died. Then some old lady came out of a hut and started screaming at me and one of the guys in my crew was going to shoot her too but I told him not to. I didn't care about the kid, but I keep seeing him whenever I close my eyes. I don't care. He deserved it. He had a little brother with him, but the kid didn't even cry or nothing. He just took stuff out of the other kid's pocket after he was dead. That's a future VC for sure. I'm sick of this place.

Here's a joke for you—Knock Knock. You say, who's there? Matt. Matt who? Matthew whose dad is a junkie and whose mom is a tramp for any guy who buys her a meal, that's who. Matthew who killed a little kid yesterday. I know it's not funny, but that's who I am.

You and Simon stick it out together. Do that for me, especially if I don't make it home. I told you all this before, and I'll keep saying it so you hear my voice when you go to sleep at night. The things that pull the three of us apart, the things you can't do anything about, like Dad and Mother and this war, there's no sense getting mad at each other about because we didn't do anything to deserve it. The things we do to each other, we have to be careful to not let them mess up our heads about our own brothers. OK? I know you hear me, Joneser, but I know you and Simon get mad over the things you can't do nothing about, so remember what I'm asking.

I bet I worry about you guys as much as you worry about me. I miss you both so much it feels like I'm the one who got shot in the gut.

I'm going to get a car and take you both for a ride. We'll go get drunk or something. Do something brothers are supposed to do.

Don't worry.

Bye for now.

Love,

Matthew

Sweat rolled down my neck.

It trickled between my shoulder blades.

I didn't know where I was leading my friend.

So I stopped when the path I was following came to an end upon a white gravel road stretching off toward the northeast. I looked both ways down along the road.

"Which way do you think?" I said.

"I'd go left," Dalton said.

"You want a drink?"

"Yeah."

We each took a drink of the tea-warm water from my canteen. We had been walking for nearly an hour and had seen nothing, no track, no mark, that showed Simon or Lilly might have come this way.

We followed the gravel road.

And we looked nearly identical, shirtless, dressed in the same tan pants tucked into our matching boots. But I was hatless, and Dalton wore his constant cap, the one with the flaps that hung down from the back to shade his neck.

I felt lost. I knew we could find our way back to the truck, but it just felt like we were looking in the wrong place. But Dalton and I kept walking forward, anyway.

And I knew he was thinking the same thing when he said, "Let's just give it a little more time before we rethink our plan, Jonah. Maybe we'll see a sign or something. 'Cause we sure don't want to get stuck out here."

"I know."

I found myself thinking about the socks I wore. They were Simon's, dingy and mud-stained from that river.

And as we followed the dirt road along at its edge, I scooted my feet and listened to the sound of the path they cut, just for a moment

238

mimicking the way I remembered Simon walking in the loose shoes he always wore, before we met up with Mitch.

In the early part of the morning is when you can see the things that move in the desert.

A white-tan rattlesnake drifted from a cholla clump out onto the road beside me, sweeping in sideways-pulsing arcs as it scooted diagonally away and vanished soundlessly across the other side.

"Do you still have that razor in your pocket?" I asked.

"I always do," Dalton said. "Why?"

"Don't know."

I looked at the perfect S-shaped tracks the snake left behind, my eyes scanning down the length of the road.

I froze.

I saw something dark, faint, moving through the brush ahead of us.

Dalton stopped, too, right beside me.

Someone was out there.

We left the road and dropped to our knees behind a thicket of palo verde. I took the pistol from my pack and held it with both hands, bracing my elbow on a knee, aiming the barrel down the road.

"What do you see?" Dalton whispered.

"I can't see him anymore."

Dalton put his hand on my back. Then we both saw the top of a black hat floating above the brush tops, like it was carried on a vacant breeze in the windless desert heat.

I cocked the pistol and held my breath.

"Please don't kill anyone, Jonah."

My finger pressed tight against the spring of the trigger, ready to shoot.

I gasped. I relaxed my grip and uncocked the hammer. I let the weight of the pistol drag my arm down to my side as I stood. Dalton didn't know what was happening. He couldn't tell. He grabbed me by the waist of my pants and tried to pull me back down when he saw the person who was walking in the road toward us.

I stood up and dropped the gun and pack down on the ground. "Simon!"

He snapped his head up and almost tripped when he took a jump to the side of the road. I ran to get my brother.

Simon looked shocked, but then his shoulders relaxed when I got close enough for him to see it was really me.

"You almost gave me a heart attack, Jonah."

I threw my arms around him, hugging hard, and Simon, dripping with sweat, squeezed me back and knocked his hat backwards off his head.

"What the hell happened to your hair?" He put his hand on my head and rubbed it.

"I cut it off."

"Yeah. I can tell. Looks like everything's been changed on you." And Simon held me back at arm's length and said, "You're all right. Oh my God, Jonah. I was so scared you never got out of the river."

I don't think Simon ever said anything nice like that about me in his life. And I think we both wanted to say something else to each other, but we didn't. We knew. And with brothers, I think that's about the best you can do.

"Who's that?"

I'd forgotten that Dalton was standing in the road behind me.

"He's a friend," I said. "His name's Dalton."

I was so happy to see my brother that I almost felt like crying. I turned back and waved Dalton to us.

Then I looked square into Simon's eyes and asked, "You okay?"

"Yeah."

Simon fell down to the roadbed and sat in the dirt, bending his knees up. He folded his arms and put his face down and began crying.

"I want to go home, Jonah. I just want to go home."

I sat down beside him and put my arm around his shoulder, watching Dalton as he cautiously walked up toward us. I knew he could see that Simon was crying, could tell he slowed his pace down a bit to give him time, to see whether or not he should even be there.

"We can't go home."

Simon's shoulders heaved. He pressed his fists into his eyes.

Dalton stayed back, halfway between me and the palo verde trees where I'd dropped my pistol.

"If we go home, they'll take us away from each other," I said.

Simon began crying harder.

"It's up to you, Simon. Do you want to stay together?"

"Yes."

"Then we will. Now stop crying."

I stood and brushed the dirt away from the seat of my pants. Then I walked back to Dalton and picked up the pistol and my pack.

"You look like a communist, Jonah," Simon said, his voice still shaky. "Where the hell did you get those clothes?"

"I gave them to him when I found him by the river," Dalton said. He held out his hand for Simon and pulled him up to his feet. "My name's Dalton."

Simon didn't say anything. He wiped his eyes with the back of his wrist, leaving a track of mud on his skin.

I held the canteen out for my brother, the pistol in my other hand.

Simon drank.

"I didn't know you brought that gun."

"'Cause I didn't tell you."

241

"You pointed that thing at me?"

I sighed. For a second I thought it was going to be another fight.

"It's okay," Simon said. "Thanks for not killing me."

He drank again.

"I wasn't going to let him kill anyone," Dalton said.

"You from New Mex, too?" Simon asked.

"Yeah."

Simon looked Dalton up and down.

"What kind of name is that? Are you an Indian?" he asked.

"Yes."

And I noticed the big cut on Simon's throat.

"What happened here?" I asked, touching Simon's neck.

Simon jerked away from my touch.

"Nothing," he said. "The car blew up."

"I saw it," I said. "And what's this on your arms?"

Simon looked at me. He turned his wrists over and showed the red wounds there.

He didn't answer me.

So I said, "And where's Lilly?"

"She's real sick, Jonah. I was coming to try and find some help. I don't know where Mitch is now. We ran away from him last night."

"Did you just leave her out there?"

"She's at an Indian's house. He's a good man."

"We have a truck." I looked at Dalton. "Can we drive it there?"

"He lives on this road," Simon said.

"Okay."

"Jonah?"

"What?"

"I'm glad you found us."

Simon picked his hat up and put it on his head, and the three of us started walking back.

When we got to the truck, Simon found a tee shirt lying on the floor among the scattered clothes, the map, Matthew's letters, and he slipped it on over his sunburned shoulders.

"Where'd you steal this truck from?" Simon asked. He knew I'd never stolen anything in my life, at least not until that money I took from Mitch.

"It belongs to my dad," Dalton said.

"We're gonna bring it back, too," I said. "As soon as this is all over. You'll like his family, Simon. They live in just about the neatest place I've ever seen."

My brother straightened out his shirt and looked at Dalton.

"Neither one of us has never seen no place," Simon said. "Until now."

Simon began picking up the things I spilled out onto the floor and piling them up on the seat.

"Jonah," he said. "Mitch had a gun in his hand. He was going to shoot you."

I froze. I guess I never really realized why Simon had knocked me into the river.

"That's why you did it?"

Simon didn't say anything.

"That's why?"

He looked at me and grinned weakly.

"Only partly. 'Cause I was pretty mad at you, too. But, I promise, Jonah, I am not doing anything bad anymore. Brothers' Rule Number Four. I promise."

Dalton climbed out from the camper and handed a tan tee shirt to me.

"You should cover up," he said.

"Thanks."

I tucked the shirt down inside my pants. Simon watched me.

"You look different," he said. "I never seen you in any clothes that weren't Matthew's first. And I never seen you without hair."

"Dalton cut my hair. Do you want him to do yours, too?"

Simon looked at Dalton and said, "Hell no."

And I was suddenly so relieved at seeing my brother, at hearing him talk like Simon always did; and I knew I never wanted to do bad things ever again, too.

I pictured the scratched images on the side of the Lincoln.

"Mitch told me he was going to kill you, Simon."

"When did he say that?"

"Right after we got in that fight at that rest stop."

I took off one of my boots and shook the dirt out of it. "I didn't want to get back in the car, and he said he would kill you if I didn't go along."

It suddenly seemed so quiet.

Dalton slid in behind the wheel and started the truck.

I brushed off the bottoms of my socks and slipped my feet back into the boots Dalton gave me.

"He killed a guy at that bar we stopped at that next day, when he got me drunk," Simon said. "When you and her were making out in the car. He shot a guy."

"He killed a guy right in front of you?" Dalton said.

"No. I didn't know it till later. I was outside taking a piss when he did it."

"You were drunk, anyway," I said.

"Dang," Dalton said. "You guys get drunk?"

"No," Simon answered. "It's not like that. I'm not going to do anything like that anymore, Jonah."

Simon slid into the middle of the seat and I climbed up beside him and shut the door.

"You're both lucky you got away from him," Dalton said.

"We're not away yet, I think," Simon said. He shifted in his seat and looked at me. "When all this is over, do you think I'm going to go to jail?"

"No. I won't let that happen. We'll just have to be careful about what we say."

"Okay, Jonah."

I balled up the clothes Simon and I left home with and put them into the bottom of the pack. As Dalton drove through the brush, trying to get the truck over to the gravel road where we'd found Simon, I looked out across the flat of the desert to where I could see the glint of the tin statue just poking up above the brush and cactus. I grabbed Matthew's letters and my comp book and placed them in the open pack, and, finally, lay the gun on top and closed the flap.

"Why are you carrying those things around with you everywhere, Jonah?" Simon asked. "He's not coming back."

"He promised he would."

The truck bumped and rolled over the brush.

"You haven't heard from him in six months."

"I have to try."

"You don't have to hide it all from me," Simon said. "It's not like you're protecting me from anything. I'm not stupid. I know what's going on."

I felt my shoulders slump.

"At last," Dalton said, as the truck leveled off onto the gravel road. "I go left, Simon, right?"

"Yeah. Left."

I sighed, "Okay, Simon."

"Are we good?"

"Good," I said. "And thank you for saving my life."

"I'm sure you would have kicked me off that bridge if you had the chance, too."

"There've been plenty of times when I would have loved to."

Simon smiled. Then he put his arm across my shoulders.

Dalton swerved the truck to avoid running over a rattlesnake. He glanced at me. He probably wondered if I thought he was crazy or something.

"How bad is she?" I asked.

Simon said, "I don't know. I don't know anything about that stuff, Jonah. It might just be nothing."

"Why'd she decide to run away with you? Did Mitch do something crazy?"

I stared straight ahead as Dalton sped the truck noisily down the gravel road. Simon turned his wrists over in his lap. I know he was trying to hide the marks that Mitch made on him.

"Yeah."

"To Lilly?"

"No."

I looked at my brother.

"Are you okay?"

"I told you I was," Simon said. "That's the place right up there."

Simon pointed at the trailer and the huts through the windshield and dust that came floating in through the windows on the sweltering air.

the watch

Mitch sits in the brush, black in the shade, ten yards back from the road.

He hums and smiles as he watches the boys in the truck roll past him.

So close.

lilly

A barking dog ran out to the truck as Dalton skidded it to a stop beside the mud hut where Walker had slept the night before.

"Watch out," Simon said as I stepped down from the truck. "That dog likes to pee on you."

The door on the trailer was already propped open in the heat. Walker came out of the darkness of the trailer's interior and stood on the wooden porch, looking out at the three of us.

"That's Walker," Simon said. "Hey, Walker! I found my brother, Jonah, and a friend."

I climbed the stairs with Dalton and Simon following, and shook the Indian's hand.

"This is Dalton," I said. "And I'm Jonah."

"You the one who beat him up?" Walker asked as he shook my hand.

I felt myself go pale, scared that he was angry or something.

"Yes," I said plainly.

"Well, he's a good boy."

"I know."

Dalton removed his cap and shook Walker's hand. He wiped the sweat back through his short black hair and Walker eyed him.

"You're an Indian," he said.

"I know," Dalton said.

"I thought you looked like an Indian when I saw you get out of the truck just now," Walker said.

"Come on." Simon pushed his way past us and into the darkness inside the trailer.

I saw Lilly lying on the bed, pale and sweating, her eyes fixed to the white frame of light at the doorway, watching us as we entered. The dog sat, motionless, on the stoop behind us.

"Mitch?" she said.

And I don't know if it was my short hair or the fact that Dalton was standing there behind me that made her say that. I went to the bed and dropped to her side.

"Hey," I said, feeling for her hand.

Her skin was damp and cool.

She held on to my hand.

"Jonah," she said. She opened her eyes wider. "Look at you. Look at your hair. You look like a little boy."

"I'm not a little boy."

"Yes you are." She tried to smile.

"I came back from my swim." I scratched the nubs of my hair and glanced back at the others. Then I kissed her mouth, but it didn't feel like Lilly.

"It doesn't hurt anymore." Her voice was barely more than a whisper. "But I don't think I can move."

I swept my hand across her clammy forehead.

"I'm going to take you away. We have a truck outside. We'll get you some help."

I held her and pressed my face down beside hers.

"I'm sorry for what I did, Jonah," she whispered. "I love you, though."

249

"I know." I closed my eyes and said, "Everything is my fault."

I just watched her. Mitch had hurt Simon, and that was my fault. And I was sure that Lilly's sickness was my doing, convinced that I broke something inside her that night at the Palms.

I wiped a dirty hand across my eyes. But I wasn't going to cry.

"It was me," she said. "I knew what I was doing all along, making Mitch crazy. But I needed him to get me away from Texas. I'm sorry for what I did to you and your brother."

I looked back at Simon. He lowered his eyes and shook his head.

"Don't say that."

"But I did," she said, so softly. "You should know better. But you're just a little boy. Even if you are a sweetheart."

"Don't say that, Lilly. It's going to be okay. I promise."

The dog in the doorway jerked, growling. Its ears shot upward and it launched itself down the stairway, barking.

"What is it?" Simon asked.

The dog's barks receded farther from the trailer.

"I don't know," Walker said.

Lilly closed her eyes and I kissed her, whispering, "I love you, Lilly."

In the darkness of the trailer, we heard two gunshots.

They sounded far away.

And outside, the dog fell silent.

dog

The numbers swirl, combine, and collapse.

He knows the exact amount of steps taken from the car to the mesa.

The ash and dried blood, the lines he's cut, the tattoo of a cartoon skeleton on his flesh.

"Stupid dog," he says. He spits on the twisted and dead animal.

out there

J ones,

    Scotty got killed. It was the craziest and worst thing ever. I can't stand it. I'm sick.

    A rat crawled inside his mosquito net, crawled up to the top, and then it fell on him. I told you how he was about those things. He started flipping out, and the rat got scared and it actually got inside Scotty's pants. He tore off all his clothes and grabbed his M-16 and started shooting at everything in sight and screaming like I've never heard anyone scream before. I guess he thought it was another prank, but it wasn't, and he even started shooting at the guys who came around to his hooch to see what was happening. I tried to get him to calm down and he took a shot at me. Then he shot a guy from our crew and almost took his arm off.

    Then a sergeant and another guy from another Duster crew opened up on him. I think they shot him about 50 times. It was sickening what they did. There was blood and brains and stuff all over inside there, and Scotty just laying there naked and blown to bits. Everyone was mad about him snapping like that, and then I was the only one who would go in there and clean it up. Because I loved him. I'm still crying about it, even now when I write this. What a waste this whole thing is. Stupid. I just can't stand it anymore. I can't stand anything, and I'm not listening to anyone or talking anymore. The guys here think I'm crazy and I am. Now I know I'm walking. I don't care what they do about it. I made my plans. What a stupid waste.

When you get this I could be dead. I'm sorry. We will always be brothers. I love you and Simon more than anything, just know that. You're my brothers. There was a time when I thought I was doing this for you guys, like I was saving the world or something, but that was stupid, too. I can't even tell you what I did this for because I don't even know. I don't think I ever will even if I make it out.

I won't ask you to pray for me. I know how you feel about that anyway, but if there's anything you can do that I might feel, then try your hardest, and I know you will always be strong and do what's right, and I will feel that, and I will hear your voice when I go to sleep.

This place is a slaughterhouse.

I know they won't tell the truth about it. I mean what happened to Scotty, and what happened to all of us too. I will see you in Arizona, Jones.

Promise me you will take care of Simon. He really looks up to you. You might not know that, but it's the truth.

Bye.

Love,

Matthew

Walker stood in the dark, hidden just inside the doorway.

"He's out there," Simon said.

"I guess so," the man answered.

I held Lilly's hand, but she didn't move.

"There's something really wrong with her," I said.

Walker said, "I think he shot my dog."

The man limped to the edge of the opening and tried to edge his way past Simon, but my brother held him back.

"Don't go out there, Walker."

"Okay. This is really crazy," Dalton said. "I never thought it was going to be like this."

Walker stood back from the doorway.

"I'm sorry, Dalton," I said. "I should have known it would end up like this when we got in that car."

Dalton paced toward the doorway, looked outside quickly, and moved back into the dark.

"We need to get her out of here," I said, standing.

"I don't have no bullets for my gun," Walker apologized.

I felt sick.

"I left our gun in the truck," I said. "I'm an idiot."

"Shut up, Jonah," Simon said, whispering. "We're in a mess and you saying that it's your fault or something isn't going to help us at all. So stop trying to take the blame for every little thing that happens to us all the time. That's what pisses me off most of all about you. You don't want to admit that it might be something else and not you who's always in control of things. It's not your fault, so shut up."

Simon looked away from me after he said it. I tried to swallow.

I turned away from the door.

"I'll go out there," Walker said.

"No," Simon said. "He was going to kill you last night. I had to beg him not to. You can't go. Maybe we should wait till it gets dark."

"I don't think we can wait that long. I don't think Lilly can," I said, glancing back at her on the bed.

"We should get the hell out of here," Dalton said.

Walker hobbled past the three of us toward his kitchen.

"Here," he said, "let's see if we can take a look at him."

Walker pulled back the corner of a red-and-black Seventh Infantry flag that draped down over the slat-paned crank window beside his shelves of food, and looked outside.

Simon and I stood close behind him.

"Can you see him?" Simon asked.

Walker shook his head. "No. And I can't see Lady, either."

The hammer pop of a gunshot cracked in the dry air and a hole tore through the thin wall of Walker's trailer, just inches from his head. The bullet knocked down a can of cling peaches, splashing sticky clear fluid across the floor.

"Damn!" Walker said. He immediately collapsed below the window's sill, panting, "Is everyone okay?"

As soon as Walker dropped, the rest of us threw ourselves flat onto the floor. And I looked around quickly, because I couldn't tell if Dalton and Simon were just ducking, or if one of them had been shot.

"We're okay," Simon said.

Walker stared up at the wall, at the small black hole that looked like a bug speck.

"I guess we don't need to see him to know it's him," he said, but it sounded to me like there was an edge of irritation in his voice. "What exactly did you two do to him that makes him like this?"

"He's insane," I said. "There is no reason."

"The hell," Walker said, obviously not buying my explanation.

"We took something away that he thinks belongs to him," Simon answered. "The girl."

"Hell," Walker said, and he swept his eyes across the floor and looked at each one of our faces. "This is all about a girl? You two fighting each other, and him out there trying to kill people, all over a girl?"

"I'm sorry," Simon told him. "I didn't mean to bring this on you."

"You either, Dalton," I said.

Walker took a breath, and said, "I know that. I got to think about this."

Then he belly-crawled back to the center of the trailer and slammed shut the open door.

"It wasn't Simon." I scooted myself back along the floor, following the Indian man, and stopped beside Dalton. "It was me."

"Shut up," Simon snapped.

And Walker said, "You boys will probably still be fighting after that guy out there puts a bullet in both of your heads, I guess."

"It's okay, Jonah," Dalton said. "Like you said, it was all written down there. I knew what I was getting into when I read your book. I guess part of me wanted to think you were making stuff up, so it would be exciting. But made up."

ascent

Laughing, he tucks the gun barrel down inside his back pocket. Laughing, he watches the trailer door swing shut, hears it slam. It is the sound of someone being afraid. It is the sound of Simon going out to take a piss at Chief's when Mitch put a hole in his head and smoked a cigarette.

"I bet we got one," Mitch says, and covers his mouth with a blood-grimed palm. "I bet we did. I hope it hurts. I hope they're real scared."

He watches the window for three breaths, that's all, to make certain there is no more movement on the other side of that curtain. His eyes scan the massive wall of rock butted up against the back of the trailer. Mitch hums the opening riff of "Jumpin' Jack Flash," over and over; his voice becomes a growl as he studies a path up the side of the mesa.

"We get up there and we can wait for Piss-kid and the other piggies to come out. They'll come out. They have to."

He hums, hunches over, low, begins moving in a wide circle around the trailer's scattered yard. The cap of the Zippo lighter clicks open and shut, absently flicking a metallic clink to match the cadence of his steps.

Flick.

running

Walker sat on the rug in the middle of the floor, looking at us. "We know what direction he's coming from," he said. "But we're going to need to get that gun of yours. I can pop out the window in the back and one of you will have to squeeze your way between the trailer and the rocks and try to make a break for that truck. There's no way I can do it fast enough."

"I'll do it," Simon said.

"No you won't," I said.

"Are you two going to fight about that, too?" Dalton asked.

"We'll do it together, then," Simon said.

I could tell the Indian was thinking things over, and I sensed he didn't have a good reason to trust us, either. Maybe it was our age, or the fact that he knew I'd beaten Simon up, or maybe it was Simon's long hair, but I couldn't see why Walker would even *want* to trust us.

"We're not going to take off, if that's what you're worried about," I said. "I wouldn't leave her."

"It's my truck," Dalton said.

"You don't think we'd split, do you?" Simon asked.

"I'm sure you wouldn't do that," Walker said. "Come on. We better hurry before he changes positions."

Walker moved to the end of the trailer and pulled down the American flag hanging on the rear wall, wadding it up and placing it on top of the glossy chrome-rimmed table attached to the inside wall. At the bottom of the window's edge he swung open two hinged handles and pulled the glass pane inward and free of its frame.

"Keep an eye out and yell if you see anything," I said to Dalton.

He nodded, and looked right at my eyes without blinking. Then I saw him bite his lip and look down.

I put my hands on the frame of the window and poked my head out. There was only about a foot of uneven open space between the trailer and the huge red rocks butting up against it; we would have to be careful to avoid being trapped in the crevice. I scanned the width of the trailer as far as I could, in both directions, looking for snakes, looking everywhere for Mitch, and when I was certain our path was clear, I turned back to Simon and gave a nod.

"Have that side door open in case we need to come back in that way," I said to Walker.

"Both ways will be open," the man said.

"Okay."

I lifted myself up to the sill, swung my legs out into the gap behind the trailer, and dropped down to the ground. Even standing up straight, the top of my head did not reach the window's opening. I grabbed the edge with both hands and looked in at my brother.

"You don't have to come. I can do it."

Simon looked me in the eyes and said, "Shut up. I'm coming."

He glanced back once at Walker and then slid over the sill and dropped down beside me. And then Dalton stuck his head out and said, "Move over. I'm coming, too."

Simon and I caught his legs and lowered him from the window.

I inched my feet forward along the ground, bracing my hands

against the cool metal skin of the trailer. I paused just at the corner, where the sunlight cut the shadow's edge.

Dalton put his hand on my shoulder and said, "Calm down."

I realized I was breathing heavily. Dalton tried to squeeze past me. "Let me go first."

I blocked his way with my shoulder.

"No."

I bit my lower lip and peered out around the side of the trailer. My heart drummed and boomed in my chest, I could feel the thick swells of blood pumping through my neck.

I kept my eyes pinned on the truck.

"Neither of you guys has to go for the truck with me. I don't even know why you came out here in the first place," I whispered.

Simon reached his hand past Dalton and shoved my shoulder, like he was telling me to run.

"Wait here and see if I make it."

I wondered what it would be like if I didn't make it.

"Okay," Simon said.

"I'm going now."

"Go!" Dalton answered.

I took off, sprinting, bent forward, aiming myself toward the front grille of the truck. And neither of them waited behind to see if I'd make it; they both came running right alongside me, matching the cadence and stride of each step I took like we were in some kind of playground challenge to see who was best.

And as we ran, the distance from the trailer to the truck seemed to stretch into an endless marathon. Each of us kept our eyes on the span of the desert, watching for the man we knew was out there, somewhere.

We made it. The three of us collapsed to our knees, hiding low at the front of the truck, panting and still trying to control our breathing so we could listen for anything that might tell us Mitch had seen us making that run.

"You guys were supposed to wait," I whispered.

"I wasn't going to argue about it with you," Simon answered.

"And I wasn't going to just stay there by myself," Dalton said, squinting into the distance. "He's probably moving."

I flattened out onto my belly and looked every way I could see across the land from beneath the rusted chassis of the truck. I pressed myself back up to my knees, dirt sticking to the front of the clothes Dalton had given me.

I looked at Simon.

"After I get the pack out, I want you guys to take the truck and go. As fast as you can."

And Simon just stared at me, a look of disbelief on his face.

"I don't care what you want me to do, Jonah, I'm not leaving."

"You want to argue now? You could go get some help."

"Who?" Simon whispered, leaning in toward me, angry. "Who would I get? The police? So I could go to jail? So they could split us up?"

I didn't have an answer. I looked at Dalton.

He said, "I'm not leaving, either. I've come this far. Let's get the girl and get out of here."

Simon inched past me and poked his head around the corner of the bumper, looking down the driver's side of the truck.

"We're wasting time," he said, and crawled out on his knees, arm raised, sliding his palm along the dull body of the truck, feeling blindly for the handle on the door as his eyes kept focused forward, scanning for movement across the expanse of open desert.

Simon's fingers wrapped around the handle and he swung the door open, ducking his head down low to the ground as it flared outward.

No sound.

I crawled up beside Simon. Dalton squatted on his knees by the bumper, watching. I was already thinking about which way we'd go back—by the window or up the stairs—trying to calculate the distance and the time, how long we'd be exposed.

Simon slid his body along the dirty floorboards of the truck and stretched his arm across the hump there, wrapping his hand around the shoulder strap on my pack. His feet and knees dangled from the open door in front of my face, and I held on to Simon's legs the way you'd hold someone upside down in a well.

"I got it," Simon whispered.

"Go," I said.

"Shut up."

"Take the keys out," Dalton said.

I heard the clink of the keys falling down. Simon pulled himself out from the truck. I slipped the pack over my arm. I looked back at Dalton, and Simon ducked as he slowly swung the door inward over his head. He jammed the truck's keys down into his back pocket and followed me back to Dalton, all of us now squatting at the front of the truck, looking out again across the dry land.

I twisted around so that the pack hung in front of Dalton.

"Get the gun."

"Okay."

I could hear Simon's nervous panting.

Dalton fumbled with the catches on the flap and carefully lifted the black revolver out. He handed it to me.

I squeezed the gun tightly in my hand, bracing my left palm flat against the ground, ready to launch myself out from our cover toward the trailer.

"Jonah!" Simon gasped. He grabbed my shoulder and pointed off at the rust-colored rock face towering up behind the trailer.

A crooked black figure was making its way up the side of the mesa, ascending, arms stretched out, and clutching at rock holds.

We all saw him.

Mitch.

I squinted, focusing my eyes.

"He's all covered in black."

"I don't think he saw us yet," Simon said.

"*Yet?*" Dalton said. "We gotta get out of here."

I took a few short, deep breaths. "You ready to run faster this time?"

Simon swallowed, but I could tell his mouth had gone dry. He kept his eyes fixed on Mitch as he climbed, sometimes stumbling, higher up the cliff's face.

I looked at Dalton and Simon. I held the gun up, pointed at the mesa, and nodded toward the trailer's porch.

"Let's go."

We burst forward from the narrow shade, dashing out across the open space between the truck and whatever safety there could be at Walker's little trailer.

Simon's feet slipped out from under him and he fell forward, sprawling out on his belly in the dirt. Dalton and I were in front, and we heard him go down. We both stopped running. I pushed Dalton's back, shoving him toward the trailer, and said, "Go!"

Then I turned around and saw my brother on the ground.

"Simon!"

I grabbed Simon by the back of his tee shirt and jerked him back up onto his feet, pulling him along as we both turned and sprinted forward. It felt like we were falling the whole way.

That's when Mitch noticed us.

He was barely holding on to the side of the steep wall he'd been climbing, but he pivoted around and watched Simon and me as we stumbled toward Walker's trailer. I thought it looked like he was smiling, too. Maybe I was just crazy and scared at the time, I don't know. But I did see him swing his arm out, pointing that chrome pistol I'd seen in the Lincoln's glove box right at us.

I twisted my fingers into Simon's shirt and tugged him toward the steps that led up to the door on the trailer. Dalton was already there. And I was suddenly angry, mad at Simon for having fallen down, for coming along with me to get the pack in the first place, for agreeing to leave Los Rogues and not fighting me into staying home when our mother left us, for never, never doing anything the easy way. And for being right about Lilly, too—that's what bothered me the most, because I knew all along how stupid I was being, and I wouldn't listen to him and I knew now that Simon loved me.

Mitch didn't shoot.

Dalton pushed the door open.

Walker stood beside the cot, watching us. I put the gun on the floor and let the pack slip down from my shoulder. I put my hand on Simon's head and looked at him, trying to see if he'd been shot because I couldn't figure out why he'd fallen down like he did.

"Are you okay?"

"My hands got scraped," Simon said, holding out his palms so I could see the bits of gravel that clung there next to those red marks on his wrists.

"I thought you got shot or something." I brushed Simon's shirt flat where I had been tugging on it.

"I thought both of you did," Dalton said.

Walker was standing there, in the middle of the floor, motionless and silent, just staring at me.

"Did you see my dog anywhere?"

We didn't answer. I felt sorry for him.

Walker sighed.

"We saw Mitch," Simon said.

"He's gone up on the side of the mesa," I said. "He's behind us now."

Walker didn't say anything. Something was wrong.

He turned his head back at where Lilly lay on the cot.

"She stopped breathing," Walker said.

I didn't get it.

Then I looked at her. She was covered with the blanket. It was over her face. Just her bare feet stuck out at the bottom of the cot. I looked back at the Indian.

"What?"

"She stopped breathing, boy," Walker repeated.

I felt like I'd been slugged in the stomach.

"What?"

I looked at Dalton and Simon. When I did, they both turned their eyes away.

I moved to the side of the bed, dropping to my knees and shakily pulling back the covers that hid her face.

I had never seen a dead person before. And I knew Lilly was dead as soon as I saw her. I almost didn't recognize her. She looked empty, gone.

She was gone.

I brushed her hair back softly with my palm, her skin already cold and waxy.

"I'm sorry, Lilly," I said, and I felt the first slick tear streak like that meteor, arcing down, heavy, trailing a line down to my chin.

I pulled the blanket away from her and placed my hand on her stiff belly. I knocked Simon's meteorite down to the floor by my knee. I couldn't believe things like this ever really happened, even if I knew they did. But it was just like all those times I'd heard warnings in my own head about things, about Lilly, and I knew about the bad things

265

even if I chose to ignore them. I lifted her shirt and put my ear down against her pale skin, taut and unyielding, trying to listen for anything that might make me understand what had happened, holding my breath, straining to hear the rhythm of her body, of blood, the *drum drum* of what it was that had killed her, anything at all contained beneath that cool and silent place.

Nothing.

I closed my eyes.

I began shaking.

"What do we do now?" Simon whispered.

Walker looked down at the gun I had dropped to the floor and said, "I better go put that window back in."

"I'm sorry, Jonah," Dalton said.

I held my eyes shut and pressed my face into Lilly's belly.

"It's my fault. It's my fault."

I began to cry, and I got angry for doing it. After all Simon and I had been through since we left home, I just didn't want to cry now. But I couldn't help myself. I felt so sorry for Lilly, for how she'd suffered. And I felt guilty for what I'd done with her, and foolish for how I just let it happen.

And the Indian turned away and left Simon and Dalton standing there, just watching me quietly in the dim of that trailer.

He stood back, waiting, then Simon lowered himself beside me and picked up his meteorite, squeezing it so tightly in his fist. I looked at him, but I couldn't say anything. And I wanted to tell him I was so sorry for all the terrible things I'd put him through.

But I just couldn't say the words.

Simon rubbed my head and put his arm around my shoulders. He put his face right up to my ear and whispered.

"Jonah?"

I shuddered.

"Jonah?" Simon whispered again and pulled my shoulders tight against his chest.

"I'm sorry, Jonah."

"So am I."

"She loved you. She told me she did. That makes it true."

And I knew Simon tried plenty of times to make me see things clearly, but I was so selfish and stupid, absorbed by my wanting things to be like they weren't, that I wouldn't ever listen to him, even if I wanted to now.

Simon kissed me on the side of my head.

"I'm sorry, Jonah. I love you, brother. You know. No matter what."

Dalton kneeled beside us and put his hand on my shoulder.

I pictured the first time we saw the girl, breezing past us in that Lincoln, blond hair whirling around her, her glasses tipped down, her smile, the stroke of her fingers. The teasing.

Simon tumbled the meteorite around in the sweat of his hand. I wondered what it would be like to look down at the earth, to fall, to burn brilliantly in the air like the image of the girl who passed by, kicking back dust like cosmic ash, and could she see that, now; was she up there above us?

I wondered.

We closed our eyes.

All hell and chaos erupted before either one of us opened his eyes again.

los rogues

They drove into Los Rogues in a pale green Ford station wagon, on a sweltering and still afternoon, the two of them making nervous conversation and joking about how none of the streets had names or how they all seemed to have the same name. The passenger tried to read off the directions written on the back of an envelope from the county sheriff's, watching, waiting, seeing just how long that curl of dangling ash on the driver's cigarette would get before giving in and tumbling down onto his lap.

They had driven around the same dirt-road loop twice, and the lieutenant colonel on the passenger side, frustrated, flipped the envelope over the top of the seat to land beside the carefully packed box of belongings they had carried with them since they started their drive at three that morning.

"I think that's the place there," he said.

Stevens turned his head to see if that really was a house tucked in back there behind those bent and scarred cottonwoods, and the lieutenant colonel nearly exhaled in relief when he saw that finger of ash finally break free and fall onto Stevens' Class A pants.

"I knew that was going to happen."

"Damn," Stevens said, and swiped at the white-gray smear on his leg. "You think that's it?"

"Yeah."

"I hate being wrong."

"I'd rather be wrong than lost," the colonel said.

Stevens twisted the wheel around and drove the car forward up the rutted drive to the nearly hidden shack, grinding the butt of his cigarette against the lip of the filled ashtray.

"I don't know what that means," Stevens said. "If you're wrong, then you've got to be lost. Right?"

"Not if you convince yourself that you're right. If you admit you're lost, you've given up."

"If you say so, Colonel." Stevens stopped the car and turned off the motor, bending forward at the wheel and looking out at the small and crumbling house. "I don't think anyone lives here. So which are we . . . wrong or lost?"

The colonel opened his door and put a foot down on the dirt.

"Neither one, I'll bet." He stood up and stretched his back, damp with sweat, and, as he pulled his jacket from the wire hanger over the back door's window, said, "Get the box, Stevens. I want to get out of here as quick as we can."

The men, in their uniforms and hats, their perfect shoes, walked across the narrow dirt strip that was front yard to the shack, the colonel holding a thin leather folder, Stevens carrying the box, sealed with tape, an ID strip glued crookedly over the top. They stood on the porch, the colonel half-expecting the deck to give way under their weight. He looked at the torn piece of cardboard tucked into the corner of a broken window, taped with yellowed cellophane that had become some sort of death trap to hordes of dried insects, petrified in the place of their final struggle.

"This is it," he said, almost in a whisper. "Look."

He pointed at a smeared handwritten card pushed into a metal enclosure on the empty black slot mailbox hanging beside the door.

"It says 'Vickers' on it," the colonel said.

"Okay," Stevens conceded. "Who in America doesn't have a telephone in their home in 1970, anyway?"

"Never had a phone in my house when I was a kid."

Stevens held the box level, bringing his knee up so he could free the hand that knocked on the frame of the warped screen door.

They listened quietly, but heard no sound from inside the house. They waited.

"I don't think there's anyone here," Stevens said, kicking his feet at the ancient rotting leaves scattered through the dust on the planks of the porch. "It looks abandoned. How much family did he have, anyway?"

The colonel opened his folder and thumbed through the pages inside.

"His address is reported here. He lived with a mother and two younger brothers—Jonah and Simon. From their DOBs, it looks like the older one is just about seventeen and the younger one's fourteen. They have a father incarcerated at Yuma."

"Incarcerated? For what?"

"It doesn't say."

Stevens put the box down at his feet and sighed.

"Are we going to have to drive to Yuma?"

The colonel snapped his folder shut.

"No. Try the door."

Stevens pulled the screen forward and it fell, crookedly tilting from the only loose screw in its failing upper hinge, the spring catch-arm swinging downward and clanking against the peeling door.

"Oh, great."

He knocked, loudly, against the front door.

"Maybe they're just sleeping," the colonel offered.

Stevens felt the perspiration spreading beneath his arms.

"Who sleeps on days like this?"

"What else would you do?"

"In this place?" Stevens said, "Enlist, I guess."

The colonel pushed his way past Stevens and wrapped his hand around the wobbling, spotted brass knob.

"Not by the book," he said. "But I've got better things to do."

"I didn't know there was a book, sir."

"There's not."

The door swung open at the colonel's nudge and the men just stood there.

"They left it unlocked," the colonel said.

"I don't imagine there's too much to keep in, or too much to keep out, either way."

"Hello?" the colonel called out. "Mrs. Vickers? Is anyone home?"

Nothing.

"What do you think we should do?" Stevens asked.

The colonel answered by stepping through the doorway and into the dark room. The windows were covered with ragged curtains; the sun, stretching low through the treetops on the hill, stabbed the smallest spears of amber light through the fraying gaps in the draperies.

"Hello?" he called out again.

The colonel walked forward into the center of the small front room, Stevens following behind and flicking at a light switch that produced nothing more than a clicking sound.

Flick.

"No electricity," Stevens said. "Maybe they've moved."

"Doesn't seem right. Everything is still here," the colonel said, moving toward a darkened hallway at the back of the room, while Stevens followed.

The colonel was right, Stevens thought. In the gray light of that cramped small room, he could see the furnishings that meant someone had been living there: an RCA television with bent rabbit ears ribboned at their tips with twisted aluminum foil, a sofa and chair, a scratched dinner table with dirty plates and glasses, one of them with an inch of water in it, and clumps of wadded, discarded clothing balled-up against the corners of the floor, looking like pale sleeping cats in the dimness.

The colonel tried the faucet at the rusted and filthy sink in the kitchen. No water came.

"Nothing's on in here," he said. "I think they left, but probably not too long ago. There's still some water in that glass on the table."

"I saw that," Stevens said. "Do you think it would be okay if I had a cigarette, sir?"

"Sure. I'll have one, too."

The men smoked in the kitchen, Stevens flicking his ashes into the sink and the colonel just letting his fall to the spotted and blistered linoleum. The colonel bit the inside of his lip. He placed his folder down on the counter, scooting smeared silverware across the tiles as he did, and began opening the cabinet doors.

Stevens watched him while he smoked.

"There's no food or anything in here," the colonel said. "It's like they just ran out of everything."

Stevens pulled open the latch on the yellowed refrigerator and nearly fell backwards from the damp corpselike stench that exhaled out at him. Gagging, he covered his mouth with his hand, the cigarette pinched between his fingers, and slammed the door shut as he turned away.

He could hear the colonel peeing in the bathroom at the back of the small shack, heard the useless lifting of the valve and the gurgling suction as the colonel flushed but no water came. Stevens walked back through the hallway, peering into the small bathroom, its mirrorless wall, the dingy bathtub without a shower curtain, the colonel's soggy cigarette butt lying crooked in the yellow fluid that just covered the bottom of the toilet bowl, stained pink with a line where the water level had once been. Stevens wanted the man to just admit that they had done all they could, that they could go home now, but the colonel seemed to enjoy examining this place where a soldier had lived once, and so Stevens kept quiet.

He lit another cigarette.

"Little wonder why they left," the colonel said.

"Or why the boy enlisted," Stevens answered. He inhaled, standing behind the colonel where the hallway ended at two opened bedrooms.

"I guess we got off easy today," the colonel said.

Stevens sighed in relief. It sounded like the colonel was getting ready to admit they were lost, or wrong; either way it meant they could go home soon.

"It never gets easy, telling someone their boy's dead," Stevens said.

"He killed himself," the colonel answered. "That's even worse."

"I know."

The colonel looked down at his hands.

"Where'd I put my folder?"

"You left it in the kitchen."

"Hanged himself."

"I know."

"That's the tough one."

"Yeah."

"'Cause no one ever knows why that happens."

273

"Yeah."

"I guess this is the mother's room."

Stevens looked past the colonel into the room, dark and square, everything tidy, the bed made up cleanly, not the smallest wrinkle on its covers. A rack of clothes hung in an open closet.

"It looks like they mean to come back. Or, at least, she does," Stevens said.

The colonel turned around and entered the other bedroom. The floor was scattered, strewn with clothes and paper. The one small bed sat low against the wall, its covers trailing off onto the floor, two sweat-yellowed pillows, still indented from the heads that had slept on them, flattened, at opposite ends of the mattress.

In the middle of the bed lay a wadded pile of clothes. The colonel guessed they were the older boy's. The clothes sat as though they were ready to be packed, but had been forgotten there.

"Looks like the boys lived in here," Stevens said.

The colonel lifted one of the tee shirts from the pile of clothes. He looked at the tag in the collar, turning the shirt over in his hands, smelling it.

"It's clean," he said. "I bet the boys ran off. Maybe she doesn't even know it. That's what I think happened."

The colonel placed the shirt back on the pile and pushed the clothes aside to make a place to sit. Then he saw the yellow sheets of paper left there on the bed.

"Here we go," he said, looking at the pencil scrawl of a boy's writing. He stuttered along, squinting to decipher some of the smeared words, as he read the letter to Stevens.

Dear Matthew,

Something is happening here, but I don't know what it is. Ha ha, I thought you would like that.

Simon and me are leaving today. I didn't tell him yet, but I am going to after I finish this letter. We are taking the horse and going to Arizona, to Scotty's mother's-house, where you said you'd be. Maybe we will run into Dad, I don't know. We ran out of food and we are pretty hungry. Also, the electricity was shut off two days ago. Mother's been gone for a long time now, and I really don't care anymore. I just know we have to get out of here. It will be better for everyone if we just leave.

I've been trying to listen to what you keep telling me about Simon. So I stopped talking to him. It doesn't help, really, because I still get so mad at him I feel like I could kill him. But what can I do, Matt? I promise I will try my hardest. And I promise I will take good care of him. And when you come back and we see each other again, we will all do something crazy like brothers are supposed to, like you said. So if you get a car, maybe you could drive us to the ocean. I'd like to see that.

I have ten dollars. We can eat for a few days on that, I guess. I am bringing the gun, too, but I'm not going to tell Simon because it will scare him. And, like you said, I need to take care of him so I will do what you ask.

Matt, I am sorry for all the bad things that happened to you over there, especially for what happened with Scotty. And I am sorry for what our life is like here, too. It makes me feel so scared and alone sometimes, like I'm a little baby crying out for mommy or daddy, but that's really not what I want. They can keep ours, you know, because we're better off without them but it still hurts to say it.

So I know all we got is each other, but there's too many things that want to keep us apart, like you said. If I could wish you back and make it real, I wouldn't be writing this letter right now. And me and Simon are another thing. I know we look for ways to convince ourselves that we are not as close as we are, and that both of us like fighting with each other, even if it always makes us both feel sorry. I'm pretty tired of that.

275

At night, when it's quiet, I hear your voice, like you said I would. I close my eyes and try to rub them so hard so I will forget what Mother and Father look like. I am carrying your letters. They are stained and smell like the place you are at.

I hope we make it.

I am going to keep track of where we go. We are going to head north to Tucumcari, because I figure that's the easiest way to maybe get a ride west to Flagstaff.

Maybe someone will feel sorry for two boys in torn hand-me-downs and offer to help us out, but I doubt it 'cause we look too much like hippies. Neither one of us has had a haircut since before winter.

We will see each other again.

Simon knows you love him.

Love,

J. (Mister Jones)

The colonel put the letter back on the bed where he'd found it. He looked at Stevens.

"Are we done?" Stevens asked.

"Looks like we got off easy," the colonel said.

"It's a long way to Arizona."

"Those boys are crazy," the colonel said. "They'll make it. Some-one'll find them."

"Yeah."

The colonel lit another cigarette, and said, "I'm tired. We did our job. Let's get out of here."

"What about the box of Vickers' personals?"

"Leave it on the floor."

hell

Drum drum.
I opened my eyes and sat up.
I covered Lilly's face.

piggies

The first rocks he throws down at the trailer are fist-size knots, porous and scab-red. They smash into the roof and it sounds pleasing, like explosions.

Mitch digs his fingers into a sliver of a crevice. He pries at a boulder, loses his footing, arms flail as he slides twelve feet down the wall of the mesa. The rocks that slow his descent scrape flesh from his back and shoulders. He spider-crawls back to his place, hurls the boulder outward, throws himself back against the cliff wall to save himself from following it.

He laughs, watching the boulder sink down into the trailer's roof. It looks like a fly caught in a bowl of pudding.

He sweats and grunts. Whatever he can lift, he sends down onto the shuddering little trailer.

"Come out, Piss-kid."

"Come outside, Jonah."

On the face of the cliff, he counts as he launches the stones skyward.

"Thirty-three. Thirty-four."

sounds

Dalton stood right beneath where the first boulders slammed into the trailer, and he tumbled backwards and fell against the door.

Walker ran from the back of the trailer, pointing the pistol up as though warning whatever thing was above us to go away. He stumbled and dropped the pistol onto the matted floor, just as the largest boulder struck, splintering the thin paneling across the ceiling and opening up a toothy, jagged slash of skylight above us.

We could hear rocks crashing in through the opened window at the back of the trailer. Walker hadn't replaced the glass, and it would have broken, anyway.

We all rolled to the edge of the floor, looking up at the sag in the ceiling, and Walker, sensing what we were doing, slid against an outer wall as well, alternating his darting, panicked eyes from the quaking ceiling to look at each of our faces.

I felt numb.

"Stop it, Mitch." Simon spoke barely above a whisper, angry, his fingers twisting into the rug, as the rocks continued to hammer, without rhythm, into the trailer.

Drum drum.

Walker stared up at the ceiling. I was certain it was going to give way under the barrage.

"What did I do? This is my home. What did I ever do?" Walker said.

Simon pushed himself to his feet and put his arm over his head as he made for the door. The roof vent had given way and collapsed, its plastic door dangling and swinging like a spider on a hair of web. Three more loud *bangs*, and Simon ducked as he twisted at the knob.

"Simon!" I gasped.

"Don't go out there," Dalton said.

Simon pulled the door inward and stood outside, fully exposed in the light of the sun, shading his eyes with his flattened hand, framed there by the darkness of the trailer's interior, looking like he was some kind of ghost.

"Stop it, Mitch! You stupid bastard!" Simon screamed up at the mesa.

Another rock arced downward, thudding into the dirt between Simon and the truck.

"Simon! Get back in here!" I looked over at Walker, who was struggling to get to his feet.

"Mitch!" Simon yelled. "Leave us alone! Lilly's dead! It's your fault! She's dead because of you! Just leave us alone and let us go!"

The rocks stopped falling.

Walker sat motionless, resting a hand on his lifeless leg, his eyes wide and frantic.

I listened to my own breathing.

It was suddenly so still, so quiet.

"Simon!" I whispered.

He didn't move.

Dalton started to get up. I knew he was going to get my brother, so I held him down with a hand on his shoulder. I launched myself up and ran to the doorway. I reached an arm out the door and grabbed Simon's shirt, and pulled him back inside the trailer.

down

Black, filthy, rusted with his own blood, Mitch raises himself up and looks down. Piss-kid, standing outside the door, yelling something. He doesn't care. It's a lie. A trick. The kid is looking right at him, but he can't see Mitch; he fades into the hematitic colors of the mesa.

His hand shakes. Not enough water, tired and sore from this climb, heaving the rocks. His hand shakes when he raises the pistol and points it at the kid.

Mitch pulls back on the trigger.

"Whore! Piss!"

Simon disappears inside.

"Next time," he says. He smiles. "Time to go down."

He tucks the pistol away and scoots down the same path he took climbing up.

plan

I kicked the door shut as I pulled Simon inside.

"What were you trying to do?"

And I remembered, in my distraction, how Simon and I had been trapped in that trailer the first night after leaving home. It seemed like such a long time had passed, but it wasn't even a week before.

Dalton was just staring up at the battered ceiling.

"We need to get that guy. There's four of us and one of him. We need to get him," he said.

"I couldn't see him," Simon said.

I looked at Simon. I let my eyes drift across the floor to where my gun had been dropped, saw Walker bracing himself against the wall, propping himself up onto his feet. And I looked again at the small bed, and Lilly, stretched out there beneath that dark blanket.

I looked at Simon.

"Jonah?" Simon said, but I didn't answer. "Jonah?"

"What do you have in mind, Dalton?" I said.

"We need to make a plan," he said. "Just like we're playing a game. We need to make a plan so we can win."

white simon

At the bottom of the mesa, Mitch wedges a foot down between two rocks and stumbles forward. The ankle pops and he curses. He catches himself, scuffing his palms, tumbling forward.

"Damn! Piss!"

He pulls his foot in toward his body and tries to stand. Pain fires upward through his knee and he nearly falls again, rights himself by hopping forward.

"He's a liar."

"White-Simon-Piss-kid is lying to me. The whore isn't dead."

He limps. Like that stupid man coming out of the dark last night. He carries the box under his arm. It is beginning to break apart at the corners. He counts the corners.

"Scared pigs."

Nothing moves in the trailer. He sees the truck, decides it will be his way out of here. His and Piss-kid's. He opens the door and drops the box there.

No keys.

Piss.

He waits behind a wall of brush, not twenty feet from the trailer.

"Why did I listen to her? If I just kept on driving and left them there, none of this would have happened. Those boys have ruined everything. They took her away from me."

He flicks the cap on the lighter.

The lighter is silver, looks like the trailer.

He listens to the bell-ring of the cap and counts.

Back and forth; five, six, seven.

evening

We could take him," Dalton said. "We just need to stand up to him. Let's just go out there and get the truck."

I stooped beneath the gap in the ceiling and grabbed my gun. I tucked it into the waist at the back of my pants. I looked at Lilly's feet.

"What caliber is that gun?" Walker asked.

"We need to cover her."

"Jonah?" Simon said.

I curled the blanket beneath Lilly's head, lifting it up; she seemed so wooden, heavy.

"We need to cover her up," I said.

"It's okay, boy," Walker said. "Here."

He passed another wadded blanket across to me.

I tucked the blanket around Lilly's feet. I knew I wouldn't see her again. And as I looked down at those rumpled covers on the bed, I thought, *You can't even tell there's someone under there.*

I was so tired. I was tired of being so stupid, so wrong about everything.

I sat down on the edge of the bed and propped my elbows on my knees. I put my fists in my eyes.

Simon put his hand on my shoulder, tried pulling me up from the bed, and I jerked away from him.

"Come on, Jonah," Simon said. "Don't sit there."

I didn't move.

I could feel everyone watching me. I felt so stupid, and naked, just like Mitch waking me up that morning at the Palms.

"Don't just sit there now," Dalton pleaded. "We need to do something."

Simon cupped his hand beneath my arm and began lifting me up, saying in a whisper, "Come on."

I swatted at Simon's arm and made a fist with my opposite hand, aiming it. And I don't know if I was honestly trying to punch Simon or not, but I knew I wanted to hit something.

"Hey!" Walker shouted.

And Simon tackled me just as my fist sailed past him. He pushed me backwards and drove me down to the floor, grabbing my arms and pinning me, sitting square on my chest and locking my wrists beneath his knees.

"Get off!" I said.

"You can't just sit there," Simon said. "You need to do something."

I struggled, pushing with both feet against the floor, arching my back, trying to wrestle my arms free from Simon's weight, but my brother was too strong.

Dalton looked at Walker, and said, "Get off him, Simon. Things are already bad enough. Let him go."

I struggled. "Get off! What am I supposed to do?"

"Give up," Simon said.

"Okay. You beat me. Now get off!" I felt tears running sideways down my face.

Simon breathed and relaxed, still sitting on my chest.

"That's not what I mean," Simon said.

Simon let my arms free and rolled away. He sat beside me on the floor, with his back turned to the little bed where Lilly lay beneath those blankets.

"The farther we go, the worse things get," Simon said.

I stretched out on the floor, staring up at the splintering ceiling, expecting it to collapse and crumple in on all of us.

"We're here. In Arizona. Look what it got us, Jonah," Simon said. "Let's go home, Jonah. You need to give up on Matthew. On everything. Let's go home."

"I can't."

Simon pulled at a blue bead on his moccasin. He exhaled a sigh, staring at the door.

"You're always saying I'm the stubborn one. You're more stubborn than me, Jonah."

We waited. The trailer darkened as the afternoon sun stretched the shadows of mesa and mountain across the desert floor. Walker pulled the flag back across the open window at the back, carefully trying to manage his way between the rocks that had scattered there over the floor. My mouth was dry. I ached for a drink, but I didn't want to say anything. It was so quiet. I kept the gun on the floor between my legs, staring across at that gray cot, the metronome of belief and doubt swaying in my mind, back and forth, ticking the time that seemed motionless in the silence, the heat of that battered home.

"When it's dark enough, we go," Dalton said.

Simon sat beside me, just watching me, tumbling his black meteorite from hand to hand. I could tell he wanted to say something. I always know when he does, but I just didn't want to talk anymore.

At the sink, Walker pumped water into a smudged glass pitcher.

The Indian drank from the rim; lukewarm water cutting two dark lines down the front of his chest where it spilled down from the edges of his mouth. He refilled the pitcher and limped to where Dalton sat, and watched as my friend drank.

"Here." He held the water out for Simon.

Simon took the pitcher with both hands and drank in gulping swallows that sounded comically loud.

"Here, Jonah."

I drank, draining the last of the water.

"You should have said something," Walker said. "You could have told me you were thirsty."

"I'm okay," I said.

"You hungry?"

"Yes," Simon answered.

The three of us sat on the floor while Walker rested in the chair, watching us eat unheated food with white plastic spoons from cans: corned beef hash and beans.

"It's been quiet for a while now," Dalton said.

"Do you think he's gone?" Simon asked.

"Maybe."

"He's not," I said, straightening myself. "He's out there."

"It'll be dark enough pretty soon," Dalton said. "I have a plan."

Simon wiped his mouth on the back of his arm. I looked at Dalton.

"When it gets dark, we'll make a run for the truck. I'll drive and Jonah sits up front with the gun in case he starts shooting at us. Simon and Walker, you two will have to jump in the camper."

"I can't move too quick," Walker said.

"Move as quick as you can," Dalton said.

Simon turned to Walker and said, "I'll help you. But what are we going to do about Lilly?"

"What do you think, Simon?" I said, agitated.

After a moment, Walker looked at me and said, "We'll come back. We'll make it right."

rat

The sun disappears.
The air finally begins to cool.
He stands there and watches.

He is dizzy, tired, his mind swirls in numbers, thoughts of Lilly, those boys, Lilly and *that* boy. Whore.

Piss-kid lied. He is trying to make me mad. Push my buttons again.

He rubs a hand on his chest. The sandy grit of dried blood and ash flake under his touch. He feels the wound on his neck, licks his fingers, touch, lick, his tongue dry as a cat's.

"Know what I'll do? I know what to do."

Nothing comes from the trailer, no sound or movement. He waits. Mitch lowers to a crouch and crawls from the stand of bushes toward the trailer. His ankle is now stiff and swollen, so he drops to his knees, scoots along the ground like a limping dog.

"Like a dog," he whispers, smiling. "Stupid dog."

He crawls right to the skirt of the trailer. He stops and listens. He can hear faint voices inside, can't tell which punk is talking.

There is a gap in the rocks beside the trailer's wheel. He puts an arm in first, moves his hand around to gauge the area, then he squeezes his body in and disappears into the black pit beneath the floor of the trailer.

Something with fur runs across his hand. Mitch almost shrieks and flails his arm dumbly in the dark. The thing brushes against his leg and escapes out the same opening he crawled through.

A rat.

prayer

Walker moved the infantry flag just an inch at the corner, then let it fall back into place.

"It's not dark enough yet," he said. "Fifteen more minutes."

Dalton inhaled deeply. "Ten."

"Okay," I said.

I looked at Simon. I couldn't tell what he was thinking.

The cans we had eaten from were arranged in a line across the top of the small stove, their upturned tops peeled back like rising metallic moons, edges jagged, toothlike.

I stood and stretched, tucking my shirt behind the grip of the pistol in the back of my pants so I could draw it quickly if I needed to. I slung my backpack over my arm. Simon watched me, sitting with his back against the door, legs straightened out in front of him. As if saying he was ready to leave, too, Simon pushed the black meteorite into his pocket, and rolled slightly onto one side so he could slide his hand all the way down behind him and pull out the keys to the truck. He handed them to Dalton, who looked around the inside of the trailer like he was trying to see if there was something else that needed to be done.

I paused over the cot where Lilly lay beneath the blankets.

Simon looked like he was going to say something, but he was silent. I held an open hand over the bedding, feeling nothing there in the space between my palm and the covered girl.

I turned and looked at Simon and Dalton, then Walker.

"Door or window?" I asked.

"What?" Simon said.

"Which way are we going out?"

"It's gotta be the door," Dalton said. "It's closer to the truck."

Simon pushed himself up to his feet. He looked tired; his eyes watered as he yawned.

"Do you want to pray or something before we go?" Walker asked.

"Why?" I said.

"I don't know," the man said, "I just thought you might."

"I do," Simon said.

And Dalton said, "Okay."

hiss

Mitch hears them moving just above him.

Their feet shuffle, there is a soft hum of indistinguishable voices muted through the floor in conversation. He rolls onto his back.

The black is so complete as he turns upward, he imagines he is at the edge of a starless universe. He reaches out, fingers pressing through sticky webs and soft balls of spider eggs.

He feels the underside of the floor. He pulls the gun from his pants and points it up, wondering if he would be able to hear the tell-tale sound of one of them directly above. He presses the barrel against the peeling laminate of the floorboard. It makes the faintest scraping hiss before he recoils his hand and rests in silence.

below

heard something," Simon whispered, looking down. He unclasped Dalton's and my hands, the creases of his palms shining with sweat.

We sat, circled, on the floor beside Lilly.

My eyes widened. I held my breath, trying to hear what Simon had, hoping it was nothing, even if I had a feeling it was something terrible.

We were completely frozen.

"I felt something under me." Simon's voice was just the faintest breath, mouthed more than heard.

I didn't move. My eyes turned to Walker.

"I have rats," Walker whispered. "Probably just a rat."

"He's under the house," Simon panted.

Walker let Dalton's hand go. "Couldn't be."

And I'd never seen Simon look so scared and so sure of himself at the same time.

flick

Flick.

No sounds come through the floor above him.

Mitch opens the lighter and drops it onto his chest. The metal case feels smooth and cool. Like that falling rock Piss-kid picked up that night in the desert.

His thumb finds the wheel, a spark explodes in the black, staining his eyes with purple smears, and a flame leaps up, fanning waves of yellow light beneath the trailer.

Near one end of the trailer, a corroding pipe elbow drips rusted water onto the dirt. A desiccated orange hose, cracked and striped with electrical tape, snakes out from between the rocks and up into the floor.

A gas line.

He worms his way on his back. The gun lies flat on his chest. He holds the lighter like a torch before him, as he makes his way toward the end of the trailer. Serpentine black coils of smoke writhe upward from the lighter and flatten out against the underside of the floor.

"Maybe we can use this."

The hose gives off the faintest smell of propane.

Mitch smiles.

He waves the lighter around to look for the way out. He watches the soot from the lighter spread a circle of black on the blistering hose. It begins to smoke and stink.

Nothing.

He burns his fingers, drops the lighter.

They're dead.

The floor creaks above him. Someone is moving up there. He looks at the blackened hose, the lighter, still burning in the dirt and spiderwebs.

He grasps his pistol, pointing it up at where he can hear the sound of weight sagging the dry plywood.

Gravity.

dark

"Well, is it dark enough now?" I whispered to Dalton.

Dalton glanced at Walker, then up at the sky through the jagged slash in the ceiling.

"I think so," he said. Then he said to Simon, "Make sure you stay with him. And don't fall this time. We might only have one chance."

Simon didn't answer. He continued to listen.

"Simon?" I grabbed my brother's shoulder.

"Okay." His voice was just a breath. "I can do it."

We stood.

I watched the door, barely seeing it through the dark, not wanting to turn back and look at the bed where Lilly was, not even one last time.

"Help me up," Walker said, extending an arm and pulling his leg beneath him with the other.

Dalton grabbed the man at his wrist, dropping the truck's keys to the floor as he did.

Then he felt the jerking impact of the bullets striking Walker's body as they tore upward through the floor. The Indian fell backwards onto me, and I crashed against the frame of the door as I tried to catch his weight.

poison

He chokes and gasps against the airless poison beneath the trailer. He rolls onto his belly, the pistol held out in front of him, and crawls, feeling his way to the hole by the wheel. Something is on fire, but it's not the gas line.

He can't breathe.

In the still silence of the night, the arms squeeze their way out from the breach in the rocks and pull the body forward on a wave of reeking exhaust. Mitch, black, stripped to the waist and smeared in ash and blood, an obscene parturition, stumbles forward and inhales deeply, spiderwebs plastered against his hair, sweating, smiling.

He circles around toward the rear of the trailer.

(jonah)

fire

Simon froze, staring at the thread of smoke curling up from the holes in the floor.

"I fell!" Walker grunted. A slug had lodged in his artificial leg. Small splinters splayed out from the blackened tear where his jeans were creased by the path of the bullet.

My hands braced Walker steady by his armpits; and I leaned over his shoulder to see where the man had been shot.

"Are you okay?" Dalton asked.

Walker rubbed his hand over his leg.

"It's nothing," Walker said, his voice hushed. "He's down there."

"No he's not," Simon said, and he pointed at the twin holes in the floor, now glowing with pulses of amber light as twisting and thickening ropes of black smoke curled upward. "We got to get out of here."

"What the hell?" Walker said.

"Come on!" Dalton said, picking up the keys.

I pushed Walker upright and turned to open the door. And I hesitated there, thinking about what we would see on the other side.

"We got to get out now!" Simon pleaded, and ran for the back window, stumbling, sightless.

"Hey!" Dalton called out, but Simon had already climbed out into the night.

I yelled, "Simon!"

My lungs convulsed. The fumes from below the trailer were suffocating. Points of flame splattered up from the bullet holes in the floor, and every bit of space inside the trailer filled with smoke in seconds.

"Come on." Walker pushed me aside and flung open the door.

(mitch)

homecoming

Simon has come home.

Mitch waits there and watches the boy climb down from the window.

"Welcome home, Simon." His voice is sandpaper. "I missed you. I love you. Why do you want to hurt me?"

He squats in the rocks behind the trailer, the silver barrel of his gun pointed level at Piss-kid's belly.

Slashes are scabbed over, the dirt-skeleton tattooed in filth.

The yellow teeth, eyes fixed on the boy.

The kid stands there and stares at Mitch.

"You said he was the bastard," Mitch says. "Look at what you did to me."

Jonah is calling his brother from inside the trailer. Smoke coughs from the window.

"Look at what you did to *me*, Mitch," the kid says. "I hate you."

"You're dead, punk."

The Indian and some other kid come around the corner. Mitch sees something reflecting in that kid's hand. He swings the pistol over and shoots. The Indian goes down. Half his face is gone. He brings the pistol right up to the other boy's head and the boy backs off and ducks behind the trailer.

Now it's just him and Piss-kid. *Push this button, punk. Just try letting that whore flirt with you again.*

Click.

The gun does not fire.

Click.

All his counting brings him to zero.

And Simon runs for the truck.

Piss.

He stumbles around the opposite side of the trailer, moves painfully, wide enough to avoid the fire that now spears outward from the underside. He sees flames through the covers over the windows.

The universe turns to numbers. Nothing but numbers. Stacking. Falling. Collapsing. Reducing.

He can't stop it.

He sees an antler of flame with four spikes that flashes into six; debris scattered on a mound of trash, eleven wads of paper and fourteen opened cans; the number one, a rusted pipe the length of his arm; counts his steps, counts his steps.

mitch

The smoke thickened inside the trailer as soon as Dalton opened the door. I saw him and Walker go out. I was scared Simon and I wouldn't see each other again, so I turned and ran back through the burning trailer to follow him.

My eyes ached and pooled with stinging tears; all I could see were my feet and the faintest outline of the window frame, where Simon had gone.

"Simon!"

I tripped, falling to all fours near the back of the trailer. I tried to breathe, but my lungs seized in coughing spasms of rejection. I kept my head down, trying to find some air, and realized I had to force myself up or I would not make it out of the smoke. I felt my way along the floor to the back wall and pulled myself up to the edge of the window, thrusting my head out, blinking to try to clear the blindness from my eyes.

I heaved myself over the sill and lowered my feet to the ground, thinking, *How long ago did me and Simon climb out this way?*

I slid along the trailer, edging my way around the back.

The truck's engine coughed in ignition.

I stepped over Walker's body on the ground at my feet. I only looked at him for an instant and had to turn away. It made me sick. I knew he was dead.

When I rounded the corner I saw Mitch, ghostlike and blackened, a metal bar in his hand, swinging an arc downward at Simon's upraised arms.

Simon dodged the swing and fell backwards onto the steps of the trailer.

"Where's Lilly?" Mitch demanded; his voice sounded slurred and groggy. He raised the pipe again, the gun hanging limply at his side.

"Mitch!" I screamed.

"Come on!" Dalton called nervously from the truck, revving the rumbling engine.

I ran toward them.

As I pulled the pistol from my waist, the metal bar came down across my head and I dropped to the dirt, the blood already seeping down into my eyes that closed on a red-smeared and flaming image of Mitch panting above me and raising the heavy pipe again.

I knew what was happening, but I could not move. I kicked my feet against the ground, attempting to push myself away and into the dark. My body felt so heavy, like it had melted into the earth. The gun had fallen from my grasp onto the ground behind me.

Dalton sprang from the truck, flashing that shining straight razor low beside his hip. He leapt at Mitch and slashed a line across Mitch's side before he could swing that pipe a second time at me.

Flames twitched and wriggled from beneath the trailer and smoke vomited out, blacker than the sky, in great billowing coils.

Simon pushed himself up from the steps. In the pulsing copper light from the fire, I tried to raise myself onto hands and knees, blood crawling across my forehead and dripping in warm blobs to the dirt between my hands, the amber glint of the gun barrel in the dirt behind me.

Mitch spun around and pointed his pistol at Dalton.

Simon grabbed my gun from the dirt and swung it across me, leveling it at Mitch.

Mitch held the pipe over his head in one hand, the gun in his other pointed at Dalton, who crouched in the dim light with his razor held in front of him.

"No!" Simon yelled.

"Simon!" I stood behind my brother on unsteady legs, a hand flattened over the gash in my scalp.

Mitch looked at Simon, smiling his gap-toothed yellow grin. He looked over to Dalton, panting, and then back at my brother, who held a gun.

"What are you going to do, Simon?"

"Get away," he said.

"Simon," I whispered.

"What are you going to do, Piss-kid?" Mitch repeated.

Mitch began slowly walking toward us.

"Ferris wheel," Simon whispered.

Then Simon kept shooting until the gun was empty.

falling objects

We knew it was the only thing to do.

We dragged the corpses into the trailer.

We had to do it fast, before the fire grew too big.

Simon was sick. He threw up all over the place after he shot Mitch. So he sat with his legs resting out the passenger side of the truck and watched as Dalton and I pulled those bloody bodies up the stairs and rolled them through the doorway.

Neither of us said anything while we did it. I think we were both in shock at the sickening scene in which we were playing parts. I wouldn't have blamed Dalton if he just abandoned me and Simon out there in the middle of the desert beside that burning house and tried to forget everything he ever knew about us.

We were covered in blood. It smeared on our hands and shirts, down the front of our pants when we pulled the bodies into the fire, each of us tugging on a leg, trailing the torsos and arms along on the dirt. There was too much blood for us to try to lift either one in any respectable manner.

And as we worked, sweating, pulling the dead as quickly as we could up the stairs and into the smoke of the doorway, I thought about everything that Matthew had written about his own horrors, and I understood how there really was no coming back from things like this.

When we were finished, we took off our clothes and threw them into the doorway as the flames rose up from beneath Walker's trailer. Then we dressed ourselves in new clothes from the camper and we both climbed inside the truck's cab.

I sat in the middle. Simon was beside the door with his head resting outside the window. The flames inside the trailer were curling over the top of the open door, lapping from the windows, rising up into the night sky.

"I'd understand if you just told me and Simon to get out of your truck now," I said.

Dalton looked at me. "Why would I do that?"

"We got you in trouble."

"No you didn't."

"Well, I'd still understand."

"Let's get out of here."

We drove away from the fire. Dalton kept the headlights turned off, but we could still see the white of the dirt road that led to the highway. There was no one around. Walker was the only person who'd seen the fire from the Lincoln out in that remote place, and now he was dead, so I couldn't believe anyone would notice what we left behind at the mesa. And, as we bumped down that road, I thought that even if anyone ever did map out the pieces of what had happened with Mitch and Lilly, that Lincoln, and Walker, there were three figures: me, Simon, and Dalton, who would never show up on that map.

"He left his money box," Simon said. "Why'd he do that?"

"He thought he was going to get away," I said. "That's all there is to it. He was going to kill us all. I know that."

"How long do you think till someone finds out about this?" Simon asked.

"I don't think anyone's going to find out for a long time," Dalton said.

"And, think about it, Simon," I said. "No one's ever going to know we ever got in that car in the first place."

We went back to the Lincoln. We picked up the blankets and threw them in the camper. Then we put that tin man back there, too.

What happened to me and Simon was unfair, but we chose most of our path, too. I know I chose to fool myself into believing things—about Matthew, our father, and, especially, about Lilly—that would never be true. And a certain part of me still wants to believe that there was something special and real between Lilly and me, a passing dream of something that wasn't Los Rogues that I got to hold on to for just a moment. But there's also that part of me that knows that someone like Lilly just floats by and does what she has to do to survive. I could still feel sorry for her, though, could still miss her.

And I did.

We were too scared to stop in Kayenta, convinced that someone would notice the three boys who happened to show up there on that bloody morning. I think every one of us felt like we were in some kind of movie or something, that all the eyes of the world were paying attention to us, watching every thing we did or said.

So we didn't say anything. And Dalton just kept on driving.

Not one of us had any idea where we were heading.

I don't know how long we had gone like that, just driving, not talking, listening to the whirr of the wheels on the grainy, hot asphalt; but Dalton finally pulled the truck off the highway and turned

down a dirt road that wound its way past a flimsy sign that said
COAL MINE CANYON.

It scared me to leave the road. I could tell Simon was worried, too, because as long as we were on the road, it was like we were invisible. Anonymous. But when we went out into the dirt of the desert, we had to be us again.

Dalton tapped my shoulder and said, "I want to take a look at that cut on your head."

I didn't even realize I'd been pressing my hand down onto my scalp the whole time since we'd left Walker's.

So I sat on the ground at the back of the camper and Dalton took a needle and thread from inside and put some stitches across the cut to close it. Simon stood over and watched him do it, but then he ran off and threw up in the dirt on the other side of the truck.

"Does this hurt?" Dalton asked.

"No." But my eyes were watering pretty good. "Where did you learn how to do that?"

"I'm learning how to do it right now," Dalton said.

He tied off the last stitch.

"Okay."

I carefully pressed my fingertips against the knots.

We washed up with the last of the water from my canteen. Simon sat in the road at the front of the truck, leaning against the bumper with his knees bent. Dalton was doing something inside the camper, and I walked around to where my brother sat.

"I'm okay, Simon," I said.

"Good."

"Are you okay?"

"Yeah. I just got sick looking at it. It looked like it hurt you."

"Not too bad," I said.

Dalton came around from the camper.

"Here," he said. "I think these will be good."

He dropped a bundle of clothes on Simon's lap.

"I don't think Simon and me would ever have gotten away, Dalton," I said.

Dalton sighed. "Let's try and find someplace to eat. I think I'm lost, but how hard can it be to get to Flagstaff, anyway?"

"Next to impossible, for me and Simon."

Dalton smiled. He pulled Simon up to his feet.

"Come on," he said. "Change your clothes, and let's get back on the road."

We drove south into Indian land, through a place called Tuba City. I wondered where the name came from. It wasn't a city, and I don't think there ever was a tuba there, either. The desert here was so flat and endless. Simon slept a little, but he jerked and his hands shot up when he dreamed about something. I knew it wasn't much of a dream.

And Dalton said, "The bad stuff is over, so let's get you and Simon to Flagstaff and then we'll see what we're going to do. Okay?"

Simon said, "Okay."

That afternoon, we drove through a place called Cottonwood. We still weren't talking to each other much, though; but it was a real nice little town that made me feel almost normal again. We ate hamburgers there. I finally used that ten-dollar bill I'd carried with us from home. I knew we were all afraid to get into that box of money Mitch left behind, because there was still too much of a bad smell on it, if that makes any sense. It's the only way I can describe it, though.

When we left the diner, Dalton followed the river up toward the hills outside of Sedona, looking for a place where he could park the truck for us to sleep. We were all so tired. Simon yawned and stretched. He put his arm around my shoulders so he could tap Dalton and said, "Thank you for the clothes. It feels good to wear something new."

"It's okay, Simon," he said. "I'm glad to help you and your brother out."

And just before the light completely faded, we drove past two hitchhikers, thumbs out and facing backwards, as they backpedaled along the road beneath the trees. They looked so much like Mitch and Lilly the first time I'd seen them that my heart went up into my throat and I looked, wide-eyed, over at Simon, like I couldn't believe what I was seeing, to see if he noticed it, too.

Simon turned to me and said, "Just don't even look at them, Jonah."

He knew what I saw.

We saw the same thing.

We had to put Don Quixote outside when we parked by the river for the night; so the three of us could get inside the camper. I sat at the table with my map for a while, but I just couldn't draw anything on it yet.

And Simon and I had to sleep head-to-foot since there were only two beds. Just like we always did.

flagstaff

We made our way along a winding and shaded road, the tires of the truck sighing like ghosts, the three of us sitting up in the cab, Simon sleeping against my shoulder despite the clattering and clanging of the metal man on the camper floor in back of us.

Jones,

If you are reading this, then I know where you are and I am not coming back.

But I am glad you found Mrs. Scott and I hope you can feel that me and Scotty are both in a better place now. I am sorry. Tell Simon that.

Joneser, I know that you understand why I had to send this letter to Scotty's mom and not to Mother. Please try to make Simon understand, too. Because none of this is your fault, or mine either, we were just unlucky is all.

When I think about it, I guess all along I knew I was never going to just walk out of here, but I wanted you and Simon to get out and see what's out there. Away from Los Rogues. Away from Dad. Away from that woman who never cared for anyone as much as she cared for herself. I know things are working out for you. I believe that.

You know what I want (besides a hamburger—ha ha)? I want you and Simon to be brothers again. You guys should do things that brothers do. Smoke cigarettes and chase after girls. Sneak into drive-ins and get drunk together. Don't ever wear a suit, and especially not a uniform. And when you get into fights, do it because you're sticking up for each other. And beat the hell out of any guy who wants to mess with you or your brother. Because I'd do all that with you and Simon if I could.

I haven't slept in four days. Since they killed Scotty. I am so tired.

I can hear shooting. I'm not even going to go and look. Nobody knows where I am anyway.

One more thing: Don't miss me. I found out that missing someone is just another way to feel sorry for yourself, like someone's done you wrong. You know where I am. You'll hear me at night. You can't look at your brother's face and not see me.

So go out and do those things I told you to do.

I'm going to rest now.

Bye.

Love,

Matthew

Dalton sat in the truck and waited for us.

He said he was tired.

We knew why he didn't want to come inside.

"I can see Matthew in you both. He was such a good-looking boy."

Mrs. Scott held up a Polaroid picture of Matthew standing beside her son.

And I could read the smeared blue ink inscription on the back: "Suicide Pact. That's the name of the track we're standing in front of. Me and Matt, 1970."

I folded Matthew's letter and put it back into the envelope. I wiped my eyes.

Simon drank his glass of milk.

"What did it say?" Simon asked. He wiped a hand across his mouth.

I looked at my brother.

"He's not coming back."

Mrs. Scott cleared her throat.

"Your father called me," she said. "He didn't know what else to do. I guess Matthew gave him my phone number. He said that some men from the Army came to talk to him. You know. In the place where he is."

She looked at each of us. Maybe she thought we were too young, or something. Maybe she thought we just hadn't seen enough of this world for us to learn that sometimes things that are real end up being scarier than dreams. I knew what she meant.

"He told me your brother's passed."

Simon put his glass down.

"We figured that," I said. I cleared my throat. "Thank you for keeping his letter for us."

"There was nothing else I could do with it. I've kept it here for three months."

Her hands shook. She pressed a tissue to the corner of her eye and looked away.

I spun the photograph around on the table where she dropped it so Simon and I could see it.

"It seems like he's been gone forever," Simon said.

"Are you boys still hungry?" Mrs. Scott looked at the crumbs from the sandwiches she gave us.

"No thank you," I said.

Simon shook his head.

"You came a long way to get here."

"We had a fun trip," Simon said.

I looked at him.

"I know your father must want to see you. It isn't that far from here," she said. "And you are both welcome to stay with me until his release. It's almost here. I would like that very much."

"We can't," I said. "We have to return a truck."

Simon leaned against the window and slept while Dalton drove the truck along the crooked highway through the hills.

I let him sleep. I wanted to talk to him, but there was no need to wake him up.

"It sure is pretty up here," Dalton said.

"Yeah," I said. "How long do you think it'll take us to get back?"

"Do you want to go fast, or slow?" Dalton asked.

"Slow."

"Me, too."

"What are we going to tell your family?"

Dalton glanced at me. "I told you I never lie to my dad. But I'll be honest, Jonah, I've been thinking about what to say, too."

I sighed. I didn't want Simon to get into any kind of trouble for things we couldn't have done anything about.

I didn't want us to be split up.

And Dalton said, "So I thought we'd just say we found Simon on the side of the road in Arizona, and that then we drove up here to Flagstaff to visit Mrs. Scott. That's the truth, right?"

He put out his right hand to me and I grabbed it.

"Dalton."

"What?"

"Thanks."

"And what are you going to say, Jonah?"

"To your dad?"

"No. In your book."

"It wouldn't be a map if I didn't put in everything that happened to us on our trip." I shifted against Simon, and he moved slightly. "What do you think your dad will say when he reads it?"

Dalton kept his eyes forward on the road. "I think he'll say you're brave; and you're a good brother."

My back itched, dripping, glued to the cracking vinyl of the bench seat, so I'd lean forward from time to time to allow the rush of dry air to cool me off. I had never seen trees like the ones fencing the highway in this part of Arizona, making shade even if it was over a hundred degrees. I liked the dark ponderosas.

I looked at my brother. Simon had kicked off his moccasins and curled his legs across the seat toward me, so the dingy socks he wore rested on my feet. At another time, this would have made me mad, I guess.

Even in a perfect world, brothers can only get so close.

Dalton pulled the truck off the pavement and turned onto a dirt road cutting a border through the tall pines toward a small lake. When he parked, Simon stirred, but did not open his eyes. I wondered if my brother was dreaming; Simon had slept so fitfully since that night at Walker's trailer.

I took my book, my map, from the backpack on the floor and slid out of the truck through Dalton's door, leaving it open so Simon wouldn't get scared if he woke up.

I put the map down at the base of a tree and followed Dalton down to the water's edge.

The lake was shaped like a sickle, a partial moon rimmed with soft green grass that quickly burned to the color of rust only a few feet away from the shore, where the trees grew. We kicked off our boots and socks, pulled up the legs of our pants and sat down in the grass with our feet in the icy water.

"Ahhh. That feels good," Dalton said.

I dipped my hands down and then washed my face and hair, feeling over the jagged knots of stitches where Dalton had sewn my scalp together with black thread. The water felt good, running down through my short hair and over my shoulders and chest, making dark circles where it pooled on my pants.

We sat like that, not saying anything, staring out across the slate surface of the lake on the windless afternoon, the sawtooth tops of the green-gray trees jutting upward on the opposite shore into a pale and dusty sky.

I closed my eyes and inhaled deeply.

Footsteps behind.

"What are you doing?" Simon asked.

"Nothing," I said. "Cooling off."

"You left this back there."

I heard the slap of my comp book hitting the ground next to where Dalton and I sat, a pencil landing and rolling off into the grass.

I opened my eyes and picked up my map and pencil. Simon, shoeless, sat down beside me, pulled off his socks, and dipped his feet into the lake.

"I thought about drawing some more on it," I said. "But I guess I didn't really feel like it."

"You need to," Simon said. "What if we die or something? No one will know how we got here."

"We won't."

"We almost did."

"Yeah."

Simon paddled his feet, making waves, and watched as I drew a line south and marked it with dots and the names of the towns we had driven through, away from a scrawled image of the burning trailer, a mesa, crosses labeled "Lilly" and "Walker," a house beneath tall trees where I'd written "The End."

"How come you didn't draw something for Mitch on there?" Simon put his finger over the map where I had drawn a dog lying down by a cactus.

"I didn't know what to put."

"Yeah."

Simon hurtled a rock out into the center of the lake.

"How about a rat?" Simon asked.

I smiled. "I'd rather leave it blank. There."

I showed Simon the map, now with a lake and three boys sitting at its shore.

"Now I can tell us apart," Simon said. "We always used to look the same in your pictures."

"Maybe I'll get some moccasins."

"Maybe I'll cut my hair."

"Don't say that," I said. " 'Maybe' is as good as setting an appointment with Dalton's razor."

Dalton laughed. "You asked me for it, Jonah."

"I like it. Now," I said.

"I guess we went past the end, then," Simon said.

"And we didn't fall off the world," I answered.

"Like Lilly said." Simon smiled and lay down, brushing his hair back away from his face.

We all stretched out in the warm grass, staring up at the sky, our feet still resting in the lapping edge of the water. Simon pulled his meteorite out and tumbled it around, over his head.

"I'm tired," I said.

"Maybe you should sleep," Dalton said. "We won't go anywhere."

Simon held the rock between his hands, its shadow stretching across my chest.

"Walker said this was lucky," Simon said.

"Maybe it is."

"Not for him."

I knew I'd never forgive myself for what happened to Walker and Lilly. If *forgive* is even the right word. But I could almost hear it in Simon's matter-of-fact tone, the way he'd cursed me that night for always taking the blame for things, like I was supposed to be in control when we both knew I never was.

"Things will be okay, Simon," I said. "I believe that things will work out for us."

"You'll like it at my place," Dalton said. "With my family. A real family. And Jonah knows you can stay as long as you want. Forever."

"We going to take Don all the way back to New Mex?"

"As long as he lays down," I said. "'Cause I'm not ever sharing a seat with him again."

I reached my hand up to where Simon played with the meteorite. "Can I see it?"

Simon didn't answer; he just handed the rock to me. And I held it over my face and spun it between my hands, like Simon had done, imagining how it must have looked out there in space.

"Jonah?"

"What?"

"Do you think anyone found them yet?"

I knew what he was talking about. He was worried about those bodies we burned in the trailer.

"I don't know," I said. "But let's make a rule right now. Brothers' Rule Number Five: We aren't going to . . ." I sighed and didn't finish the words.

"Not going to what?" Simon asked.

I sat up. I looked at Dalton, then Simon. "We're never going to forget how we got here."

"And everything's going to be good now," Dalton said.

I held out my hand. "Yeah."

And Dalton and Simon grabbed my hand.

Simon swallowed. "Are you gonna be okay? About Lilly?"

"I'll be okay."

"She was nice."

"I guess."

I looked across the lake. I closed my eyes and I swear I could hear the sound of tires on gravel and smell the dust of the road, exactly the way it was the day I first saw Lilly floating past us like an angel.

"You said you figured out about Matthew."

I stared at the meteorite. It was so black.

"I don't know. I guess I knew but I didn't want to think about it. You felt it, too, didn't you, Simon?"

"Yeah."

I sighed.

"And what are we going to do with all that money in that box?" Simon asked.

"First thing I'm going to do is buy a bag of rice."

"You don't even like rice," Simon said.

Dalton laughed, "It's for my dad. I'll tell you that story."

"I'm not gonna lie, Jonah," Simon said. "But I kinda wished I could have a cigarette right now."

"Then the second thing I'm going to do is buy a bag of rice. 'Cause first I'm going to get you some cigarettes at the next gas station," I said. "I don't care."

"Cool."

"Here." I handed the meteorite to Simon and sat up. "And when we get back to that bridge in New Mexico, both of us are going for a swim."

"Heck," Dalton said. "There's a perfectly good lake right in front of us."

I stood up. "I'm jumping in."

And Simon said, "Then so am I."

I drew a map.

I believe we knew all along what we were trying to find wasn't there. And now I know why Simon was so angry with me until the day we met up again on that dirt road by the mesa. Because he knew I was trying to keep him fooled, like he was the little boy, when, really, it was me who was fooling myself into thinking we'd find something—just because I wanted it to be there.

I went out looking for Matthew, but I found Simon instead.

And maybe he found me.

I don't know.

Maybe brothers need to do that, to deal with the most horrible things, just so they can see what they're really made of, what's really between them. Because sometimes, I think that's a force that's more powerful than all those other things we can't do anything about.

I drew a map.

acknowledgments

My older brother, Patrick, volunteered to serve in Vietnam when he was seventeen years old. And I still have the letter he'd written, saying to tell my younger brother, Steve, not to worry—that he promised he would not get killed. It's a terrible thing when brothers make such requests and answer with such promises.

I rode through the Southwest with two of my best friends, Mike Bowen and Steve Tureaud; and I had to endure being in the backseat of Mike's car the whole way home from Mexico, sitting alongside a life-size tin statue of Don Quixote that Mike picked up there (legally). The car was not a 1940 Lincoln Cabriolet, though.

Before he died, my father-in-law, Don Letney, bought a 1940 Lincoln Cabriolet. Now the car sits in a garage. I always planned to put that car in a book, so here it is, and now I suppose we'll have to take it out and put that car on the road, where it belongs. It really is an amazing vehicle.

I do not believe in luck, but I am very fortunate to be represented by an incredible agent, Laura Rennert. She isn't just a skillful agent, she's about the smartest person I've ever run into when it comes to writing and telling stories. Thank you, Laura.

Thank you, Kelly Milner Halls, for making me write again.

And thanks to all the "friends," too. Like my good friend Lewis Buzbee said to me, there's a reason why it's called Feiwel and *Friends*. Thank you so much, Jean Feiwel, for being, like, the coolest person I have ever met. And thanks, Elizabeth Fithian, Allison Remcheck (officially, my first fan), Liz Noland, Rich Deas, Jessica Tedder, Dave Barrett, Caroline Sun, Ksenia Winnicki, and everyone else who works in one of the most architecturally beautiful buildings on Manhattan.

Finally, I have a piece of paper, a sign, taped on the wall of my office that says, "What would Liz do?" My greatest thanks go to my editor, Liz Szabla. She may be the most amazing and talented editor that has ever loved working with stories, but, above that, she's a friend. Thank you, Liz. You may remember that when you told me how much you loved this book, my answer to you was that if it was any good at all, it's 'cause you, Liz Szabla, taught me how to write. I do believe that.

GOFISH

QUESTIONS FOR THE AUTHOR

ANDREW SMITH

What did you want to be when you grew up?
I think I always wanted to be a writer when I grew up. The problem was, growing up when I did, most families were overly concerned about having stable futures and working in industries that would always expand—like warfare and stuff. After all, I am a child of the Cold War. So my parents were not very enthusiastic when I revealed my future aspirations to them. In fact, I think I recall them saying something like, "But what do you *really* want to be?"

When did you realize you wanted to be a writer?
I always liked it when my teachers would give creative assignments that dealt with writing stories or illustrating things. And I actually am a pretty decent artist, although I really wish I could paint better. But becoming a writer probably became a certainty for me when I was in high school.

What's your most embarrassing childhood memory?
When I was in kindergarten, I sat next to a boy named Chip. Chip had to pee really bad, but he was too afraid to ask the teacher, Mrs. Bailey. So Chip just peed under the table, all over

the floor, and, of course, he denied it was his. I was ethically torn by the situation. We were sitting two-to-a-desk, Chip was my friend, and I had an irreconcilably feverish crush on Mrs. Bailey.

As a young person, who did you look up to most?
When I was a kid, I looked up to my brother Patrick the most. He was older, and we shared a bedroom (there were four boys in my family) until he enlisted in the army—when he went off to fight in Vietnam. Patrick drove a 1959 Cadillac—a gift from our aunt—and he used to drive the three of us younger boys around with him and his tough-guy high school friends on their crazy adventures, and we listened to AM radio stations and daringly used words like "bitchin'" when we talked.

What was your first job?
My first real job—where I actually collected a paycheck—was writing for a local newspaper in Southern California. Beginning reporters are called stringers, and in those days, stringers got paid by the inch of copy we wrote (newspaper columns, typically two inches wide, had about fifty words per inch). I often say that getting paid for writing by the inch is very likely the origin of my predilection for big words and long sentences.

How did you celebrate publishing your first book?
It honestly wasn't much of a celebration for a couple reasons: First, publication takes such an interminably long time. From the time you get an offer to when you actually sign contracts may take several months. Then, when the book is actually in the stores is usually more than a year after that. But the biggest reason for a non-celebration was that I wrote—and continue to write—in secret. Nobody knew what I was up to, so my family and friends really didn't believe much of anything had actually

happened. In fact, I didn't tell my wife that I had written a book until after I received an offer for representation from my agent. And when I finally told her, she was so relieved because she thought I was having some kind of online affair due to the hours and hours I'd been spending quietly working on my computer. Now, I think my writing is more of a bother to my wife and kids. Maybe they'll want to celebrate when I decide to quit.

Where do you write your books?

I write my books in my upstairs office at home. It is a perfect writing place. It has a deck and lots of windows looking out at mountains and trees and my horses. When I travel, I carry a laptop with me and I work on my writing by emailing bits and pieces of my work back and forth to myself.

Where do you find inspiration for your writing?

Inspiration is a moving target. If you sit still, you'll never find it, and you'll get really old waiting for it to bump into you.

Which of your characters is most like you?

Well, to some extent, all my protagonists are part "me," but if you had to isolate one individual character, I think there'd be no doubt about it: I am most like Simon Vickers, from *In the Path of Falling Objects*. He always takes risks without seriously considering the consequences, and I think he has an attitude—maybe due to naiveté—that nothing bad will ever happen to him. He likes to push buttons and then acts indignant when the people around him get pissed off. Yeah . . . that's me.

When you finish a book, who reads it first?

When I finish a book, I read it first. That's when I try to read it like I didn't have anything to do with it having been written. I am not a writer who shares what I write with friends and family, though.

So, when I finish a book, I usually send it directly to my agent, Laura Rennert, and my editor, Liz Szabla. Then, immediately after that, I get sick and start asking, "Why did I send that to them? Why? Why? Why?" and I start calling myself every version of stupid I can think up. Then I get really grumpy until I hear back from them—an interminable and agonizing wait, even if it's only a few days long.

Which do you like better: cats or dogs?
I am entirely a dog person. Still, we do own four cats who are all very good at keeping down the rodent population around the house and then making little shrines of death on our front walkway.

What do you value most in your friends?
I like my friends for their intelligence and sense of humor. I also truly value the fact that my friends understand that I am a fairly quiet and reserved person who can go for long stretches of time rather quiet and isolated.

Where do you go for peace and quiet?
I live in a very peaceful, quiet location—and I really couldn't have it any other way. Although there are certain cities that I absolutely love (Los Angeles, New York, Chicago, Boston, London, to name a few) my ideal getaways usually take me to secluded places that are not very crowded.

What makes you laugh out loud?
I most often find myself laughing out loud at things we say when I'm hanging out with my wife and kids—or when I'm joking around with my very funny friends: John, Casey, Brian, Steve, and Jeremy.

What's your favorite song?
I wonder how many people can confidently answer that question. My favorite song changes about every other week. But I can offer, as a means of getting around the question, that if there ever were perfect "soundtracks" made for *Ghost Medicine* and *In the Path of Falling Objects*, I would like to have the following artists contribute: The Felice Brothers, Bob Dylan, Bon Iver, and Johnny Flynn. Now, if there were a soundtrack made for *The Marbury Lens*, I would like to hear what Radiohead, The Cure, and maybe a reunited Pink Floyd would come up with for that monster.

Who is your favorite fictional character?
"My" favorite fictional character is, naturally, one of my own—a kid named Stark McClellan. You haven't met him yet because he's in a book I wrote called *Stick* that is not yet published. But the reason that I like him so much is that he has this really dry (but definitely not cynical or sarcastic) sense of humor in the way he looks at things, and he has this remarkable ability, I think, to see a kind of wonder in everything—even if he's surrounded by cruelty and ugliness. I admire people who are like that.

What time of year do you like best?
I definitely prefer summertime. Still, there is a lot to be said for sitting by a fire while snow falls outside, reading a great book.

What's your favorite TV show?
I do not watch television at all. I am incapable of sitting still and having information, noise, and visuals pumped into my skull. I know this is a shortcoming on my part and that I am missing out on something, but I just don't ever do it. My friends think I'm a snob, but it has nothing to do with my looking down on the medium. They're all dumb, anyway.

If you were stranded on a desert island, who would you want for company?

A television. Just kidding. There wouldn't be anywhere to plug it in. This is a trick, right? You left out the phrase "besides your wife," right? Okay, so if I couldn't have my wife OR my kids with me, then I'd probably be just fine by myself. I am an incurable loner at heart.

If you could travel in time, where would you go?

I would very much have liked to live in California during the 1880s. I know that's a random choice, but I've always had a fascination for that time period, which is only part of the reason why I set a portion of *The Marbury Lens* in California during that decade. There were so many interesting political, social, and religious movements in America at that time, and those tremendous transformations in the ways that people looked at themselves and the universe—coupled with the anxious feeling of being right on the razor's edge of this incredible twentieth-century future—really made for some potentially amazing adventures.

What's the best advice you've ever received about writing?

People who make it a practice to give advice about writing tend to give the *worst* possible advice. Here are my top three pieces of idiotic nonsense people will tell you about writing:

1. You have to have a thick skin.
2. "Show" don't "tell."
3. Don't quit your day job.

Those are all really wrong and meaningless, in my opinion. The only rule in my writer's code is *there are no rules*.

What do you want readers to remember about your books?

I want my readers to find some personal connection to what I write. It's hard for me to say just how much it means to me when I get letters or email from readers telling me how they've been impacted by one of my books. That's the greatest thing in the world, and it seems like every one of those letters always tells me something different about how that connection was made.

What would you do if you ever stopped writing?

I would probably be an inconsolable grump, the worst neighborhood grouch in the history of neighborhood grouches. I can't see myself quitting.

What do you like best about yourself?

I'll tell you what I like *least* about myself: I take everything personally. I know that's a critical weakness for someone who writes professionally because everyone in the business seems to repeat this *you-need-to-have-a-thick-skin* mantra (see above), but I can't help it. I actually lose sleep over the littlest things people say or do.

What is your worst habit?

Evasiveness. When I don't want to talk about something, I'll craftily change the subject. My sixteen-year-old son, who is afraid of insects, is far braver than I am when it comes to riding on roller coasters.

What do you consider to be your greatest accomplishment?

Here we go again with the "bests" questions. I think I am a good father. I believe my kids will look back on some of the things we've done together as a family as some of the greatest memories in their lives. That said, I am also very proud of all the books I've published—as well as those that will be coming out in the future.

Where in the world do you feel most at home?
Oddly enough, I feel most at home *at home*. I am a bit of a recluse, I suppose, and I greatly prefer the quiet of the countryside (where I live). I have never been able to understand the "dream" of living in a house that sits in a tight row of clone houses, surrounded by row upon row of other houses, in a neighborhood where you constantly hear the sounds of traffic and sirens.

What do you wish you could do better?
I wish I could speak Italian better. When I was a child, my mother could not speak English, and I spent many years in Italy, so I naturally picked up the language when I was young. Now, it's difficult for me to form the words although I still can understand it very well.

What would your readers be most surprised to learn about you?
When I was a little kid, my family lived in a very old house that was actually haunted. And to be completely honest, I frequently saw the ghost of a little boy in it, but never told anyone until after we moved away, and then my mother told me that she saw ghosts in it all the time, too.

Jack ends up in the wrong place at the worst possible time.
He gets kidnapped.
But he eventually escapes and ends up
somewhere completely unexpected—MARBURY.

THE MARBURY LENS

ANDREW SMITH

Jack will never be the same again after looking through

THE MARBURY LENS

guess in the old days, in other places, boys like me usually ended up twisting and kicking in the empty air beneath gallows.

It's no wonder I became a monster, too.

I mean, what would you expect, anyway?

And all the guys I know — all the guys I ever knew — can look at their lives and point to the one defining moment that made them who they were, no question about it. Usually those moments involved things like hitting baseballs, or their dads showing them how to gap spark plugs or bait a hook. Stuff like that.

My defining moment came last summer, when I was sixteen.

That's when I got kidnapped.

I am going to build something big for you.

It's like one of those Russian dolls that you open up, and open up again. And each layer becomes something else.

On the outside is the universe, painted dark purple, decorated with planets and comets, stars. Then you open it, and you see the Earth, and when that comes apart, there's Marbury, a place that's kind of like here, except none of the horrible things in Marbury are invisible. They're painted right there on the surface where you can plainly see them.

The next layer is Henry Hewitt, the man with the glasses, and when you twist him in half, there's my best friend, Conner Kirk, painted to look like some kind of Hindu god, arms like snakes, shirtless, radiant.

When you open him up, you'll find Nickie Stromberg, the most beautiful girl I've ever seen, and maybe the only person in this world, besides Conner, who ever really loved me.

Now it's getting smaller, and inside is Freddie Horvath. That's the man who kidnapped me.

Next, there's the pale form of the boy, Seth, a ghost from Marbury who found me, and helped me. I guess he was looking for me for a long time. And the last thing on the inside is me. John Wynn Whitmore.

They call me Jack.

But then I open up, too, and what you'll find there is something small and black and shriveled.

The center of the universe.

Fun game, wasn't it?

I don't know if the things I see and what I do in Marbury are in the future or from the past. Maybe everything's really happening at the same time. But I do know that once I started going to Marbury, I couldn't stop myself. I know it sounds crazy, but Marbury began to feel safer, at least more predictable, than the here and now.

I need to explain.

"Hey, kid."

I felt a hand on my shoulder, shaking me.

"Kid. Are you okay?"

A face leaned in close to mine. I could feel the warmth of breath.

"Do you need any help? Are you hurt or something?"

"Huh?" I put my hand up to my eyes. My head hurt. The guy was looking right into my eyes, like he was trying to see if anyone was really home.

"Did you take anything tonight, kid?"

I wasn't sure where I was, had to think, remember. The man in front of me smelled like cigarettes and coffee. He was dressed all in green, a doctor or something. I thought I must have been in the hospital, but it was too dark.

"Where are we?"

"Yeah," he said. I heard him sniff at me. "How much did you drink?"

"Huh?"

"Can you sit up?"

"I'm drunk."

The man pulled me up. His hands felt warm, careful. When I sat up, everything in front of me spun like a compass needle in a hallway of magnets.

"Do you know where you are?"

No.

"I was at a party. I was trying to go home."

The man looked over both shoulders. I thought he was trying to see if there were any other kids there, that maybe they'd know what to do with me. I could hear music coming from somewhere. I remembered, the park was in front of Java and Jazz. I heard jazz.

The man was still looking right into my eyes.

"Are you going to throw up?"

"No."

"Where do you live?"

"Glenbrook."

I tried standing, but it felt like there was no blood in my head. I fell back onto the bench.

"I'm a doctor at Regional. I'm headed that way. I can take you home, if you want."

The man pulled me up from my armpit. "But you have to promise not to throw up in my car."

"No. I'll be okay," I said. "It'll be okay for me to walk."

He let go of me. "Are you sure? It's no problem."

"I'll be okay," I repeated.

The man turned away. I fell down, caught myself on the pavement, and landed on my hands and knees.

He turned back. "I think I'd better call someone."

He started to unclip a phone from the waist of his loose green pants.

"No," I said. "Do you think you could drop me off?"

He smiled. He helped steady me on my feet. "Sure."

He said his name was Freddie Horvath. He even gave me his card, which, I guess, was supposed to prove something. I didn't know what to do with a doctor's business card. I slipped it into my wallet, which I dropped when I tried putting it back in my pocket. Freddie laughed and picked it up, handing it to me.

"I remember what it was like, being a kid, too. You'll be all right."

He was nice, and I trusted him. But I was drunk and stupid.

I fell asleep again in Freddie's Mercedes. I woke up when my head snapped forward. The car stopped somewhere. I couldn't recognize the place, and had to think, again, about where I was, piece together the blurry sequence of disjointed events from the party: walking in on Conner and Dana, and ending up, somehow, asleep in this car that was now parked in front of a dark ranch-style house that I had never seen before.

"Stupid," Freddie said. "I left my ID badge at home. I'll be right back."

He pushed his door open. I could have sworn he was wearing an ID badge when he found me on that park bench.

"Where are we?"

"Don't worry," he said. "We're probably less than a mile from your house. I'll be right back. Can I get you some water or something? You look like you could use it."

My head pounded. My mouth was paper.

"Thanks," I said.

He closed the driver door and walked around beside the car. I watched him as he came up and pulled my door open.

"Want to come in?"

I knew I was stupid, should have never accepted his help. But I rationalized that he was a doctor. Still, all I really wanted was to get home; and I wanted to speed him along, too.

"It's okay," I said. "I'll wait here."

Freddie smiled. "I'll be right back, John."

John?

I never told him my name. At least, I don't think I did. I figured he must have looked at my driver's license when I dropped my wallet in the park, because I'd never say my name was *John.*

I felt in my pocket. My wallet was still there.

I nodded and said, "Thanks."

Freddie came back out in a minute, a plastic badge dangling from his breast pocket and a bottle of drinking water in his hand. He got in and started the car and passed the water to me.

"Are you going to be okay?" he asked.

I was so thirsty. "Yeah. Thanks."

I opened the bottle and drank.

I was unconscious before we made it out of Freddie's driveway.

That's how I ended up in that smoky room.

Freddie smoked constantly.

And it wasn't until maybe a full twenty-four hours had dissolved invisibly past me — Sunday night — when I started to soberly realize that I was in a situation that seemed unreal, like something you'd only see on TV, something that would never happen to me.

But it was real.

Something hurts on my foot.

That's the first really clear thought I have: *Something hurts.*

I sit up. There is a constricting tightness around my ankle, cutting into me if I pull against it too much. That's what holds me there. I'm lying on a bed. There are no sheets on it. I can feel the swirling grooves stitched into the mattress.

My hands are free. I sit up and rub my ankle. The binding feels like one of those heavy-duty zip ties, the kind cops use. That's what it is. I feel the trap mouth where the toothed band has been fed through.

I see a slit of light along the floor. A door.

I run my hands over my body. Check everything. I don't feel like I've been hurt. I don't feel like he did anything to me. He didn't. I am sure of that. But I'm lying there, stripped of everything I remember wearing, except for my boxer briefs, the same ones I put on when I got dressed for Conner's party.

How long ago was that?

I try to think, feel around the bed to see if I might find my clothes, my wallet, something I can use to cut this goddamned strap off my leg.

Nothing. I track my fingers along the edge of the bed as far as I can, my hands blindly squeeze between the mattress and the foundation, probe the cool bare floor underneath. It is clean, but I can reach pretty far. I push my hand up inside the box spring. Something metal is there. I slide my fingers behind it and begin pulling.

Black shadow moves beneath the door.

Someone is out there.

I flip myself back up onto the bed. My ankle burns. Just that moment of exertion leaves me gasping for breath. I am sweating, my eyes wide; and I watch the light at the door's edge.

It opens.

I shut my eyes.

I heard him walk up to the edge of the bed. He put his hand flat on my chest.

"I know you're awake, John."

I opened my eyes.

"How are you feeling?"

And I thought, *What an idiot. How do you think I feel?* I wanted to scream, howl, but I kept my mouth shut. Mostly, I had questions. I kept hearing them over and over, but I didn't want to say them.

What the fuck are you trying to do to me?

"I bet you're thirsty," Freddie said.

I was.

"Would you like a drink of water, John? Do they call you Johnny, or just John?"

Jack, asshole.

"I promise it's only water this time."

He walked out the door, leaving it open. My eyes adjusted to the light. He was wearing those same doctor's scrubs. I saw the name badge, too. He didn't even try to lie about his name. That was bad, I thought. And he looked big, like I'd never be able to fight him, even if I was pretty strong.

In a minute Freddie Horvath came back through the doorway, pushing one of those adjustable rolling desk chairs in front of him. There were some plastic bins on the seat that had things in them — I couldn't tell what they were — and a bottle of water, the same brand he'd given me the night before.

A cigarette pointed at me from his mouth. The smoke curled back through the uncombed hair that hung down over one eye. I tried to take in as many details about him as I could, but looked away every time his eyes landed on mine. I thought he was maybe about thirty. Maybe younger than that. His mouth and eyes looked dead, like he was bored.

He took the things from the chair and put them down on the floor beside the bed. He took a drag from the cigarette and pulled it away from his lips, exhaling streams of gray from his nostrils.

"I know." He smiled. "A doctor who smokes."

He held the water bottle in front of him and sat down.

I could reach your fucking throat.

"Thirsty?"

I put my hand out, but Freddie jerked the bottle away.

"First lesson, John." He drew another hit from his cigarette and said, through the smoke, "You have to ask me."

I looked at him, his name badge, the water.

He sat back in the chair.

"Ask me for it."

"Can I please have some water?" My voice sounded sick, far away from my body.

"That's nice," he said. "That's how you do it."

He handed the bottle to me.

"See?" Freddie said. "It's sealed. No tricks."

I drank, and spilled some of the water down my neck onto the mattress.

"What did you do to me?" I said.

"I didn't do anything. You did it to yourself."

I capped the bottle.

If that's what you think, asshole.

"This thing really hurts my ankle." I thought about what he'd do. I wanted to be careful. "Will you take it off, please?"

Freddie leaned over the bed. He put one hand beneath my heel and the other on top of my foot. The way he turned my foot in his hands and looked at me told me he really was a doctor.

"Stop pulling against it," he said. "I can put something on it so you don't get an infection. Tomorrow, maybe I can switch it to the other side if you want."

I wondered if he was going to make me ask for that, too. He reached down to the floor. I heard him moving things around, the sound of a plastic lid being pulled open. He took the cigarette from his lips and tilted it toward me.

"Smoke?"

I looked away.

"Didn't think so. You sure can drink, though."

He put the cigarette down somewhere. I couldn't see. He squeezed clear, greasy cream from a silver tube onto the tips of his fingers and wiped them around the burning cut on my ankle. Gently. I looked at the window, wondered what was out there.

"Does that feel better?"

I didn't say anything. I took another drink and recapped the bottle.

"You need to pee? I bet you need to pee, John."

I needed to piss so bad, it felt like I was going to burst.

"My name's Jack."

I looked right at him, trying to see if he'd have any reaction to that. I couldn't tell anything from his eyes. He scared me. I knew I'd have to play along with him so he wouldn't hurt me, but I wanted to lash out and hit him as hard as I could. The only way he'd think my name was John was if he'd looked through my wallet. I wondered what he did with it, with my clothes. How he got me into this room. I knew what I'd done to myself to get here, and I realized nobody would even miss me yet.

Six chilling tales

AVAILABLE FROM SQUARE FISH

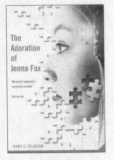

The Adoration of Jenna Fox
Mary E. Pearson
ISBN: 978-0-312-59441-1
$8.99 US / $11.50 Can

*What happened to Jenna Fox?
And who is she, really?*

The Compound
S.A. Bodeen
ISBN: 978-0-312-57860-2
$8.99 US / $11.50 Can

*Eli's father built the Compound to
keep his family safe. But are they
safe—or sorry?*

Dead Connection
Charlie Price
ISBN: 978-0-312-37966-7
$7.99 US / $10.25 Can

*Can Murray's ability to talk
to dead people help him find
a missing cheerleader?*

Holdup
Terri Fields
ISBN: 978-0-312-56130-7
$8.99 US / $11.50 Can

*The most dangerous thing at Burger
Heaven should be greasy food,
not a maniac with a gun.*

The Love Curse of the Rumbaughs
Jack Gantos
ISBN: 978-0-312-38052-6
$7.99 US / $8.99 Can

*Ivy has two great loves, her mother
and taxidermy.*

Zombie Blondes
Brian James
ISBN: 978-0-312-57375-1
$8.99 US / $11.50 Can

*All of the girls in Hannah's
new school are blonde and
popular—and dead.*